Stampede County

It all started when Careless O'Connor, that mighty legend of the Old West, stopped a bunch of land-grabbers from driving an old man and his daughter out of Stampede. The land in question had been given to the Kiowas but the Indian agent had been killed so nobody could safeguard their interests.

Such was the record of Careless that the Kiowas trusted him enough that he could at least pursue the land-grabbers and bring them to justice without resistance from the Indians. But the land-grabbers packed a mighty punch and some of the best farmlands in the country were at stake.

The question was: could Careless keep the Kiowas in check long enough for him to defeat the marauders and bring peace to a troubled land? As ever, it was the law of the gun, where justice was administered by hot lead!

Stampede County

Gordon Landsborough

A Black Horse Western

ROBERT HALE · LONDON

© 1953, 2003 Gordon Landsborough
First hardcover edition 2003
Originally published in paperback as
Kiowa Man by Mike M'Cracken

ISBN 0 7090 7312 7

Robert Hale Limited
Clerkenwell House
Clerkenwell Green
London EC1R 0HT

Typeset by
Derek Doyle & Associates, Liverpool.
Printed and bound in Great Britain by
Antony Rowe Limited, Wiltshire

1

THE BIG MAN

A lone rider suddenly appeared along the trail, far up the bare, red hillside. The early morning sun reflected upon saddle decorations, blinking back a bright, silvery light.

At once a man swore, riding alongside the crazy, lurching prairie schooner.

'Kiowas!' he shouted.

There were five men riding with the wagon, five men dissimilar physically yet all looking alike in that they were hardfaced, brutal-looking, suspicious-eyed – and not too clean.

At the shout they came spurring round into a milling knot about the spokesman, their grim eyes watching that lone figure up on the horizon. An old man sat upon the high seat, his foot stamping on the crude brake and halting the ancient wagon. He was spare and pale, in the way that city clerks grow.

There was nothing muscular about this Western pioneer, and he had the pallor that comes from working always indoors, yet he held an air of toughness, and his faded grey eyes watching that growling, nervy little group of horsemen, were filled with indignation and barely suppressed wrath.

He called, sarcastically, 'looks like you're skeered of one Injun – jes' one Injun, huh?' Plainly he wanted to irritate the men.

At his words the canvas behind his head opened and someone looked out and up the trail. It was a girl. She was dark, blue-eyed; a good-looking girl, with honey-brown cheeks that spoke of much time out of doors.

She saw that one rider, sitting his horse far up the mountinside, then her eyes flickered contemptuously towards their escort. 'They're only good for handling old men and defenceless girls,' she said, and then disappeared back within the wagon.

But all the same, they didn't move until they realized that that distant rider was coming down the trail towards them and was alone. Then they shouted roughly to the old driver to 'Git 'em rollin'!' and they leaned from their saddles and dragged on the raw-leather bridles of the two horses and got their old legs into movement, the wagon creaking protestingly behind the pair.

A few hundred yards up the trail that first blue-chinned rider who had spoken shoved back his sweat-stained, broad-brimmed hat and growled, 'He ain't no Kiowa. This fellar's a pale-face.'

They watched the rider approach. They saw he was riding a big black stallion that carried saddle and bridle decorated with silver in Kiowa fashion. That was why they had been deceived, from a distance.

He seemed to loll in his saddle, riding 'lazy,' as these five would have said. A big, casual, untidy-looking *hombre*, with a shirt that had once been blue but was faded grey by long exposure to the fierce Texan-Border sunshine: with torn and trail-stained jeans slopping over riding boots instead of being tucked inside them.

An inelegant figure of a man, and the face under the old, shapeless, droop-brimmed hat wasn't an oil painting, either.

With the screech of wooden blocks skidding on iron-rimmed wheels, the leader of the escort, that scowling man with the bruised left eye, shouted, 'What'n the tarnation are you doin'?'

'Stoppin',' said the old man calmly.

'I didn't tell you to stop,' roared the man. 'Git goin' agen. You don't stop till you're run out of the county, you an' your trouble-makin' daughter.'

The big fellow had drawn rein, right in amongst the men. They weren't taking much notice of him, because he looked so slow and half-asleep, squinting against the warm morning sun like a man not yet fully wakened.

'Don't he want to go?' he asked.

Nobody answered him.

The five horsemen began to shout at the horses and tried to get them started up the steep trail again, but they plunged in vain against their harness, for the old man was standing on the foot-brake.

The big, brutal-looking leader of the quintet lost his temper. He was the kind of man who habitually resorted to anger to get his way. Before anyone knew what he was doing, he had jerked his rifle out of his saddle boot and thumped the butt on to the foot of the old man.

At once the wagon jumped forward, because of the release on that footbrake. There was a crashing sound from within the wagon as it jolted into motion, followed by a despairing cry from the girl.

The old man stood up and shouted in pain and anger, but his assailant only laughed and goaded the horses forward with the barrel of his gun. . . .

His hat flew off. In that same instant that he realized he was without headgear, the startled man heard the report of a rifle. He wheeled, his jaw going slack with astonishment. That big-looking *hombre* was pointing a rifle towards him – and it was a Sharps. More, the big fellow didn't look at all lazy now.

Instead, they saw grey anger glinting from those narrowed eyes in that face that was as dark as any

8

Indian's. They heard a deep, angry growl: 'You didn't ought to have done that. He's an old man. What's he done wrong, anyway?'

Horses went rearing back on their hindquarters as startled men pulled round to face the man with the Sharps. The old man suddenly, gladly, stabbed on the brake and brought the wagon to a halt. Again there was a crash from within the wagon, and again a despairing cry from the girl. But this time the old man called back cheerfully, 'It don't matter, Pru. We got a friend now.'

The girl came out through the canvas front of the covered wagon at that. She wore the traditional dress of the frontier, yellow buckskin shirt, fringed up to the elbows, buckskin trousers of a slightly darker colour. They looked tight on her, as if she had once been caught out in the rain and had then incautiously dried herself before a fire.

The grey-eyed, scrub-chinned leader of the men shouted furiously, 'What's this, a hold-up? You aim to get yourself strung up, mister?'

The big galoot said drily, 'I don't aim to do anythin' so uncomfortable. I jes' figger here's an old man an' a gal mebbe wants helpin'.'

The girl called: 'Mister, we sure are grateful for that Sharps o' yourn. These no-good, low-down critters were running us out of Stampede County.'

The blue-chinned escort leader worked himself into a fury and began to sidle his horse towards the man who covered them with that dreaded Sharps repeater.

'You get on your way,' he bellowed savagely. 'This ain't none of your business. By heaven, you poke your nose into what ain't none of your affair, an'—'

'An' what?' There was a grimness to the big *hombre*'s tone now that stopped the angry, bullying flow of words. This big, careless-looking, lazy-eyed man had deceived them by his first appearance; but this man wasn't lazy, wasn't careless when it came to handling a gun.

He seemed tired, suddenly, of fencing verbally with these men, for abruptly he demanded of the teamster, "Old timer, do you want to be run out of Stampede?'

The old man said, 'Nope!' emphatically. Then he drew in a deep breath and exploded, 'Goldarn it, all I want is to get back to my print shop an' start gettin' into people's hair again.'

The big *hombre* on the black stallion chuckled. Then his rifle muzzle jerked, indicating the trail behind the wagon. 'Git,' he ordered tersely. 'Skedaddle. Ol' dad here don't want no company no more – not yourn, sabe?'

The men looked at each other, and it seemed there was minor consternation in their glances. As if plans had gone wrong, and they were worried about the consequences. Then they looked at that blued-Sharps' barrel and began to pull their horses round. Then a hand flashed and came up flaming. One of the men had risked a quick draw on a Colt.

The bullet smacked past the big rider on the big black stallion. Instantly he kicked his horse into a mighty lunge forward, jumping for the shelter of that wagon; his Sharps ripped off – once, twice – and the five horsemen spurred madly for the cover of some timber along the trail. The girl noticed it, and approved. She also realized that neither of those two rifle shots had been aimed at the men – just near them.

She saw the rider urging his mount alongside the wagon; saw grey eyes that were no longer narrowed and lazy-looking, but wide with urgency. He was shouting, 'C'mon, get out of that wagon. That canvas won't stop bullets—'

He held his arms wide. The girl hesitated. He grabbed her and pulled her across his saddle bow. He was a man who didn't stand on ceremony, evidently, when action was indicated. The old man saw what he wanted, grabbed the cantle and hoisted his old limbs behind the big *hombre*.

At once the rider spurred his heavily laden horse in line away from the canvas-covered wagon, to where a gulch opened up off the trail and afforded cover for them.

They all dismounted in a hurry. The Sharps and a revolver holstered on the big man's belt were all the weapons they had. The girl sat down and looked at the big man, lying prone a few yards from them. She shuddered. His shirt, without

11

buttons, was kept closed across that mighty chest because fence wire had been looped through the buttonholes.

She called, 'You got yourself into this trouble, mister, because you took it on yourself to interfere in our business.'

He grinned back at her, a cheerful smile from such a battered face. A bullet suddenly zipped right where his head had been a fraction of a second before. But he'd jerked it down under cover, as if seeing the suddenly raised rifle that pointed towards him from that copse of trees by the trailside.

He said, drily, 'Looks like they've got us nicely bogged down.'

As if to confirm his statement, a voice came floating up the valley towards them. It echoed between the steep-sloping, almost bare, valley walls. 'You folks'd better come walkin' out with your hands up. We've been told to run that old man an' his daughter clear outa the county, an' that's what we aim to do.'

The old man looked round unhappily, then rubbed his chin with a dry, rasping sound. 'I figger we're sure gonna be thirsty afore long,' he opined. His grey, faded eyes looked at the black stallion, magnificent in its Indian harness. 'You got any water in that cantina, son?'

'Nope.' The big man was lifting himself to look down the trail. 'I figgered on makin' Stampede around noon, an' couldn't be bothered to fill up at the last stream.'

The old man was saying, dolefully, 'That sure was mighty careless of you, mister.' And then the Sharps smacked two swift bullets down the trail.

'They're closin' in on us.' The big *hombre* slipped fresh rounds into the magazine. 'Guess they aim to drive us into Texas, not wait for us to go on our own accord.'

He knelt, now, and began to fire whenever he saw a movement. The white powder-smoke drifted into their nostrils, acrid and biting at such close quarters. The men along the trail were experienced frontiersmen, however, and they moved quickly when they moved at all, and never came out of cover unless it was to dive into new cover only a stride or so away. They were coming steadily up the valley, getting nearer to the mouth of the gulch in which they were hiding.

The girl was watching that big, flat, Indian brown face, and suddenly she realized that the stranger was perturbed. She caught his sudden, calculating glance up the rock-strewn, narrow gulch that seemed to bore into the steep mountain side.

He heard her say, softly, 'There's no way of escape that way, not on horseback.'

He looked at her, his face smiling grimly. 'Nope. We're kinda trapped here, I reckon.' He looked speculatively up the steep mountain slopes. 'Keep a watch up there,' he ordered. 'I figger they're tryin' to work into a position above us. If they get up there—' He shrugged.

The big *hombre* relaxed, sitting on the side of one mighty limb. He reloaded, looking at the pair, intent on the mountain slopes behind them. They heard his voice drawl, 'Mebbe someone would tell me what it's all about. What've these galoots got agen you?'

The old man sighed. He didn't take his eyes off the danger spot, high up beyond the gulch, but he started to talk.

'They're on to somethin' big an' greedy an' dirty, right now, them folk in Stampede,' that dry old voice continued. 'Them? Two – three dozen mean *hombres* that hit the town in the last month or two, since the Staked Plains began to open up to settlers. They've got ideas on grabbin' land here, around the Wichitas.'

That information seemed to startle the big *hombre*. He said, 'That's agen the law – Indian Agreement, anyway. This is Kiowa country, not to be settled in. If they want land, there's plenty two – three hundred miles west, on the Staked Plains.'

'That,' said the old man in triumph, 'is what I wrote in the *Stampede Citizen*. An' that's what all the ruckus is about; that's why you're right here 'longside me, fated to get a bullet in your big head or die of thirst.'

The big *hombre* grinned comfortably. 'Mebbe,' he said. Then he said abruptly, 'I didn't know they had noospapers so far west.'

The girl then took up the story. Her father was a printer at Blytheville, on the Mississippi. He wanted to see new lands, and he had a feeling that better opportunities awaited pioneers away from the long-settled basin of the Mississippi.

He'd packed up his precious printing plant and come out West. Three or four months ago he'd found this prosperous trading town of Stampede, on the edge of the fabulous cattle lands of the new state of Texas, and it had seemed a good place for him to set up business.

He started a paper for the whole county, the *Citizen*. It had come out weekly, for a while, and then—

'Then dad began to write against the land-grabbers,' Pru said. 'I reckon they objected to what he had to say of their tactics. He said, sure as shot they'd be starting another war with the Indians, because they were fencing in Indian territory.'

The big *hombre* demanded abruptly, 'They've got an agent, haven't they? What's he doin' about it?' His manner was suspicious, for many Indian agents were in active league against the people whom they were paid to protect.

'Joe Ponder?' The girl shook her head, recognizing his suspicions. 'He was murdered last week. We wrote about it.' She shuddered. 'He was found – scalped.'

'Injun trick.' The big man growled. He was beginning to be uneasy at the silence down the valley. He hadn't seen any movement for some time.

He called a warning. 'They're up to some tricks. Watch out, you two.'

At that the old man said, 'Fellar, I figger somethin' moved back up the mountain. I've been watchin', but I ain't seen it come agen. Might be some of them varmints though.'

At once, that big man came back where he could watch up the mountain slope. The girl saw that quick movement out of the corner of her eye, and marvelled that a man so big could move so swiftly, so lithely. Continually he belied that first impression of a big, casual, lazy *hombre*.

'What happened when you started to rile them land-grabbers, old timer?' The big *hombre* was sighting his rifle up the slope.

'It happened this morning.' There was a quaver of indignation in the old man's voice. ' 'Bout four, before the sun was even thinkin' of gettin' up, them fellars came a-knockin' at my door. They had guns. All they said was, 'You've been in this town too long, old man. Pack your things an' head any way you like, but get outa Stampede County.'

'That galoot shouted somethin' about bein' told to run you out of town,' the big *hombre* said drily. His finger was slowly tightening, but they couldn't see what was at the end of that Sharps' barrel. 'Looks like someone put 'em up to chasin' you out of Stampede.'

'I don't know anythin' about that. We jes' packed the old machine, type an' paper into the wagon – an' git. Now I figger it's all jumbled at the back of the wagon.' He began to say things under his breath that could have been muffled cusswords.

Then that Sharps jumped, a crash echoed from the barrel up the narrowing, rock-walled gulch. The smoke blew into their faces, and they heard a distant yelp of pain.

Three bullets came screaming near to them, ricocheting like furious wasps from off the nearly rocks and bouncing harmlessly towards the sweating, nervous horses harnessed to the prairie schooner. The noise disturbed the beasts and they began to turn round and trot down the trail.

'There goes the water,' the girl cried in dismay.

'There goes my type!' howled the old man, as a crashing sound came from the wagon.

They had all scrambled into cover with the first of those shots, and now were crouching between two tall dark-red rocks that stuck up like teeth from rich, red soil of the gulch bed.

The big *hombre* shuttled rounds rapidly into the magazine and fired three times up the hillside. He couldn't see what was happening along the trail, now, and for all they knew their enemies might be coming up at the double right behind their backs. It made the girl's spine tingle to think of it. Without saying anything she tugged the heavy Colt out of the man's belt and faced towards the trail. She saw a movement and fired, and a man ducked back out of sight.

Then guns began to blaze from the trail behind them. Someone was shouting. For five gunmen, they seemed to carry a lot of guns. But with that shouting, the firing stopped.

There was no more firing after that. Then their straining ears caught the sound of horses' hoofs beating rapidly down the trail to the east of them. They looked at each other, then, not understanding.

The old man said suspiciously, 'Goldarn it, what're they up to?' And all thought, 'This is a trap, a ruse to get us to come out into the open.'

So they remained where they were, huddled between those two rocks.

But the most nerve-racking part of that wait in the gulch was the uncertainty – not knowing what was happening all around them.

After a time Pru whispered, 'I heard something – on the trail.'

At that the big *hombre* sighed, shifted his position and said, 'Reckon mebbe I'd better get it over with.' He suddenly lurched to his feet, rifle gripped hard against his side, ready for action. The girl found herself jumping up with him, the Colt ready to support him.

Her eyes opened, seeing what she did. Involuntarily her mouth opened in a scream of fear. Her gun came up.

Right across the mouth of the gulch, sitting their horses silently, were a dozen warriors of the Kiowa tribe.

2
BACK IN TOWN

The big *hombre* saw the Indians, clad for the most part in deerskin shirts and breech-clouts. Saw a dozen or so in line across the gulch before them, saw a jostling mob of Indians back of them on the dusty, rutty trail.

He knew them to be Kiowas, because of their silver-decorated saddles and bridles. No other Indians in that part of the West knew the art of silver-making like the Kiowas.

Out of the corner of his eye he saw Pru lift that heavy Colt. His hand swept down and knocked it to the ground. His own rifle he held at arm's length, out from his side, to show that his intentions weren't hostile.

He growled, 'Don't do anythin'. Fightin's useless – there's too many of 'em.'

He was watching those suspicious-eyed, brooding Indians. Now he called, '*How!*' and then began to walk forward, taking the girl with him. There was a chief among them, a very important chief and perhaps chief of all the Kiowas. The big *hombre* knew he was a powerful man, because of the way the others sat back from him, and because of the proudness of his bearing, sitting stiff-backed on his pinto.

This chief looked across at the big *hombre*'s horse and growled, 'Red man's horse?'

'Nope, mine.' The big *hombre* was standing in amongst the Indians now – right in amongst them, so that they were all about the man and that girl.

The chief appeared to doubt the words. 'Him Kiowa saddle. Him Kiowa bridle.'

'Kiowa,' returned the big man easily, levelly, 'my friend. Kiowa give harness to me.'

There was a stir among the Indians at that. Few Kiowas were ready to acknowledge friendship with any white man, or to make presents to them. One of the braves, plumed with a black crow's feather, called something in the harsh language of the Kiowas that was so near to Cheyenne in its guttural unpleasantness. The big *hombre* must have understood some Kiowa, for his head lifted immediately and he called, 'I don't tell lies. I'll tell you who that Kiowa was.'

They waited. The big *hombre* took his time and then said, 'It was Man-with-Thumb.'

That information seemed to startle the Indians. The girl heard the sharp exclamations and then found the Indians crowding even closer, their faces inflamed with anger. The chief imperiously held them back, but his own face was dark, as if he shared their passions.

'Man-with-Thumb him dead. Man-with-Thumb killed by white man. How come Man-with-Thumb give harness to paleface?'

The big *hombre* merely shrugged and said, 'Man-with-Thumb had favourite wife, Brown Woman. Brown Woman came to Texas, riding Man-with-Thumb's horse. Brown Woman came to me and said, "This is your harness. Man-with-Thumb, my husband, always said, If Man-with-Thumb is killed, take my harness to my white friend O-Kon-Or. He will understand." '

But O-Kon-Or didn't explain what he understood by the gift.

The chief looked thoughtfully at O'Connor. 'Man-with-Thumb was friend with O-Kon-Or?' His manner said, 'He must have felt mighty friendly to have left you his silver-decorated saddle and bridle when he died.'

The big *hombre* nodded. 'Yeah, Man-with-Thumb came huntin' with O-Kon-Or many times. Once O-Kon-Or saved him from bein' killed by a grizzly b'ar.'

'A grizzly—' That shocked the Kiowas. To them a grizzly was a sacred beast – sacred but savage beyond all other creatures and to be feared. Their fear of the animal was such that no Kiowa dared mention its name unless he was himself named after it.

A brave spoke up eagerly, 'This is all true,' he

declared. 'Man-with-Thumb once told me that on a hunting expedition he nearly lost his life to' – he couldn't use the word, so he ended 'Him-who-is-all-hair-and-walks-like-a-man.'

Then he added the final corroboration. 'Man-with-Thumb said white man who was his blood brother fought . . . him . . . with fists and drove him away and saved Man-with-Thumb's life.'

Pru sighed, relaxing. She felt that now the danger was passed. O-Kon-Or was a blood brother of a Kiowa. They could not harm a brother of the tribe.

She was right. Now those savage, ferocious masks of anger relaxed. Only the chief did not relax. Big chiefs never relaxed.

O'Connor took advantage of the easing of tension and walked the girl out through the Indians. He whistled and his horse came walking across, slow, proud and majestic, a king among stallions.

The old man breathed out a tremendous sigh of relief as they came up. He went quickly across, catching up with the stallion, so that they all met together. The old man gripped his daughter fervently by the hand. 'By gosh, Pru, I sure thought we was all goners that time.'

She squeezed back, her relief apparent. He saw the shine in those bright blue eyes, and they were looking round at big O'Connor. 'Dad,' she whispered, 'this is a man. He never turned a hair, with all those Indians around him.'

Big O'Connor came up, that slow, lazy smile on his flattened brown features. 'We'll ride down after the wagon, Pru, you'n me,' he drawled. There was that glint of humour in his grey eyes. 'The old timer c'n walk.'

'Me walk?' The old man was indignant. His pale face came jutting forward belligerently. 'You oughta be ashamed o' yourself, makin' an old man walk.'

O'Connor nodded comfortably. 'Sure, sure. Right now I feel ashamed o' myself. But I'm kinda tired this mornin'. I reckon I'll ride.'

He mounted, reached down and lifted her across his saddle bow again, and he did it easily, as if her pliant young form weighed nothing in his mighty grip.

The old man took hold of a stirrup leather. He didn't want to be left behind. Then they started to walk down the trail to where they could see the wagon and horses about half a mile ahead. The Indians were talking together, but when O'Connor began to ride down the rutty trail they fell in behind him.

In time Big Chief Fighting Bear and some of his minor chieftains came riding up alongside O'Connor's black stallion. By the look of things they had been conferring together. Now Fighting Bear said, 'Red man him plenty fed up of paleface. Paleface him promise not to fence red man's hunting-grounds, but now everywhere Kiowa country is being stolen by white men.'

The chief's copper-coloured cheeks seem to stain darker with anger.

O'Connor looked at him then asked, 'Why're you tellin' me this, chief?'

'You are blood brother of Kiowa. Man-with-Thumb called you man-among-men, my braves tell me. Kiowa are surrounded by enemies – want friends. Chief Fighting Bear ask O-Kon-Or to be friend of Kiowa, fight for them against bad white men.'

Those words seemed to electrify the girl. He saw that her warm, impressionable young heart had been stirred by that plea of the harassed, worried Indian chief.

'Oh, Mister O'Connor,' she begged. 'Please do as Fighting Bear asks. Take the place of their dead agent, and fight for them against the land-grabbers.'

Even the old man got excited. 'You've got to do it, fellar,' he was urging. 'The things they're doin' to these pore Injuns is a shame. Back there you heard what happened when I started to write agen the land-grabbers. They sure up an' started to run me outa the county. Wal, I reckon that's what they aim to do to the Kiowas – run 'em clear outa the Big Bend country. They want war agen the Kiowas so they c'n walk in an' grab their lands. An' these Kiowas ain't got much chance, I tell you. What're bows an' arrows agen six-shooters an' rifles?'

They had come to a halt now, while that old man pleaded with the big fellow to take the part of the

Indians against the avaricious whites.

When he had finished there was a lot of growling and grunts of approval from the Indians. O'Connor heard it, but he also heard a few savage voices say, in Kiowa, 'The red man has courage that few white men possess. If the white man wants war, let us paint our faces and take the war trail.'

He even heard one voice say, 'All white men are dogs. Let us take three scalps now!'

O'Connor's eyes looked lazy, but they were quick to spot the last speaker. It was one of the minor chieftains, a man with the red blood of anger under the copper hue on his cheeks. He was the one with the solitary black crow's feather. He made a mental note of that face and then turned to his white companions.

'What c'n one man do agen so many? An' why pick on me?' he protested mildly. 'Me, I like to take things kinda quietly. I ain't no fightin' man.'

He spoke like a man who genuinely believed what he was saying. Then he caught the scornful gaze of the girl on the saddle bow before him.

She said, 'Mister O'Connor, you don't know the things that have been done against these poor Kiowas. Not only are they robbed, but they're murdered, too. Everything is being done to get them to take to the warpath again, just to give these greedy conscienceless land-grabbers the chance to wipe out the tribe and take their country as their own.'

Her hand waved to the rich red soil of this country that was already being known as Oklahoma. 'This is some of the finest farmland in the world. Some day it's going to be worth a hundred dollars an acre – and the Kiowas' hunting-grounds cover several million acres.'

'The prize is big, O'Connor!' that was the old man speaking up to him eagerly. 'Big enough to have brought together a bunch of the most ruthless adventurers in the West.'

The big fellow shoved back that disgraceful battered old hat. 'Jumpin' rattlesnakes,' he protested. 'You tell me all this, an' you expect me to go gunnin' agen that mob.'

Pru said coldly, 'I do expect it of you, Mister O'Connor. If you run out on these poor Indians, I'll be ashamed of you.'

'Yeah?' The big fellow had quite a wicked sense of humour. 'About five minutes ago you'd have given a lot to have run out on these poor Injuns, I kinda recollect.' Pru glared at him, so he ended meekly, 'OK, I'm with you. I'm a Kiowa man in this fight.'

Chief Fighting Bear called out a translation to his followers, that the blood brother of dead Man-with-Thumb was to be their friend.

O'Connor began to move his horse down the trail again, and now they came to the wagon. Here the trail descended sharply, between high banks that went steeply up into tapering mountain ridges. There were trees clothing the lower slopes, right against the trail, mostly spruce and Douglas firs.

28

But the big man's eyes had focused upon something brown that moved slightly behind the trees, a quarter of a mile or more down the trail.

He thought, 'Someone's watchin' us.' And he decided it would be one of the gang who had tried to run the old man and his daughter out of Stampede.

The girl slipped off his horse and pulled herself over the tailboard into the wagon. Big O'Connor looked within when he heard her cry of concern.

The wagon was knee-deep in paper and sheets of card; type trays and stone jars of printer's ink were mixed with the debris, and at least one jar had come open and there was black, oily ink marring the clean paper.

He heard her voice, and for a second it was filled with despair. 'Oh, heavens, this will take days to sort out!' Then her manner changed. 'I'll sort out that type even if it takes me a year,' she said belligerently. 'And when that's done we'll bring out the *Citizen* and really get into the hair of the land-grabbers.'

Big O'Connor had to admire her spirit. It took some courage for an old man and a girl to ride back into a hostile town with the determination to again bring out their newspaper. He started to pull away, when his eye fell on a small, single-sheet newspaper. He saw the words *Stampede Citizen*, and picked it up.

The old man was up on his high seat, ready to resume the journey back into Stampede.

The old man's dry, emotionless voice spoke out. 'Me 'n Pru reckon to go back to Stampede an' rile them land-grabbers even if we've got no friends in the town at all. But I figger I'd feel happier if you were there in case we needed a friend, big fellar.'

O'Connor looked at those silent Indians, watching him from a few yards back up the trail. Then he looked back at the old man silhouetted there against the blue Oklahoma sky, and he growled, 'Durn it, why does everyone want me to be their friend today? How did people manage afore I rode up from Texas?'

When he found the Indians were falling in behind the wagon, O'Connor dropped back alongside the chief. 'Why you go to Stampede?' he asked. Idly he unfolded the newspaper and his eyes skimmed the small headlines.

'A fence was put across the Cutthroat Gap,' Fighting Bear said sombrely. 'That means no buffalo can come through into Kiowa hunting-grounds.'

Game, especially buffalo, needed room if they were to survive. Start to fence them in and they were trapped and helpless. O'Connor thought, 'That's the idea, of course. Shut out the game, an' in time the Kiowas'll have to move out of the country to where the range is free an' open.'

He asked, 'Why didn't you tear the fence down?'

'Fifty white men guard that fence, and they have good rifles.' He looked at O'Connor's Sharps. 'Him got plenty rifles like yours, O-Kon-Or.'

Then he told O'Connor that these men were already marking out the land for settlement, that houses were being built for permanent habitation.

O'Connor was listening and reading at the same time. When he'd finished a fighting article against the land-grabbers, he turned to a smaller article. It read:

'People are saying that Indian Agent Joe Ponder was the victim of a Kiowa outrage. People are always blaming the Kiowas for crimes, but is it reasonable to think that the Kiowas would kill their best friend?

'The *Stampede Citizen* goes on record with the belief that Joe Ponder wasn't killed by any redskin, but was put out of the way by the land-grabbers. They took his scalp so as to put the blame on the Kiowas.

'This, citizens, is murder – the murder of one of our best-respected townspeople. We, the *Stampede Citizen*, demand that every effort is made to bring Joe Ponder's assassin to justice. And we say, "Look to our midst for his killer. He's someone among us, right here in Stampede County."

'Who is the killer of Indian Agent Joe Ponder?'

Big O'Connor whistled at that and folded the paper away.

Chief Fighting Bear was saying, 'We go to town marshal in Stampede. When treaty was made between Federal Government and Kiowas, we were told, "never take law into your own hands. Go to law officer and get him to give justice." '

Big O'Connor saw movement to that brown horseflesh part-hidden by the trees down the trail. Mechanically, almost, he said to the chief, 'That was good advice, Fighting Bear. It is as well that you do things according to the law.'

Fighting Bear's hard, purposeful face lifted to the bigger man's. Harshly his voice rang out, 'Why, then, doesn't the white man obey these same laws? Weren't they made for red man and for white? Or just for the Indian?' His tone was bitter.

O'Connor said, 'They were made for both. You keep to your side of the bargain, chief, an' leave it to your friends to make the whites keep to theirs.'

Then he spurred up alongside the pugnacious little printer, standing hard on the brake pedal so as to hold back the heavy wagon down the steep, loose-surfaced slope.

O'Connor shouted up, waving the small news-sheet. 'Hey, you, Sorensen—' He'd seen the printer's name in the paper. 'When did this come out?' The old man shouted to his horses to get them round a bend in the trail. The heels were locked and screaming, and O'Connor just caught the brief reply to this question – 'Yesterday.'

Then a horseman shot out on to the trail far below them and went riding crazily towards distant Stampede. The Indians became alert at once and started to shout. A few instinctively kicked their mocassined heels into the well-covered ribs of their nimble hunting ponies, as if to go in pursuit. For he was a lone white man, and not an Indian

32

there had a doubt that his intentions were hostile to the red Kiowas.

Fighting Bear shouted them back, and they fell to the rear again. The younger men were muttering and angry and flashed mutinous looks at their stern chief. Big O'Connor saw among them the minor chieftain who wore a black crow's feather in his oily forelock.

'That Black Crow's a mischief-maker,' he thought. He also thought, 'That rider down there spells trouble for us – a heap o' trouble.'

On the plain below them they now saw the sprawling frontier town of Stampede, a trading post until a few months ago. They saw a puff of dust that travelled rapidly across the prairie towards the sun-bleached, crazy shacks that made up Stampede township, and they knew it to be thrown up by the galloping hoofs of that lone white rider. He was on his way to warn the town of their coming.

The big *hombre* looked at the chief, his face smiling but in a way that was lacking in humour. 'They'll be waitin' for you, chief, when you get to Stampede. You still want to go an' see the town marshal?'

Chief Fighting Bear looked at O'Connor. 'You are Kiowa blood-brother. O-Kon-Or will advise.'

So Big O'Connor said, 'Let's go an' see what happens. That fence'll have to come down. Maybe the town marshal can do somethin' about it.'

Then he stood in his stirrups and spoke in the language of the Kiowas.

He called, 'O Men of the Kiowa Tribe, we go in peace to speak with the white man about that fence that keeps back the buffalo from your hunting-grounds. Let no man touch his weapons unless he is attacked first by the white man. Do as I say, and we will defeat these land-hungry Easterners and throw them out of Kiowa territory.'

Not all were ready to obey this white man who had so recently come into their lives. But Chief Fighting Bear seemed to have trust in O-Kon-Or, and now he shouted back that that was his will, too. He called out to the Crazy Dogs to police his warriors, and at that O'Connor was satisfied.

In his hunting trips with his good friend, Man-with-Thumb, he had learned not only the language of the Kiowas, but also many of their customs. He knew that the finest, bravest, most responsible of the warriors belonged to a Kiowa society known as the Crazy Dogs. These men led the tribe in battle; if it came to retreat they stayed behind and gave their lives so as to enable their womenfolk and children to escape. And at times like these, they acted as policemen, watching the younger, hot-blooded braves and ensuring that whatever orders were given by their chief they were carried out.

O'Connor saw warriors pull out from the crowd of Indians and take up positions all around the trotting calvalcade. He felt satisfied.

Then he saw a black crow's feather riding among the Crazy Dogs, and he lost some of the satisfaction.

34

Black Crow was a Crazy Dog. Black Crow could upset everything if he wished to.

Ahead of them, Stampede was like an ant heap disturbed by the snout of a grub-hunting, winter-hungry bear. They could see men racing across the open spaces between the shacks. They all carried rifles and were taking up positions on the perimeter of the township.

O'Connor called up to the sweating old printer, 'We'll go on ahead. Some o' these people won't think twice about shootin' an Injun, I figger.'

He shouted to Fighting Bear to drop back with his men, then went on with the wagon, entering the township ahead of the Indian deputation. Reluctantly the Indians reined back and allowed the swaying, creaking prairie schooner to go forward.

O'Connor, his rifle out now, saw white men ahead, crouching behind cover for the most part, guns pointing towards the big mass of red men, now beginning to circle out on the prairie. But several men were boldly coming out into the open mesquite, though they all carried rifles in their hands and most had Colts attached to their belts.

The big *hombre* shouted to the printer, 'You want to watch out for yourself, too, old timer?' The old man looked down at him, as if thinking about those words of warning. Then he called out, 'Why, big fellar?'

Right at that moment a rifle cracked fire from

behind that group of advancing Stampede citizens. Old man Sorensen fell from his high seat into the red dust of Oklahoma.

3

THE TROUBLE-
STARTER

There was a minor turmoil for a moment after that shot. The Kiowas at once swung in savage, threatening line, prepared to charge upon their natural enemies if that shot had been intended for them.

One of the citizens in that deputation advancing towards the covered wagon turned and shouted angrily at the rifleman. No more shots followed.

Big O'Connor had reached down and grabbed the wagon horses' loose-trailing reins and halted them. Looking back he saw Pru scrambling out over the tailboard and then running in haste towards her father.

Old man Sorensen suddenly sat up. O'Connor rode round to him. The old man looked a bit ashamed and said, 'I figgered that was a bullet intended for me, big fellar, comin' right after what you were sayin'.'

O'Connor's grey eyes twinkled. 'That was some-one who got kinda nervous an' pulled too hard on a trigger,' he drawled. 'It wasn't intended for nobody, but you acted kinda scared an' fell off your high perch.'

The old man rose, trying to hide his annoyance, dusted his reddened pants and stamped off towards the wagon, cussing mildly under his breath.

The man from Texas started to ride to meet the deputation. One of them was that blue-chinned, scowling-faced man who was leader of the gang who had tried to run Sorensen and daughter out of the county. The others looked to be ordinary citizens.

Among them, two men stood out. One was young, a lean, six-footer, brick-red as if he saw most of life from on top of a saddle. A good-look-ing man in a tough way. He wore a marshal's shield.

The other was a rugged individual, nearly as big as O'Connor, nearly as broad across the shoulders, but thicker-set across the thighs. He was hatless, for all the heat from that rising, summer-hot sun, and he was spare of hair, and his face was nobbly and he didn't look a beauty at all.

He wore black store pants stuffed into riding boots, and he had a fancy grey vest on, with a heavy gold watch-chain dangling from one pocket. He was without collar and tie, his vest was unbuttoned, and he had the air of a man who hadn't found the time to finish dressing. O'Connor was to realize later that Justin Foraiger never did find time to finish dressing, and always looked like this—

O'Connor drew rein, fifty yards ahead of the wagon, and waited for the deputation to approach. He saw that the marshal was looking past him, as if in surprise at seeing that prairie schooner out there on the mesquite.

The town marshal said, 'I'm Pete M'Clelland. When people get to listenin' to me, I kinda act as a law officer for the county.' His narrowed eyes squinted back to that mob of Indians, waiting behind the wagon. 'Who are you, stranger, an' why d'you bring Injuns so close to a town?'

His manner was hostile. Now he looked at the Kiowa bridle on that black stallion and his young face had a mean and hard look to it.

O'Connor drawled easily, 'My name's O'Connor.'

Someone in that little crowd said, 'That don't tell us nothin', stranger. What's the handle to your name?'

That disgraceful old hat was shoved back from the big brown, sweating face. O'Connor said, 'I kinda never use my first name. Mebbe that's because no one else ever uses it.' He rubbed his chin as if not understanding the ways of men and said, 'But mostly people call me Careless O'Connor. I never figgered out why.'

Those citizens looked at his buttonless shirt, which gaped now and showed a mighty, hairy chest. They looked at his torn pants and the bit of rope that acted as a belt under his ammunition belt and holsters.

But when their eyes fell on that single holster they grew thoughtful. There wasn't anything careless in the way that gun was carried, strapped down on to the faded blue jeans around that mighty leg. This big guy wasn't careless when it came to essentials.

M'Clelland snapped, 'That still don't tell us anythin'. What about these Injuns?'

Careless O'Connor faced up to that truculent young marshal. Deliberately he said, 'They're my friends. I'm blood brother to a dead Kiowa. What've you got to say about that? I figger someone's got to look after them. I figger someone should stop this land-grabbin', an' I reckon it should be you, marshal. What're you doin' about it?'

M'Clelland snapped, 'That's my business, but if you want to know, I don't let any land-grabbin' go through if I know about it.' His head jerked towards the Indians. 'Is that why they've come to Stampede today? To tell of land-grabbers?'

Careless nodded. 'That's why they came, like good little Injuns obeyin' the White Father. When they accepted peace terms they reckoned to keep their part of the bargain. Mind you,' he told them, 'there's some among them Injuns that

40

don't hold with parleyin', an' if they're riled much more they'll break out an' take the war-trails.'

That mean-faced, blue-chinned *hombre* trumpeted loudly, 'Let 'em. Just let 'em try'n get tough with us, fellar, an' see what happens to their hides.'

Careless lifted his eyes to meet those mean, unpleasant ones. Deliberately he said. 'You'd like that to happen, wouldn't you, *hombre?* That's what you're aimin' for, crowdin' in on these redskins like you're doin'. You want to start an almighty ruckus so you c'n wipe the Kiowa out an' grab all their territory. But it won't happen, not the way you want it. The Kiowa are entitled to their lands an' to protection, an' I aim to see they have both.'

Suddenly, almost as if spitting the the words out, that mighty, hairy-chested man with the Texan drawl snapped, 'Tell the big boss – the fellar back of you an' your gun-totin' rannies – what I've just told you!'

The gunman must have recognized that he had opened his mouth too much, and to cover his sudden anger at finding himself so smoothly tricked, characteristically his hand dived for his gun.

Marshal Pete M'Clelland went plunging head-first out of his saddle in an effort to smack down that gun-drawing hand.

He was fast, leaping from his saddle, but no

man can move as fast as a bullet. As he dived he saw the hand lift the smooth-worn Colt. Saw it begin its short journey that would halt when it was pointing level with the big, barrel-chested *hombre*'s heart.

That gun hand was moving like lightning. Then the falling M'Clelland saw the hand jerk back, saw the revolver fly out from fingers suddenly numbed and incapable of holding the gun any longer.

M'Clelland landed on to a man so dead that he fell under the marshal's weight without even a fraction of a second's resistance.

Big Careless O'Connor was looking at a smoking rifle held by the massive, nobble-faced galoot who seemed to have come out when he was half-dressed.

M'Clelland stood up. He seemed dazed, but whether from the shock of finding a dead man in his arms or from actual contact with the sun-baked ground they never knew.

He looked at the galoot with the smoking rifle, then looked at the *hombre* with the Texan drawl. O'Connor had his revolver in his hand.

M'Clelland said, 'He's dead. Bluey Arrigo got his, that time.' His eyes were grim as he surveyed the pair with smoking guns. 'I don't go for gunplay. You saw I was tryin' to stop it. Why did you have to shoot him down?'

Careless eased himself in his saddle, then drawled, 'I wanted to go on livin'. Why else? I was

42

the target, an' I didn't reckon you could stop that gun hand in time. I aimed for his gun-hand, an' I don't reckon I miss.'

He looked at M'Clelland, still standing straddle-legged across the blue-chinned corpse. 'Mebbe you c'n settle the matter, marshal,' he suggested. 'One bullet got Bluey through the heart, I reckon, way he went out. You c'n tell if it's a rifle or a Colt bullet.'

M'Clelland stooped and pulled back the shirt on the dead man. There wasn't any waiting for a decision; McClelland could tell a rifle-bullet wound when he saw one.

He looked up, eyes seeking Foraiger's. The guy's right, Just. His bullet took the gun out of Bluey's hand – yours went through his heart an' killed him.'

Just Foraiger ran a heavy hand over his nearly bald head and his eyes were coldly wondering. 'Guess I don't shoot as straight as I did, Pete. Guess I sure am out o' practice.'

M'Clelland came walking over to his horse. 'You don't need to worry, Just. We all know you don't like gun-play, an' there won't be any trouble over this. Bluey pulled trouble on hissel'. You tried to help O'Connor here.'

' I reckon I owe you both a lot of thanks,' said Careless. 'Some day, mebbe I'll be in a position to level accounts; until then, *amigos, muchos gracias.*'

Even so, his eyes lingered on that heavy face of

Justin Foraiger. The thought in his mind was, 'Why did you kill Bluey Arrigo?'

For he knew that Justin Foraiger hadn't aimed for Bluey's gun-hand. A man with a rifle, so near to an opponent, didn't miss by a yard, and that's what it amounted to.

Some more men came walking out from the bleached and warping buildings that was the county town of Stampede. They were heavily armed and suspicious. They wanted to know what had happened to Bluey, and Careless recognized a few faces among them – the rannies who had been with Bluey, back along the trail.

He turned in his saddle and gave a quick signal to old man Sorensen to drive through into the town. He thought there was going to be trouble in a few minutes' time, and he didn't want the old man and the girl out on the prairie if bullets and arrows began to fly.

As he drew level with the group around the body of Bluey Arrigo, old man Sorensen must have recognized some of his abductors among the crowd. It got him worked up and mad, but now he couldn't stop the horses so he had to content himself with shouting, 'Them varmints tried to run me'n Pru outa town this mornin', Pete. I demand you clap 'em in gaol.'

The marshal pulled his eyes away from that tense line of Indians out on the prairie. He looked at the speaker, and his eyes were aflame with anger.

'What sort of town is this?' he almost bellowed. 'I'm law officer here. I'm the guy who says when anyone's got to be run outa town. What's the idea, takin' the law into your own hands?'

Careless was watching the marshal. He knew he would have to have friends to accomplish the mission that had brought him into Stampede, and this marshal might be a powerful ally. He was sure the man was straight, and by the way he spoke he seemed fully aware of his responsibilities as a peace officer.

The rannie was unrepentant. He challenged M'Clelland boldly, sure of himself. 'You talk too much, marshal,' he said contemptuously. 'This town thinks Sorensen's a trouble-maker. If he kept his big trap shut we'd all be able to set up in nice farms on land that's wasted on these hyar redskins.'

There was a growl of approval from the men all around him. Careless saw the light of greed in their eyes.

'Some of us decided we'd put the Sorensens across the border into Texas. They wasn't hurt none, an' we never even swore in front of the lady.'

The smile switched from his face suddenly.

'Then this big ape rides up an' draws a gun on us.' Cunning showed in his eyes. 'He'd got a big mob of Injuns to support him, an' we had to pull out.'

Marshal Pete M'Clelland spoke harshly. 'Next

time you do a thing like that, Shep Dewey, I'll fix a gaol somewhere an' clap you in as the first client.' He got good and mad again. 'I'm warnin' you, all of you, that while I'm marshal I'm gonna see that justice is done. Remember that, an' don't start takin' the law into your own hands.'

He looked at the big *hombre* who seemed half asleep as he slouched in his saddle. His voice sounded gruff. 'Reckon I'm grateful to you for stoppin' these galoots, O'Connor. You did right.' But Careless wasn't deceived. He knew that Pete M'Clelland was saying 'Thank you' for stepping in to protect Pru Sorensen and bring her back to Stampede.

He nodded and then said drily, 'This talk don't get us nowhere. These Injuns want me to speak for 'em, but you don't let a guy say what's on his mind. They complain that land-grabbers have strung a fence right across Cutthroat Gap an' are marking out places for farms. That fence cuts the Kiowa huntin' grounds in two, an' you know what'll happen. Apart from losin' more an' more ground all the time to land-grabbin' farmers, that fence'll just stop the natural movement of game. There'll come a time when there won't be any game this side o' the Wichitas, because buffalo an' deer won't stay so near to settlements. It'll get eaten if it does,' he ended drily.

'Let the Kiowas go west, then, an' follow the game,' growled one of the group round Shep Dewey.

'Nope, they're not gonna be shoved around like that. A promise was made to them, that if they buried the hatchet these lands around the Wichitas would be theirs for all time. I reckon that's how it's goin' to be. I aim to fight for the Kiowas, an' first thing, I'm gonna tear down that fence in Cutthroat Gap.'

A growling voice sounded alongside him. 'I'm with you there, O'Connor. These Injuns have right on their side.'

It was Justin Foraiger. O'Connor was surprised, but concealed it and said, 'Pardner, I'm right glad to hear you say that.'

Then Pete M'Clelland said, 'There's none of you will do any fence-bustin'. That's my job.'

Instantly Careless shot at him, 'You aim to tear that fence down – an' keep it down?'

'If it's there, like these Injuns say.'

An angry growl went up from the white men, seemingly from all except Justin Foraiger. There was a sudden threatening movement, as if they would try to stop the marshal. The Stampede citizens began to crowd forward, their guns lifting. Careless didn't turn, but he heard a cry from among the Indians.

Careless instantly started to turn, recognizing that Foraiger and M'Clelland had this crowd in hand between them. He heard a startled man shout, 'Look out, here's the Injuns!'

He saw a few – only a few – of the Kiowas riding towards them, lying almost flat across their horses' necks. One was Black Crow, a Crazy Dog who should have been policing the younger braves, but instead was leading them on to madness.

The other Indians were being kept back by their chief and his loyal Crazy Dogs, but Black Crow had started his charge, thinking to wipe out the group of citizens on the prairie before they could do much damage with their weapons, and then retreat at headlong pace before the Stampede people could retaliate with their rifles.

Instantly, O'Connor wheeled his mount and went racing to meet the Indians. They saw Black Crow lift himself erect and, riding without hands, string an arrow into his short bow and let fly at the Texan. But O'Connor had shifted his position and wasn't a target now. He was riding Indian fashion, running his horse across the front of the advancing Indians, hanging on to the neck of his stallion, one foot hooked up around his saddle horn, so that no part of his body showed as a target for the bitter, hating Black Crow.

It was all done in a matter of seconds. They saw that big, capable Texan swerve his horse right at the last moment when it looked as though the stallion would collide with Black Crow's pony. They saw a startled Indian swept clean out of his saddle by a powerful right arm as Careless hurtled past the pony – almost they heard the thud as the two bodies smacked hard earth together.

The rest of the braves who had followed Black Crow, startled at the unexpected attack, pulled out in a circle, probably only then realizing that the rest of their comrades were being held back by the soldier warriors, the Crazy Dogs; and rather aimlessly they rode back to join their fellows.

Big Careless hoisted himself to his feet. Then he hoisted Black Crow on to his. He grabbed the Indian with his huge hand round the back of his neck and propelled him across towards the rest of the Kiowas. Fighting Bear and some warriors rode up to meet him.

'Get this trouble-maker out of the district,' Careless ordered. He didn't seem to have any fear of the Indians, though he was alone among them. 'He's a Crazy Dog, all right.'

At that moment Black Crow seemed to recover his wits and strength and with a convulsive movement dragged himself free of Careless' grip. His face, contorted with pain and hatred, turned on the white man, and then he broke away and ran towards his horse. Other Indians brought Careless his mount.

Fighting Bear looked straight at the Texan. 'O-Kon-Or saved many Indians from being killed then,' he said simply. 'Black Crow is a mad man and would lead his young braves to disaster. O-Kon-Or humbled him. O-Kon-Or must watch out. Black Crow heap bad enemy. Him try to kill O-Kon-Or now.'

Careless climbed into his saddle. 'O-Kon-Or can watch out for hissel',' he retorted. Then he told the chief, 'About that fence, Fightin' Bear. Leave it to the marshal o' Stampede County. I reckon he's a good fellar, an' he's promised to drag down that fence if he finds one across the gap. If he don't do as he says, I'll tear up that fence with my own bare hands,' he promised. 'Now take your men back to your village, chief. These *hombres* back in the town are just spoilin' for a fight – don't give 'em an excuse!'

Fighting Bear inclined his proud head. 'That is good advice.'

Then he circled round Careless' mighty stallion and called to his men and led them back on to the trail that led into the hills.

Careless rode back to where a tense group of white men had been awaiting the outcome of his parley with the redskins.

M'Clelland was more friendly. 'That took some doin',' he said. Then drily, 'You're kinda tough on the people you call friends, O'Connor.'

'Some of 'em.' Careless' grey eyes swept that little party, alone now on the dusty prairie. 'I'd be just as tough on white men that went loco like Black Crow just then. I don't hold with trouble-makers, no matter the colour of their skin.'

It was a pretty pointed hint, and Shep Dewey and his fellow rannies knew it was directed towards them.

The party began to walk back into the town.

Careless rode warily, though he seemed casual enough up there on his big horse.

The street was thronged with men, and they were all talking and calling out and wanting to know what had been happening out there on the plain.

'The heck, I was agen goin' out to parley with them Injuns,' Careless heard someone say nastily. 'There's enough men in Stampede to drive the varmints clear across to Californi' if need be.'

A roar greeted the remark. M'Clelland lifted his hand. When they were quiet, he called: 'But what if the Comanche, Crows, Blackfeet an' Shoshoni figger on joinin' in? They're friends o' the Kiowas, an' they're a powerful bunch o' Injuns.' His voice rose, and he shouted: 'I figger they'd all take the war trail, an' then we'd have a big Injun war on our hands. Don't be such danged fools! Keep your fingers off the triggers o' your guns when you see an Injun, an' then we won't have trouble.'

Justin Foraiger added a postscript. 'Ef you don't,' his powerful voice growled, 'I'll shoot them danged fingers off myself!'

Careless saw a board on which someone had burnt a sign with a branding iron – 'Sorensen, Printer.' He got down from his horse and hitched it to a rail in front of the clap-board building.

The front door behind the fly screen was locked, and Careless had to go round to the yard at the back to find the Sorensens. The wagon was backed up to the rear door, and the girl and her father were transporting cases of type and stacks of paper back to their original position in the workshop.

Pru called: 'Friend, you help dad tote this stuff into the print shop, and I'll rustle some coffee and eats.'

Careless said: 'Now that's the kind o' it talk I like to hear. The stuff's as good as in.'

He hefted a big package of paper and took it inside. Two trips later he suddenly said to the old man: 'Pop, you haven't said a word since Pru left us. What's on your mind, old timer?'

Old man Sorensen sighed. Then he looked O'Connor straight in the eyes, and said: 'I figger we're licked. It's no good comin' back to Stampede after all.' He fished into his pocket. 'Didn't you see these tacked to every door down the main street?'

He pulled out a square of paper and handed it to the big Texan. Careless saw crude pencil lettering on the notice.

'Any man seen reading the *Stampede Citizen* will be shot on sight.' It was signed, 'The Oklahoma Farmers' Union.'

Careless said admiringly: 'Now that's the queerest Farmers' Union I've ever heard tell of. Reckon it's another name for the land-grabbers, don't you?'

Careless sat down on the back porch and shoved his hat from off his sweating forehead. His brown face wrinkled in thought. Then, so unexpectedly mildly, he said: 'Dad, you go an' print that paper. I'll figger out a way of sellin' it.'

The old man sighed. 'OK, I don't mind. But you're gonna start a whole lot o' trouble.'

Careless rose. 'I sure am,' he announced calmly. 'I'm aimin' to walk down this main street with the first copy an' let everyone see it's got one reader, anyway!'

4

WHAT CARELESS FORGOT

Pru's eyes were unnaturally bright as, a day later, they looked at the worn soles of those big boots. Her soft lip was trembling, and her cheeks were flushed. She looked pretty – prettier than usual – though she probably didn't feel pretty right then. Careless exclaimed: 'You seem kinda het up, Pru.'

'Het up!' She was so indignant, she nearly stammered. 'You should be het up, not me!' There was a sob in her voice. 'Careless, you big egg, drop this idea, won't you? Please, for my sake?'

O'Connor dragged his mighty limbs off the table top and dropped them on to the board floor. He shook his head obstinately.

'Not for your sake, nor for anyones,' he retorted firmly.

Careless rose and went across to where old man Sorensen was standing, apron round his middle, that first damp copy of the *Citizen* in his ink-stained fingers. He took the paper from the old man's hands and looked at it. Approval came to his big, brown face.

'You sure gave 'em some mighty hard knocks,' Careless said, reading.

'That was Pru,' the old man said, blinking up at the Texan. 'I tell her what's in my mind, an' she kinda puts the words together.' He waited for a while, until the bigger man had finished reading the small sheet, then he said: 'Look, Careless, I figger you didn't oughta stick your neck out like this. Goldarn it, you read that notice; they'll be waitin' for you!'

Pru crossed to the cobwebby window of the print shop. She went back, troubled, and told them what she had seen. 'They've heard you working the press, dad, and they're out there, waiting for the fun to begin.'

Careless didn't seem to be listening. Admiringly he said: 'You sure pack a hard punch in that pen o' yourn, Pru. The things you had to say agen them land-grabbers—'

'Didn't you hear me?' demanded the girl, furious with him. 'They're out there; just waiting for you to show up reading a paper.'

Careless glanced at the last paragraph as if still not hearing her. His face was grim and thoughtful. 'An' you did what I told you – you wrote that the killin' of Indian Agent Joe Ponder could be laid at the door of the big fellar back of all this land-grabbin' organization. That was good work, Pru.

That'll bring the big fellar out into the open if anythin' does.'

Pru took him by the arms and shook him. Or she tried to shake him, but it seemed like trying to rock a church steeple, he was so solid.

'Oh, Careless, please listen! Please don't go through with this,' she pleaded. 'They'll – they'll kill you!' She gulped through her tears. 'And I like you so much. Won't you wait at least until Pete M'Clelland comes back from the Wichitas?'

In mild surprise, he asked: 'Now, why would I want Pete M'Clelland alongside me? All I'm goin' to do is walk down that street readin' the *Citizen*. I want to show the town that a fellar can read any paper he wants, even the *Citizen*.'

His tone changed. Almost peremptorily he demanded of old David Sorensen: 'Tell me again the people you reckon to be ringleaders behind this land-grabbin'. There's Clay Colbert, who runs a freight line to the Mississippi—'

Sorensen went through the list of bad men who were capable of anything so long as there was money back of it.

Frank Waite, whose general store stood to profit by a settlement on Wichita land. Rube Seoll, who ran the livery stable and was reckless enough for any enterprise. Dapper Lew Tullet, who ran the hash-house and was a little, strutting man who wanted to be a big shot. And a lot of other greedy, conscienceless men.

When he'd finished, Careless said: 'That's a lot –

a whole lot, pop. But it don't cover every citizen here in Stampede. I figger we'd find plenty of supporters if only we knew them an' could talk to them.'

'That's why you want me to keep on publishin' the *Citizen*?' Sorensen was shrewd. 'That's why you're gonna risk your life right now to make sure this paper gets a circulation?'

Pru shook her head slowly, lines of worry on her pretty face. 'If you're thinking of just giving the paper away, of throwing it around—' She stopped.

He said gently: 'Go on, Pru. Finish what you're wantin' to say. You were tryin' to tell me—'

'That we can't afford to give the paper away.' Pru faced him courageously. Careless hitched up those disgraceful, faded old jeans that anyone else would have discarded long ago. But they were comfortable, and he wasn't bothered about appearances.

They heard him drawl: 'You don't worry 'bout revenoo, Pru. You've got yourself a new circulation an' advertisement manager. There won't be many free readers o' your paper. Now I'm goin' out to let Stampede see there's a new edition o' the *Citizen* waitin' to be read.'

They watched him go down the two worn steps on to the dusty, rutty, unpaved main street.

Deliberately the big fellow went walking up the street, challenging the entire town as he did so. For fluttering in his left hand, for all to see, was that first new copy of the *Citizen*.

On the verandas men set down their chairs on to their four legs. Then they rose and seemingly without hurry began to move indoors.

Some of the men were getting under cover before the lead began to fly, he knew, but he also knew that others were going indoors to spread the news that here was one man openly defying the edict of the Oklahoma Farmers' Union ... the land-grabbers.

It was miraculous how swiftly that street became deserted save for big Careless O'Connor. But without looking he knew that just as many people had their eyes on him – he knew that round the corner of every door and window men watched him.

Then he heard a door slam behind him. He wheeled swiftly. Pru was running down the street towards him, her hair streaming back from her face so that he saw the anxiety on it.

He shouted, 'Get back!' but she came running up to him. He jumped swiftly forward, catching the girl by her shoulders in a grip that made her wince. When she looked up she saw anger in those grey eyes. 'Go back!' he repeated. 'You might get hurt.'

Pru exclaimed: 'I won't let you risk your life alone. I'm going to stand by your side. They – they won't shoot at you for fear of hitting me.'

'Darn it!' exclaimed the big fellow wrathfully. 'I don't want to hide behind a woman's skirts!'

Only then did she really quite understand that she had upset his plans, that he actually wanted someone to take a pot at him. Then before she knew what was happening, she found herself being hurled across a board sidewalk into an open doorway. As she fell she realized that the big fellow was falling, too.

She caught a glimpse of him, his big body twisting as he hit earth like a great cat. A Colt was out in his right hand; it was firing before he hit the ground. Then dust spanged up near Careless' feet, and she heard the ragged roar of a revolver that had been fired inside a building.

Careless hadn't lost his grip on that copy of the *Citizen*, but she saw him crabbing sideways, firing up at a second storey window as he did so. She heard a cry of pain, and then a revolver fell from a suddenly shattered window and dropped amid tinkling glass, first on top of a sloping veranda roof, then into the dust of the main street.

She sat up. She was in time to catch a glimpse of a pain-contorted face reeling away from an upstairs window at the Drygulch.

She gasped. Careless had rolled on to his feet and was plunging towards the batwing doors of the saloon. She saw a mighty boot lift and kick the saloon doors open, and then he was lost to sight. She sat there waiting for the shooting to begin. She didn't have to wait a long time.

Men reeled away from the slamming batwings as Careless came jumping through the doorway. They hadn't been expecting this swift intrusion, and O'Connor had the drop on them.

Probably a couple of dozen men were in there

drinking even so early in the evening. They were cow-wranglers, in from the back ranges, farmhands, and a few farmers, the inevitable hopeful prospector, and a few drifters who had entered town because of the rumour that Kiowa lands were to be had for the taking.

There wasn't a man there with his gun out, though, and when they saw the Colt in Careless' big fist there wasn't a man who thought of going for his revolver.

Careless got his back to the wall and began to walk sidelong against it. When he came to a window he ducked and passed beneath it – he wasn't inviting any bullet in the back from any of the buildings opposite. His gun never wavered from the drinkers in the Drygulch, and they, for their part, never took their eyes off that blued barrel, never moved a muscle as they stood like frozen statues and watched the big fellow walk straight down to that narrow, steep flight of wooden steps alongside the bar.

Careless looked up the stairs. Someone came out of a doorway above, and he heard a groan of pain. Then out of his eye-corner he caught a swift movement. He dropped on one knee and fired – once.

The barman had started to pitch a heavy glass at him. The bullet shattered the glass in the barman's hand, and he pulled it down to his side as if it had been stung. But only the glass had suffered, not his hand.

Careless looked at the fat, sagging-chinned barman, and his head shook sorrowfully. He didn't say anything, however, and a mightily relieved barman saw the long-legged Texan suddenly go up the stairway.

At once everyone in the bar relaxed. Glasses crashed down on to table tops. Men shouted. The barman was calling throatily: 'He cain't get down! There ain't no other way outa the building, 'cept down them stairs!'

Careless found himself on a bare landing. Three doors led off from it, no doubt the private quarters of the owner of the Drygulch, Bert Hobson.

He saw a man leaning with his back to the wooden wall of the passage, gripping his wrist as if his hand was in pain. He was a tall, thin man, dressed much like a Mississippi gambler.

Careless squinted down the barrel of his six-shooter. It would be empty now, he remembered, but he didn't think anyone else would know that.

Careless covered the man. This would be Hobson, he thought. It had been his guess from the beginning that it was Hobson who had opened fire upon him; for clearly upstairs rooms would be private quarters, and these were over the Drygulch.

Now, gently, Careless said to the man: 'That wasn't kinda sociable, Hobson, firin' on me down in the street.'

Hobson snarled: 'You was warned! You ast for

trouble, walkin' the main street with a paper in your hand!'

'But you got the trouble instead,' Careless pointed out. He heard men crowding to the bottom of the stairway, and knew he was cornered. His empty gun waved. 'Your pardners are kinda worried on your account, Hobson. Mebbe you'd better go down an' reassure them.'

At the top of the steps Hobson looked first at that unwavering gun and then into the big, flat, battered face above it.

His hoarse voice whispered: 'What're you gonna do with me? Shoot me in the back?'

Careless came slowly up to him, and Hobson began to retreat fearfully down the stairs, his back to the wall. The big *hombre* never said anything. Instead, he pushed forward the copy of the *Citizen*. Hobson released his injured wrist to grab the proferred paper.

Down below they saw his tight, black trouser legs come into view. Their guns covered him.

Careless walked down the stairs, shoving the craven Hobson before him. The tense, armed men below saw the saloon keeper come sidling down the stairs, saw the big *hombre* from Texas with his gun pointing right between those puffed up little eyes.

They parted to let the pair through. Big O'Connor walked forward as if the bar-room was empty. He prodded Hobson right up against the long, unpainted bar, and then said: 'I figger you c'n read, Hobson?'

The saloon proprietor tried to cover his cowardice in front of his followers and friends. 'Sure I c'n read,' he said thickly.

Careless nodded to the paper. 'Then read a bit o' that – aloud!' he ordered.

Hobson looked at that gun and complied, but his face was venomous. Haltingly he read out:

' "STOP THE LAND GRAB!" ' He cleared his throat. " 'Rogues lead and fools follow," ' he read. ' "Greedy men covet the land that was given in solemn pledge to the Kiowas, and reckless of the consequences they are moving in and fencing it off as their own.

' "So far the Kiowas have shown admirable restraint, even though at least one of their number has been killed in minor disturbances. But how long will this last? How long will it be before they paint their faces and put on their war bonnets and beat the drums of war?

' "And will they be alone if they do take to the war trails, or will their brothers of the Crow, Comanche, Blackfoot and other tribes keep out of the fighting if it starts between white man and red?

' "You risk all you possess and your lives, too, by promoting this state of war. Come to your senses, citizens of Stampede, and don't go running with the wild men. Instead, stand up against the land-grabbers. Their selfish plans are against your better interests." '

Careless reached out and took the paper from Hobson's hand. 'That'll be enough,' he said. His grey, narrowed eyes didn't miss a reaction on those tough faces about him. Some remained unchangingly hard, but on one or two came a flicker of doubt as Hobson's hoarse voice read out the denunciation against the land-grabbers.

Careless said admiringly: 'You're a mighty fine reader, Mister Hobson. Now I figger an edi-cated man like you would like to be a subscriber to a paper like the *Stampede Citizen*. I reckon ten dollars'd cover a year's supply,' he said easily.

The revolver came forward another vicious eighth of an inch. Hobson swallowed hard, then said: 'Louie, you give this big—' He looked into grim, grey eyes, and the insult died. 'Give this gentleman ten dollars.'

The crowd gasped as the barman handed a ten-dollar bill across the liquor-soaked counter. Then it was their turn. Careless surveyed them, and they met his grim-humoured eyes with lowering looks.

He said gently, 'I figger there's other fellars here that can read. Now maybe Louie could take orders an' go across an' buy copies for you right away.'

Someone called: 'If Bert Hobson's gonna read the *Citizen*, I figger I can. Get me a paper, Louie.'

'Me, too!' chorused other eager voices. The truth was, most of the men there wanted to read the paper, only they hadn't dared show their eagerness before because of that ban put upon the *Citizen* by the Oklahoma Farmers' Union.

A doubtful Louie dried his hands on a sacking

apron, then went out. He was back in a few minutes with a bundle of *Citizens*. Sourly he distributed them, collecting a quarter for each copy. 'I had to pay for 'em,' he growled. 'That old fellar wouldn't give credit.'

Careless was satisfied. He even said a nice thank you to Hobson and those men inside that saloon. Then he reached out and collected a revolver from a nearby rannie who was using both hands to hold up a *Citizen*. The cow-wrangler looked surprised.

'What d'you want my gun for?' he demanded. 'What's wrong with that 'un?' He looked at O'Connor's. Careless was stuffing his own revolver into his belt.

An astonished audience heard that lazy, drawling Texan voice say: 'My gun's kinda empty. I didn't get around to re-loadin', I guess.'

He was backing towards the door. That revolver in his hand was certainly loaded this time, they knew.

There was a gasp, then an oath, and someone exclaimed in a strangled voice 'Goldarn it, we've been had for greenhorns! He stood us all back with an empty gun!'

Realization of the way they had been bluffed came to them with those words. Then the cow-wrangler who had just lost his gun began to laugh. Two or three others joined in. Careless' audacity had won him friends.

A foot stabbed up like lightning. A pointed shoe crashed into his gun hand. The Colt flew up and almost hit the low ceiling, and then clattered to the floor a few yards away.

Careless had forgotten something – that Bert Hobson was a man who fought with his feet. And now he was unarmed and helpless, facing a crowd of men he had humbled.

Hobson was screaming, 'Shoot him down, the doggoned renegade!' Guns lifted to fire point-blank at the big cowboy.

5

GHOST OF THE TRAIL

They still talk about that fight in the Drygulch Saloon. If it had gone on five minutes longer, spectators swore that the place would have come apart at the corners.

Careless would have been shot to pieces but for an unexpected intervention. That bow-legged, sheepskin-chapped cow-wrangler who had just lost his gun, snatched up a table and hurled it broadside against the men with the guns.

He shouted: 'Fair play! Give the big lug a chance, can't you?'

Two or three other men jumped across to the rannie's side, their guns coming out and pointing. In one glimpse Careless realized that every cow-puncher in the room had suddenly become a supporter of his. He couldn't have chosen better allies.

They stood back against a wall, their guns threatening Hobson's friends and supporters. That stopped the gun-play.

Careless saw the rush coming. Saw angry, suffused faces, savage, gleaming eyes – saw range-hardened fists swinging.

He picked Hobson up, gripped by the throat and the belt. For one second they saw the Texan giant with that struggling, yelling saloon proprietor held high above his head. Then he tossed the man right on to the leaders of the rush.

They were still falling towards the dirty floorboards of that flimsy, clapboard saloon, when Careless came leaping over their struggling bodies, his fists stabbing towards the men who had been following behind the leaders.

Careless fought like a mighty fury. His great swinging fists swung and chopped down two men as if they had been smacked with a piledriver. Then he picked up a runt of a bar-fly and sent him hurtling on to a cowering Louie, trying to protect his glasses behind the bar.

But three or four men came leaping in, trying to smother the mighty Texan by clinging to him. One gasped hoarsely: 'Get him to the ground! Pull him down!'

They tried to get the big man down, but it was harder than wrestling with a wild prairie steer. His fists kept stabbing in, smashing into their ribs and knocking the wind out of them. Even when he just pushed out, he knocked them from him like a man brushing away winter-numbed flies.

But more were jumping on to him. As fast as he knocked them away others jumped him. Seven or eight men were clinging to him at any one time.

The weight began to take its toll. The giant gave once or twice at the knees, but each time recovered and fought back ferociously. The spectators cheered themselves hoarse at the doors and windows. One man against many – but what a fight!

A red fury seemed to grip the Texan at that thought. By gosh, he decided, he wasn't going to let himself be bested by a mean, ornery runt like Bert Hobson!

Those delighted spectators saw that mighty giant, men clinging all over him, deliberately run backwards, carrying the weight of men with him. There was a crash that shook the entire building as half a ton of struggling men thudded against the clapboard wall. Then they saw Careless reel forward, away from the wall, his arms now fastened round the bodies of the men in front of him.

They saw men fall away from the giant – those men who had been clinging behind him in the struggle. They were stunned or knocked uncon-scious by that tremendous impact.

Then those spectators really let themselves go in a mighty cheer. Careless had rampaged forward, holding on to his opponents. There was another mighty crash as the human battering ram hurtled against the far wooden wall.

Careless seemed to bounce back, big though he

was. And now more of his opponents were falling to the ground. The few who were still left in the fight pulled out then. This giant from Texas was a killer. Numbers didn't seem anything to him.

Careless pulled himself away, walking towards the door. As he passed the cow-wranglers, he called: 'Thanks, pardners!'

The one in the woolly chaps said: 'It was a pleasure. Any time you're figgerin' on havin' a scrap, call me an' my pards. We sure like a li'l excitement occasionally.'

Only smouldering-eyed Bert Hobson was in the way. Big Careless lifted a mighty hand as if to smack out at him. Hobson turned tail and fled. There was a roar of laughter from the spectators at the window. Careless had a feeling he had made many more friends that late afternoon.

At the door Careless paused, his chest heaving as he laboured to get back the breath lost in that titanic struggle. He tossed the loaded revolver back to its owner, then went out on to the crowded main street unarmed.

They parted to let him go through, and though most were against him, still running with the land-grabbers, they cheered him all the way down to the print shop. The West liked a man who could fight like that.

Pru came running across to meet him.

Careless said soothingly: 'You didn't ought to have worried, Pru. Fellars like them don't know how to fight. Now, if they'd been Texans—'

He put his arm round her to console her, and he found that it felt nice. She had soft, warm shoulders, and it did a fellow a lot of good to feel her nestling in at his side. He decided he would try putting his arm round her more often.

She made him sit down on a box in the print shop, while she fetched a cloth and some water to bathe his bruised face. Old man Sorensen detached himself from his machine, a smile on his thin, peaked face.

'You sure are a circulation manager,' he chuckled. 'Blest if I know what you did, but right after you'd gone Louie the barman from the Drygulch came in an' bought an armful o' papers.' He chuckled even more. 'He gave me ten dollars for a subscription from his boss, too. Now, how did you make that mean-eyed gamblerman Hobson go agen them Oklahoma Farmers? Did you – fight a bit?'

Pru came in and got busy on that big, battered face.

Careless admitted: 'Wal, there was a bit.'

The old man looked at the Texas giant on that box, and said admiringly: 'I figger a fellar like you could mebbe handle any two galoots in town. In fact, I reckon I'd put my money on you agen even a couple of Clay Colbert's freight totin' buckaroos – an' they're the toughest eggs you'll find in all the county.'

Pru said: 'You won't find any takers in this town, dad. Not after they saw what Careless did to the

Drygulch boys.' But she didn't explain.

Then the old man told how right after Louie's purchases a whole queue of Stampede citizens had suddenly shown up, all wanting to buy the *Citizen.*

'Goldarn it!' he chuckled. 'They cleared me out as fast as I could run the paper off. Now I'd better keep on running so as to supply the rest o' the county tomorrow.'

He took out his watch and frowned.

Careless called abruptly: 'What's worryin' you, pop?'

The printer finished off another sheet, then turned, blinking uncertainly, his thin old face corrugated in a frown.

'M'Clelland. Before he rode out with his dep'ty, he told me to expect him back before sundown today. He said: 'If I don't show up, you'd better come lookin' for me'. Wal, he ain't showed up.'

Then his eyes lifted towards that big *hombre,* dwarfing the box he sat on.

'I reckon you're the man to take over from here,' he said simply. 'I figger you'd find him if anyone could.'

Just then a short man in a crude, tarred slicker came in and asked for a paper. He looked like a teamster, and he was as broad as he was long. They waited until he had gone out, and then Careless asked: 'You figger he's run into trouble?'

'M'Clelland told me he was expecting it. He was ridin' through Injun territory, an' some Injuns are mean after the killin' of a few Kiowas by land-grabbers recently. They shoved some Injuns off a valley by Cool Stream,' he explained. 'It was right on the border o' Kiowa territory, an' they got a crooked lawyer to argue that it wasn't included in the treaty with the Kiowas. Some Injuns got killed.'

'I know,' said Careless softly. 'An Injun woman came all the way down to Texas to tell me about it.'

For one of these murdered Indians was his old friend and blood brother, Man-with-Thumb.

He rose. Sorensen was saying: 'I figger he'd find trouble, anyway, if he found that fence. From white men this time. M'Clelland's a good law officer, an' he wouldn't stand for land-grabbin'. He's got guts, an' I reckon he'd straightway order 'em to tear down their fences an' clear out o' the country. I figger he might even try to back up his argument with his guns. Now we've got to figger who's kept M'Clelland inside the Kiowa reserve – an' what's happened to him.'

Careless heard the quick intake of breath, and when he glanced at Pru he saw her gripping her hands hard against her breast. He thought: 'She's got a soft place in her heart for that M'Clelland fellar. She only knows it, though, when it seems he's in trouble.'

'You're going to look for Mack?' Pru asked quickly, hopefully.

'Sure! I reckon I've got a circulation for this edition, an' you won't need me for a day or two. So I'm ridin' out of town right away tonight.'

He was going out to his horse, when he caught a

movement in the near darkness along the side-walk. For a second he had a glimpse of a very short, very broad man running along the street.

His brow furrowed. 'That guy took a long time to move away from the door,' Careless thought. 'Now, was he listenin'?'

He went round to where his horse was stabled with Sorenson's. Within minutes he had saddled up and was ready to ride.

There wasn't much light along the main street, for just at the moment the moon hadn't risen, and the stars weren't strong enough as sources of illu-mination. The only effective light came from the new-lit oil lamps inside the saloons and shops and gambling dens.

Careless rode with his head down, peering side-ways against the lights. He caught the red glow of a cigarette end from the shadows to his right. Then he saw that someone else was smoking right opposite from the first man. He drew rein.

Something moved in the darkness between the two smokers. He saw shapes . . . men. They were coming slowly forward to meet him. Then they stepped right into the rays of oil-light from one of the windows. He saw half a dozen men. They were crudely dressed – dressed in a way that wasn't usual even among casual Westerners.

They all looked broad of shoulder. It gave Careless a clue. That broad-shouldered teamster man who had been last in for a newspaper – these men were somehow like him.

76

Careless saw the thick sticks and the long-lashed whips in the men's hands. Saw the hard, glinting lights in their eyes, and knew they had been waiting for him.

He spurred his horse and brought it wheeling round in a flurry of small stones that rattled against the clapboard buildings. He wasn't going to get himself within range of those long teamsters' whips. They could do clever things with whips, these teamsters. They could, for instance, catch a man around the wrist and jerk him from his horse. And Careless didn't think it would be healthy to be dragged off his horse at the feet of those other men with the truncheon-like sticks.

He went back almost as far as the print shop, and then spurred his horse down a side street.

Men were strung in a line across the end of it. Broad-shouldered men – men with savage, angry eyes, and sticks and teamsters' whips in their hands. This time he realized that some carried rifles, too.

He got out of that alley quicker than he had gone into it. When he reached the main street again, he saw that the mob he had first run into were marching steadily down towards him, closing in on him.

He wheeled left and pounded down towards the far end of the main street. Back of him the men were shouting.

Bang ahead he saw plenty of light. Some of it illuminated a loading stage on which was painted in huge letters. 'Clay Colbert, Freight Hauler'. Strung across the road from the loading stage was another mob of men.

He was trapped, and his enemies were closing in on him. From a distance he heard a voice call out: 'You big ox, we warned you not to have anythin' to do with that blamed *Citizen* paper! Now you're goin' to suffer!'

The main street seemed alive with running teamsters now. They were shouting exultantly, seeing the big man on the big black stallion apparently helpless before them.

Careless didn't even bother to draw his gun. He turned the head of his horse and sent it mounting the wooden steps of a nearby building. It had batswing doors, and O'Connor guessed from that that it was either a gambling parlour or a saloon.

It was a gambling parlour. The players looked up in astonishment as Careless came ducking in through the broad doorway on his mighty horse. Careless saw the usual roulette and faro tables, and the many poker games, at the tables down the wall. He also saw a back way out, but the door was closed. He spurred his horse forward, and men shouted and fell back as tables crashed over. The thunder of hoofs upon the raised wooden flooring was tremendous. It brought a man running in from a sideroom. He grabbed a sawn-off shotgun.

Careless never even looked at the players. He was too occupied in keeping his head clear of the swinging oil lamps. When he was right across the room, he leaned down from his saddle and tried to open the back door. It was locked, however, and the key wasn't in the lock. The door didn't look too strong.

Careless promptly wheeled his mount, kicked, and shouted – and the well-trained horse promptly brought back its hind legs in a mighty kick that almost tore the door from its hinges. Careless shouted again and again. The uproar was tremendous.

The stallion's hind legs smashed the door right off its hinges. Careless saw darkness outside, and began to turn his horse. The man with the shotgun shoved the stumpy barrel right into his face and called: 'I don't allow violence in my premises, mister!'

Careless drew rein. He looked beyond the gun at the owner.

Justin Foraiger.

Careless remembered then what he had learned about Foraiger since coming to Stampede. Foraiger was said to run the straightest gambling house in the West.

Foraiger's cold voice broke in on his thoughts: 'Guess it ain't usual for a man to come a-ridin' into a room on a hoss. An' bustin' a door down's kinda unfriendly. Guess you're gonna pay for this damage afore you ride out, mister!'

The gun jerked. Careless looked beyond the crowding gamblers to where the batswings still teetered on their hinges.

It was galling, with the way of escape gaping right behind him, but that ugly shotgun was holding him there – holding him to receive the assault of his enemies outside.

Then Careless' eyes dropped a fraction, He saw a familiar face.

Instantly his mind was made up. Careless called to the cowboy: 'Pardner, I sure need help right now. I've got to fight my way out of town. You gonna join in the ruckus?'

That woolly-chapped cow-nurse hitched himself round the middle, squirted tobacco juice deftly into a cuspidor, and said: 'Sure am, pardner.' And in that same instant his Colt came out in a lightning draw that prodded Justin Foraiger in the middle of the back.

At once someone yelled: 'Yippee!' The cowpuncher had his friends with him. Four or five men in high-heeled riding boots went stomping awkwardly through a side door. Careless heard a horse blow and then the creaking of saddle leather. The punchers had gone for their horses.

The bow-legged puncher grinned. 'Drop your gun, Just. You don't need it no more, I reckon.'

His gun pressed a little harder. Justin Foraiger's shotgun slowly lowered. His face turned on the puncher, and it was cold enough to freeze sea-water.

Men were pounding towards the batswings. Any moment now they would be inside the gambling joint.

Careless' gun roared, and a lamp went out. The woolly-chapped cowpuncher grabbed for a stirrup as the stallion plunged into the blackness. Careless heard him shout: 'We'll be back to pay you for the damage, Just.' Then they were in the blackness of the night.

Some guns blatted red from behind them. Then forms came cannoning from a yard. Careless felt the grip on his stirrup release, and got an impression of a man mounting a horse that suddenly loomed up. Men were shouting all around him.

Careless bellowed: 'Shut up, darn yer, an' follow me!'

For he had seen men crossing behind the gambling saloon. Justin Foraiger had held him up just long enough for his enemies to move round to cover the back way.

A rifle suddenly roared right ahead of them. It was fired from between two buildings which threw out the sound and magnified it. Careless kicked hard into his horse, sending it leaping madly towards a dimly-seen alley that gave back on to the main street. As he thundered through, Careless heard pounding hoofs behind him, and knew that his allies were hard upon his heels.

They came crashing on to the main street, and after the darkness of the alley it looked almost as light as day – looked especially light now, because every door was open, letting the lamplight fall on to the street. Men were coming out, wanting to know what the ruckus was all about.

Guns flamed, glass crashed. Careless heard his followers give vent to a mighty 'Yipp – yipp – yippee!' They, at any rate, were enjoying this battle.

They fought their way all down that main street. Every time a gun flashed in the darkness, the punchers' Colts roared back viciously, sending their enemies under cover to escape the fury of a second fusilade.

Then they were through; they were right at the end of the main street, with gunfire coming only from behind them now, and not from all sides and in the front.

They rode for an hour, and then turned off the trail. Halting their blowing horses, they sat for a while and listened. There was no sound of pursuit. Careless called: 'We'll bed down here till daylight. You got blankets an' food?'

'We got everythin',' the woolly-chapped little puncher retorted. It turned out they'd been driving beef from the Staked Plains to the garrison at Fort Smith on the Arkansas River. They'd made their delivery and now were taking it easy back to Texas.

Careless said: 'It was a good break for me, your comin' south at this time o' the year.' There weren't many people in Stampede who would have thrown in their lot with him quite so readily as carefree punchers.

They hobbled their horses and then unsaddled. That seemed safe enough, but they didn't risk lighting a fire, so they ate a cold supper in the dark, and then got into their blankets.

He got their names, before they went off to deep, trouble-free slumber, under that warm, soft Oklahoma sky that made blankets superfluous.

The puncher in the woolly chaps was Bandy Phelan. Another was Crop Johnson. The other three had shorter names – Ed, Two-gun, and Smiler. They seemed a careless, happy-go-lucky bunch of hard-riding, hard-living beef-herders, and Careless thought with satisfaction, before going to sleep, what a stroke of luck it had been, getting their sympathies.

They slept apart from each other, which is the way on the range. For one thing, with all that space around them, there was no need for them to crowd together. And they didn't want warmth, and in case of Indian attack it was an advantage to be spread out.

Careless had put his blankets close to a sweet-smelling juniper bush. He went to sleep instantly – and just as abruptly awoke a couple of hours later.

He lay there, instantly alert, wondering what sound could have wakened him. Around him he heard the deep regular breathing of his new pard-ners. They hadn't been disturbed.

And then he saw it. One by one the stars began to blot out. Something was moving between him and the night sky. Suddenly he felt a warmth assail him, as of the presence of some heated body, and in that same second he realized that something monstrous was standing over him.

6
THE VICTIM!

He had a curious thought: 'If that juniper wasn't scentin' the air, I'd know what this thing is!' For cattlemen like Careless O'Connor could tell most beasts, from a grizzly to a coyote, by their smell.

He didn't lie there thinking, though. Simultaneously with the thought his legs came lashing out of the blanket, and he rolled away from that mighty bulk. Instantly the beast was gone, before his hand could even get his gun out of its holster.

His pards jerked upright into instant wakefulness, hands clawing for guns. They heard a violent crashing as of a heavy body bursting through the undergrowth. Careless, crouching, gun out, heard Bandy call: 'What's that? Everyone all right?'

Careless called back: 'I don't know – don't think any harm was done. I woke, looked up – an' there was some mighty big animal standing over me!'

'A b'ar?' That was Crop Johnson, guessing.

'Nope.' Careless dismissed the idea. 'Our hosses would sure be screamin' blue murder if a b'ar came while they was hobbled.' But they hadn't made a sound. That was curious, mighty curious. Cow ponies were usually as good as watch dogs, where other animals were concerned.

Careless was mightily puzzled. He knew it had been some animal intruder, but he couldn't figure out the species. Neither could his pards. They went to sleep after about half an hour, but this time they left a man on guard.

The men would have liked to have stayed in their blankets till dawn, to see what tracks the curious intruder had left; but Careless had them in the saddle and on their way a good hour before daylight. The moon was up by now, and it was imperative that they made as much ground into the Wichitas as possible before the torrid summer sun made travel in the airless valleys a nightmare.

Three hours after sun-up, they halted for a welcome rest. Their horses especially needed it, for the way had been mostly uphill, and at times very rocky. They dismounted, in a fertile little oasis that pocketed the side of the red sandstone canyon.

Within a few minutes of their resting, Crop Johnson suddenly pointed northwards, away beyond the rim of the canyon. He said briefly: 'Look!'

They saw a puff of white smoke go spiralling gracefully into the blue Oklahoma sky. At an interval later, a second white cloud ascended, to be followed by another and another.

Careless eased his big body into a more comfortable position on the grass. He was tired and wanted a rest and didn't intend to forfeit it, not even for smoke rings in the sky.

All he said, laconically, was: 'Skywritin'. Reckon we've been seen, so we might as well make some cawffee.'

Bandy got a fire going. While they drank, they watched that canyon rim to the north of them. Crop Johnson, who had good eyes, suddenly told them: 'I c'n see Injuns up by that tumblin' tree.'

They saw the tree he meant. It had grown too near to the edge of the canyon, and some of the soil had at last crumbled, throwing the oak almost at right angles to the face of the canyon wall. Somehow, though, its roots clung on. Standing back among the roots they saw the Indians. As they looked, more Indians suddenly appeared and joined their fellows, and then all stood and stared silently down at the half-dozen Texans with their horses below.

The smoke writing started again. Careless knew a little of it, from his travels with his blood brother, Man-with-Thumb. After a time, watching this more distant signal, he was able to say 'That's from Fightin' B'ar. He says we're to be watched, but no harm's to come to us until he an' his Crazy Dogs see what we're up to. He's gonna come fast.'

He was rising. Bandy Phelan jumped at him, with all the strength in his wiry body. Careless felt a hard shoulder ram into his thigh, and it hurt. He went crashing on to his face, caught off his balance, but instantly, cat-like, he started to roll to his feet. His fist lashed out. Bandy stopped it on the side of his head and went out cold. Only then did Careless realize that it was his brother Texan who had jumped him.

Startled, he came lurching to his feet. He saw the other men diving for cover. An arrow zinged into the grass and protruded quivering. Three or four more suddenly smacked into the earth round about where they had been sitting.

Careless thought: 'Somebody ain't takin' any notice of what Chief Fightin' B'ar has told them.' And he knew it would be that Crazy Dog, Black Crow, and his hot-headed young followers.

He shouted: 'Git movin'!' Stooping, he hoisted Bandy Phelan across his broad shoulder and ran zig-zagging towards his horse. High above them they heard a yell from the Indians, and a shower of arrows came hissing down. But the range was long, and shooting was inaccurate in consequence.

Bandy began to stir on Careless' shoulder. The big fellow hoisted him into his saddle. Bandy gripped and held on, though only half-conscious, but Careless knew he would be all right. A Texan only fell out of his saddle when he was completely unconscious – or drunk or dead.

They mounted in a flurry of hoofs, their horses panicking at their frantic haste and wanting to bolt. They shot out on to the canyon floor and started westwards again. After a few minutes Careless pulled his mount down to a walk. The Indians had disappeared from the canyon rim. Perhaps they would be mounting, and beginning to ride parallel to the top of the canyon. It would be rougher going along the top – it always was – and they wouldn't be able to fire over the edge without dismounting, so, all things considered, Careless didn't rate the Indian menace very highly.

Half an hour later he changed his mind. Bandy was all right by now. He had a lump the size of a turkey's egg on his chin, but he bore no malice.

'I thought you'd gone loco!' Careless said. 'Brother, I'm sorry I hit you. But I won't forget that you mebbe saved my skin from bein' punctured that time!'

Bandy saw the danger first. They were trotting along the canyon floor. The canyon wall to their right started to diminish in height. Then they saw that winter rains had eroded one part of it, so that it was a broken mass of sandstone and green, cling-ing bushes.

Bandy called: 'Hey, thar, big fellar! Don't you reckon them Injuns might be comin' down to the canyon bottom that away?' He was thinking that a surefooted Indian pony could probably find a way down that broken canyon wall.

Instantly Careless was alert. He dug heels into his horse and sent the big black trotting forward at increased pace. He took his Sharps repeater out of the saddleboot, too, and thumbed back the safety catch. The eyes of the Texans were all towards that broken canyon wall. Crop Johnson, peering from under his broad-brimmed hat that shaded a sweating face, was first to see the danger again.

He shouted something, and went racing ahead. Then they saw bobbing plumes as men rode down a steep arroyo into the canyon. As they thundered after Crop, they counted those heads – about thirty, they thought. That was quite a big band to run against.

Then they saw disaster ahead. A group of Indians ahead of the main body, suddenly raced their lithe ponies across the flat, scrub-covered canyon bottom. They had lost the race!

Instantly Crop Johnson, still in the lead, began to circle, as if to turn away from the danger. Two-gun and Smiler reined in, dragging their mounts on to their haunches.

Then big Careless O'Connor went jumping his horse forward. They heard the big *hombre* yell: 'Keep a-goin'. Fight your way through. Six ain't many!' And then they heard him shout: 'Don't you shoot to kill unless you have to!'

The mighty black went thundering away towards that group of mounted Indians. Immediately Bandy Phelan followed, and then the rest came spurring behind him. That was the kind of man O'Connor was. When he took the lead, men followed, trusting implicitly to his leadership and fighting ability.

Careless sat back in his saddle, levelled his Sharps, and spanged two quick shots low over the heads of the Indians in their path. More Indians were spilling from the arroyo.

Then Careless swerved his horse, as if about to charge to the left of the group. That altered their aim, and they got in each other's way as their ponies jostled in their frantic efforts to sight the palefaces. Right at the last moment Careless came back to his original course and charged straight at the Indians. The first of the main party from the arroyo came racing in at that moment, hunting spears levelling to the mad charge of those agile ponies.

Careless crashed right into them. His gun was roaring over their heads – but the Indians weren't to know that. It brought them low down on their ponies' necks to save their heads. The other Texans had their six-shooters out and were making a lot of noise. One of them couldn't have been so careful, for an Indian fell from the saddle with a howl of pain.

In a moment they were all mixed up together, Indians and Texans. Careless saw brown bodies, eager, excited, copper-coloured faces. Then his rifle, swung by the barrel, crashed among them, beating a path through their ranks. Tomahawks rose – and were shot out of their owners' hands. Spears flashed, were parried, and then their owners sent hurtling from their saddles as the fighting became hand-to-hand.

He hadn't wanted to injure these Indians, for all they had started the attack on them. But he wasn't going to let his comrades suffer at the hands of Black Crow's young hot-heads.

His Sharps spat fire and he felt the bump on his shoulder. A horse somersaulted and the nearly-naked rider went down under the hoofs of the other horses. Careless drew a bead and fired, and a bare-chested warrior clutched his shoulder and toppled slowly out of his saddle. Then Two-gun came with a run out from the tangled ruckus of ponies, Indians and Texans. His guns were empty, and he came wheeling round to Careless' side, reloading. The sweat was pouring from his young face, and the shirt was black where it stuck to his back.

The Indians from the arroyo were streaming round in a wide circle, brandishing their weapons and screaming their war whoops. Bandy Phelan battered his way out, holding a reeling Crop Johnson in his saddle. Crop had taken a nasty bang on his head, and there was an awful mess of blood down his face. Ed and Smiler were right behind, guarding their injured comrade. Only two of the

Indians were left in their saddles; the rest had been unhorsed.

Careless shouted, 'Keep a'goin' now, pards. We've got to keep ahead o' them varmints, or we sure won't have any hair left to part.'

Crop wiped his eyes clear with his sleeve. Careless saw anxious eyes peering at him. Then Crop shouted, 'Did they take my scalp?'

Careless shouted, 'Nope. Reckon they knocked a few brains out, that's all.' Crop looked reassured and in a moment was riding unaided.

Now it became a running battle down that canyon, but it was no easy fight for the Texans. The trouble was, these Indian ponies were fresh, whereas their own had come a long way that morning.

Those Indian arrows were deadly missiles, too, and in time, when the racing ponies came within range, the winged shafts began to zing perilously close to their ears.

All at once they came out on to an abrupt hillside that shelved from the canyon into a wide plain. Ahead of them, about seven or eight miles, they guessed, they saw a range of hills. A V-cleft in the middle of the range was their destination – Cutthroat Gap.

Bandy Phelan dropped back to Careless' side. 'We can't go down there,' he shouted, waving his hat towards the plain. 'Our hosses are too tired – they'll soon catch up on us on the plain an' head us off.'

Careless had had that thought in mind. Instantly he ordered, 'You go ahead, Bandy. Go to them land-grabbers an' fetch 'em back to help us.' The land-grabbers had no right to be in Kiowa territory, but if they were there they might as well become useful.

Then he shouted to the rest of the men, 'Stop at the end of the canyon. Git down an' hold these redskins back while Bandy rides for help.' The land-grabbers wouldn't know whom they were helping.

Careless and his men came leaping from their saddles right where the canyon widened on to the plain. Here was a tumbled mass of rocks that would provide good cover. They let their horses run on because they hadn't time to tend to them . . .

Careless had a momentary impression of a solitary horse, saddled and bridled, cropping the spare grass on the sloping hillside down which Bandy was thundering.

Then he went streaking for cover as a screaming horde of Indians came pouring round a bend in the canyon. He dived between two rocks. A man was there.

He hadn't time to look at him. His Sharps was leaping to his shoulder, stammering fire at those racing, exultant redskins. Two-gun was roaring away with his Colts; the other men emptied their Henry breech-loaders and then grabbed Colts.

Out of the corner of his eye Careless saw that that the other man was a white man. He was lying on his face. He was very still.

The Indians pulled madly on their reins, bringing their wild little ponies round and fleeing suddenly before those deadly guns.

The Kiowas didn't retreat far, however. And even that retreat was strategical. They saw the Indian braves leap from their mounts and begin to run back towards them. But now they ran.

From cover to cover, one moving to draw the fire, while others came up from a different direction.

Careless thought, 'This is bad – mighty bad. They'll be on to us in no time, creepin' up behind them blamed rocks!'

The rocks that provided shelter for the Texans gave good cover to the advancing Indians.

Careless turned to look at his companion, down behind that big boulder. His comrades heard a sharp exclamation from him. Smiler called, 'You in trouble, Careless, you old war-hoss?'

They heard Careless call, 'Nope. But there's a fellar here, an' he's dead.'

7

AT BAY!

He was a stranger. Careless called out this information, and Ed dropped down from his perch on top of a saddle of fallen sandstone to have a look at the fellow. One look and he said, 'That's Regan. M'Clelland took him along as dep'ty.' He turned the head to examine the wound.

'Don't know how he came by that. Could be Injun or white man.' He was thinking of the land-grabbers. 'There's plenty people with guns around these parts, even a few Injuns.'

Careless screwed round and looked at that other horse, cropping grass again with their own tired mounts away across the prairie. He was thinking, 'He tried to get back through the canyon – mebbe he wanted to get back to Stampede to tell us of the trouble he an' M'Clelland ran into. But that wound told on him.'

Careless got back into position, his Sharps reloaded while he was thinking. He said to Ed,

'There's been enough of this, Ed. Too much killin' altogether in Stampede County. But killin' a man who's representin' the law makes the crime worse. That's somethin' that shouldn't ever be done.'

Ed stared down at the body, then slowly began to climb out on to his perch again. Careless heard him say, 'We'll get the fellars that did this, Careless. I never did like fellars who shot people from behind.'

For that was where the bullet had come that had slain poor Deputy Regan, a man doing his duty as a law officer. Two-gun and Smiler opened fire just then with their rifles. Two-gun always preferred to use Colts, but at this range six-shooters weren't much use. Their firing was slow, because their Henry rifles only fired a round with each loading. All the same, they were accurate with their guns, and a brown body suddenly came twisting out from behind a rock and then lay still in the open.

Two-gun ripped off a swift shot. A foolhardy brave came tumbling from a high point up the canyon wall.

The Kiowas were climbing the broken canyon wall, where it widened out on to the open prairie. They were trying to circumvent them. If the Kiowas got through and came up between them and their distant horses, it meant the end for the Texans.

And by the look of that tumbling Indian, it

seemed that some were already well on their way to surrounding them.

The Kiowas were brilliant at moving behind cover. Occasionally the defenders behind those rocks at the end of the canyon caught a movement – a black forelock lifting momentarily above cover, a plume ducking for shelter, a bronzed limb showing, or even a whole body as an Indian glided like lightning from one boulder to another.

A party of braves stationed themselves in a crack up the wall of the canyon to their right, and began to pour arrows down upon the hard-pressed little party. That made Careless and his men hug cover as if they loved those crumbling red sandstone rocks. It gave the Indians along the broken wall to their left chance to slip past them.

They only knew this when arrows began to ping into their cover from the rear. Careless stood up then and bolted for closer cover.

He shouted, 'We're trapped. Them varmints is between us an' them horses o' our'n!'

Crop Johnson, a rough bandage around his head, yelled back, 'Ef that danged Bandy Phelan don't come soon with help I reckon we'll be goners.'

Indians were slipping by very quickly now, because the Texans could hardly lift their heads for a second without a cloud of arrows coming smashing on to their defences. Careless saw the swift movements and thought, 'Black Crow has got many followers.'

Careless took risks, kneeling up and emptying his magazine before falling into cover and reloading. Probably, more than all the other guns, his Sharps slowed down that encircling movement. Even so he didn't stop it, and there came a moment when they knew they were completely surrounded.

His men began to worm their way back to his side now, as they became increasingly close-beset. After a while they were all huddled in one cleft between two huge rocks, fighting desperately, and yet unable to stay that never-ceasing advance by their enemies.

The trouble was, they were hopelessly outnumbered, with far too many enemies to watch at once. The sun was merciless upon them, too, and they were suffering agonies of thirst . . . and their water-bottles were tantalizingly within sight, on the backs of their horses grazing in the distance.

Every man was wounded by this time. Crop Johnson was having an unlucky day and had stopped a winging arrow in the flesh of his right forearm.

Ed and Smiler both got hit in the shoulder, but it didn't stop their firing. Two-gun got a broken arrow in his face which hurt a lot; it hit the rock before him, snapped in two and the feathered end slapped into his unprotected face between the eyes.

They took to their Colts now, and the smoke went up in clouds.

Then Careless, his knuckles bleeding from an arrow wound, saw a black crow's feather. After that he held his fire. If it was the last thing he did, he wanted to stop Black Crow, the trouble-maker.

Somewhere an Indian began to call out. It might have been Black Crow, shouting orders. Careless couldn't tell what was being said, but he guessed at the words. He said, grimly, 'Someone out there's callin' on the Kiowas to finish us off. Stand by, they're comin' in!'

The Kiowas came in with a rush that said they weren't going to be stopped by anything. And they weren't. The brown bodies were leaning into the cleft between the rocks where they crouched.

Careless saw hideous, blood-lusting faces, heard the screams and war cries as the Indians came jumping down upon them.

He holstered his empty Colt, grabbed his rifle and went charging in at the warriors. For a few seconds he held them at bay in the narrow end of the rocky cleft.

But the end was inevitable. They were too many for the Texans. Careless, beating back their first attackers, saw a second wave of leaping, screaming warriors flooding in among the rocks towards them. The flood of brown bodies parted and ran on either side of their rocky shelter.

Careless beat back a couple of fanatical warriors, then, panting, waited for the next attack to begin.

Ed shouted, 'What'n heck . . .'

Crop Johnson was calling out from behind him.

Careless couldn't understand it. The Indians were picking themselves up and running. They were all running – running back into the canyon where their ponies were.

He wiped the streaming sweat from his face, his chest heaving mightily as he gulped for air. Then he saw figures . . . horsemen . . . and understood.

Bandy was back with the reinforcements they needed. He was tearing in with a party of at least twenty white men. He had come just in time. The Texans had been able to hold out just long enough.

They went flat on their backs then, trying to recover from that last ferocious battle. Then Bandy Phelan came trotting in with their horses. His small, wrinkled, good-humoured face was wreathed in smiles. He was proud to think that he had won the race to save his comrades' lives.

They stood up and shook his hand, and slapped his back until it hurt. But Bandy had a sense of proportion. 'What'n heck, I did nothin',' he protested. 'I jes' ran away an' fetched a passel o' land-grabbers, while you—' He indicated the scenes of combat all around them.

They mounted, and began to ride tiredly across

the sun-drenched prairie to the distant Cutthroat Gap. After a while their rescuers pulled out of the canyon and began to overtake them. They were a tough, hard-bitten lot, professional gunmen, most of them, Careless' sharp eye judged. That put them down as hired help, and he wondered who had done the hiring.

His wonder increased as they neared the fence across the gap. He had expected it to be a pole fence, but this was something much more efficient.

He saw stout posts sunk into the ground, and something caught the sunlight and came reflecting off it. 'Wire!' The thought leapt into his mind immediately. And when he came close enough to see that long fence that stretched from one mountain to another, completely across the pass, he realized that it was the newly invented barbed wire that was beginning to be seen on the range in Texas.

Barbed wire . . . That meant money. Barbed wire had to be bought, and brought in by expensive freight haulage. He was looking towards a cluster of buildings that were just going up. High-wheeled bois d'arc wagons were standing close by them. He thought, 'When I get closer I'll see there's a name on them, an' that name'll be Clay Colbert's, the freight hauler.'

It was. Clay Colbert was doing all right out of this land-grabbing, if only by hauling in tons of barbed wire. But he might be interested in more than haulage, Careless thought. Maybe he was the galoot behind the land-grabbing operation.

He frowned as he looked upon that cluster of buildings, nestling at the foot of the northern range of the Wichitas. These weren't homesteads going up – this was one mighty ranch.

He could see the ranch-house, and it looked big and imposing for all it was still without roof. This was a palace among ranch-houses, Careless decided, his brow thoughtful. And he saw the outlines of stables, barns and the beginnings of pole corrals. Whoever planned this, planned generously.

Now, who was the King Grabber? Who was big enough to hire men on this scale, transport timber, wire and building material into the heart of the wilderness? He was big, whoever he was – big enough to think he could do things and get away with them.

One of the gunnies jerked a question to him as they rode in among the raw-wood, pine-smelling buildings and the stacks of timber.

'You drivin' them steers in from Big Spring?' Big Spring – that was three hundred miles away, inside Texas. Careless played dumb for a second, because he saw here a clue and he wanted to follow it up.

Dismounting stiffly, he grunted, 'Steers?'

'Sure, the stock.' He was a black-eyebrowed, red-faced galoot with an impatient air. 'The boss is expectin' men in, Chimp says. He's in an all-fire hurry to get cattle eatin' off the land afore winter closes the passes.' He looked at the mighty, sweat-and-dust stained Texan and said, 'You're cattle-men, ain't you'?'

'Sure – but not the men you're expectin'.'

They'd all hitched their horses by now and were tramping slowly, wearily towards a brush wind-break that served as cookhouse during the build-ing operations. The men wouldn't need a roof for a couple of months yet, Careless knew.

A bullet-headed cook came along with a big can of coffee, and the men drank gratefully. Then he came back carrying a board on which was sliced buffalo meat and brown bread.

A black-eyebrowed galoot drifted across to them. Careless read the questions in that suspi-cious, pointed-chinned face and murmured a warning to his comrades. 'They're comin' around to questions,' he said.

'You fellars didn't say where you're from.' It was an abrupt statement, without any attempt at polite-ness. That wasn't the Texas way, where a man's busi-ness was his own and he didn't have to be ques-tioned about it. The Texans' hackles rose immedi-ately.

They got up, knowing that any moment there would be a show-down. Careless dusted his jeans. The way he slapped them, it looked as if they would come apart any minute.

'We didn't,' he agreed.

The galoot hadn't much sense. He snapped,

'Reckon it's time you did. Strangers ain't wanted around here. The boss says we've got to run 'em off the range. We thought you were the drovers, else we wouldn't have bothered to come out an' help you.'

'That's comfortin' to know,' drawled Careless. He jerked his head towards the heavy, middle-aged man in a four-wheeled dray. 'That the boss?'

'Him? That's Jones, the hardware merchant from Stampede. He supplies the wire. He's out measurin'—' He halted. 'What'n heck's it got to do with you?' he demanded.

Deliberately Careless insulted him. 'I always speak to the boss – never with the boy.'

He appeared to be turning a contemptuous back on the black-eyebrowed man, but he was watching that face all the time.

He kicked the gun out of the man's hand before it had quite cleared the holster. In the same movement he sprang at the galoot and gripped him hard by the throat.

'Don't draw on me!' growled the big fellow. He shook him. The teeth nearly came out of the galoot's head. 'I don't like it – kind of sensitive, I reckon, 'bout guns being drawn on me.'

There was a commotion from the other gunnies at that, and they came running up as Careless hurled the galoot away. Skippy Jones got down from his seat and came up to the gunnies.

'What're you doing to these men?' demanded

Jones. He looked fat and prosperous – looked a greedy kind of man.

Careless' reply was tough, even though he and his buddies were surrounded by a suddenly suspicious, hostile mob of professional gunmen.

'If you're not the boss you don't need any answers.' He looked round. He had manoeuvred so that his back was to a pile of stacked boards, and the other Texans had moved in with him.

'Where's the boss?'

A squat, bow-legged man, grey-haired and with a grey stubble running round his chin and down to a matted chest, pushed his way to the front of that hostile crowd. He seemed to spit words: 'I'm Chimp Ayzed, foreman in charge o' these men. I give the orders round here, an' no one needs to know who the boss is. I don't know who the boss is, either. I don't need to know. But I want to know what you fallers are doin' here on this land.'

Careless was using his eyes all the time. He told Chimp: 'We're looking for someone.' None of these men would know of the ruckus back in town last night, he thought – there hadn't been time for the news to travel out to these land-grabbers.

'Yeah?' Chimp's brows came right down over his eyes.

'Yeah. He was a fellar who came to clear land-grabbers outa Kiowa territory.' Careless spoke boldly. He'd seen something—

The gunnies got their hands on their guns at that. Their eyes were hard and merciless as they looked at Careless O'Connor and his Texas pards.

Chimp rasped: 'You'd better speak plain, mister. What fellar are you talkin' about?'

'The town marshal o' Stampede.' Guns came out then. But Chimp tried to bluff.

'I never saw the marshal out so far from town. He ain't never been here.'

'And you never saw Regan, M'Clelland's dep'ty?'

'Never saw him this side o' the Northern Range. Why?'

Careless shrugged. 'M'Clelland set off to come here, an' he's missin'. We're lookin' for him. We found his dep'ty, though.'

There was a sharp intake of breath at that, as if they hadn't expected that news.

Careless' eyes were grim and hard.

'The way I figger it,' he said, measuring his words slowly, 'Regan got into some fightin'. He stopped lead, but not enough to lay him out cold immediately.'

'So?' Skippy Jones was waiting for what was to come.

'So he galloped away, shakin' off his pursuers.' He had a guess. 'Mebbe he gave them the slip in the dark last night. But ridin' like that couldn't have done his wounds any good. He must have passed out from loss of blood – and never came round.'

'You mean – he's dead?' Skippy Jones licked his lips.

'Yeah. And the man that shot him from behind is a murderer, an' I sure hope he swings for it!'

Careless looked at Chimp and said: 'I want to speak to the boss – the big boss. I've come for M'Clelland, an' I aim to find him!'

Chimp said slowly: 'You aim to get yourself in trouble, big fellar, shootin' your mouth off like that!' He gave an almost imperceptible sign to his his gunnies. Careless saw it. He was standing right on the corner of that big stack of planking. 'You know too much, an' we ain't gonna let you go a-roamin' on your own, doin' damage with that tongue!'

His guns flashed in his hands. His men leapt forward to grab the quintet. Then his right gun barrel stabbed flame towards the Texan.

8
A LOOP OF STEEL!

Chimp fired because he saw the quick, stabbing movement of the big fellow's right foot. But he saw it a fraction of a second too late.

That mighty leg lunged forward, kicking a protruding plank from the pile of stacked-up boards. It started the pile falling; the startled gunnies, slap in front of the big stack, saw the whole pile begin to crash down towards them. Then springy planks came lashing out from the pile, jumping yards as the falling tons of wood impelled them out of the main timber mass.

The gunnies roared with anger – an anger which turned almost instantly into panic. They wheeled and began to race beyond reach of those lashing planks that seemed to pursue them like live things. Most succeeded, though a few got bowled over by the timbers.

When they turned, the planking, settling into a groaning, breaking, tumbled heap in front of where it had been stacked so neatly before, they were in

111

time to see five nimble-footed cowboys hoofing it across to where their horses were standing.

More than that, the gunnies' own horses were standing with the quintet's. With rising wrath they were in time to see the five Texans mount and then ride into the rest of the horses, stampeding them and sending them galloping out on to the prairie.

Careless and his companions didn't spend much time in turning the horses loose, but headed at a steady trot towards the north mountain range. They didn't fear pursuit, even though their horses were fatigued still.

They rode into the nearest foothills, climbed for half an hour, and then stopped for the rest of the day in a position on a hillside which gave a fine view over the Gap.

Right then all they wanted was a long, long sleep. Careless took the first spell of two hours on guard. Nothing happened to disturb him, though shortly after his buddies had settled down he saw distant smoke signals from the direction of the canyon.

He didn't know the meaning of those signals this time, but he hoped they spelled trouble for Black Crow.

He found himself nearly dropping off to sleep in the warmth of that steep, pine-clad hillside, and he was glad when it was Bandy's turn to take over. Crop Johnson didn't do any watching because he felt bad.

Just on dusk, Smiler made some coffee on a tiny fire that was well-screened and gave off no smoke. He woke them, and they all drank gratefully and felt better. Then they readjusted their bandages and were fighting fit all at once and ready for the trail, even Crop Johnson.

They all thought that with night Careless would lead them secretly through the darkness to tear down that fence and burn the picket posts. That was the way things had been done in Texas, when fencing wasn't popular.

But Careless, kneeling by the tiny fire, coffee-can in his hand, had other ideas.

'M'Clelland,' said Careless confidently, 'is there if he's anywhere.'

His long, brown finger was pointing towards the distant, unfinished buildings of King Grabber's ranch-house.

'Didn't you notice anything when you were down there with them huskies? Only one building was completed. That was a tiny hut – the kind of place you'd keep stores in. There was a fellar sitting with his back to the door when we rode up. He never moved from the place the whole o' the time we played games with his pards. He had a rifle across his knees too.'

The other Texans sat up at that. 'You mean—'

'That fellar could only be a guard. Okay. Who was he guardin'?'

Then he started to give them his plan. When it was dark they would go down to rescue M'Clelland, if he was in that hut. If they had the law on their side, he argued, anything the land-grabbers did against them was also against the law.

That argument didn't wipe away all the

pessimism. Ed grunted that they didn't seem to hanker much after law in these parts. Regan had been bumped off, and M'Clelland—

Careless stopped him again on that word. 'I've got a hunch we're gonna get more dep'ties in a short while than ever King Grabber thought of.'

They didn't know it, but he was thinking of smoke signals then.

After smoking a curly or two, the punchers lay down for a further couple of hours' rest, until complete darkness had fallen. They didn't intend to move until about an hour before midnight, and being seasoned rangemen, they promptly grabbed sleep, willing themselves to waken at the required time.

Careless probably woke a minute or so before his fellows. But then he was the leader of the party and wanted time for thinking. He lay there, instantly wide awake.

Suddenly his head came round. Then he started to lift himself gently on to his elbow, pushing back his single blanket as he did so. His hand closed about the butt of his revolver.

For he thought he had heard a sound from slightly below him.

It was more instinct that alerted him than realization that something had moved in that screen of bushes which were a black, shapeless mass in the night light.

His hair suddenly stood on end. He had forgotten that thing that had stood over him the night before. Perhaps it had followed them; perhaps that monstrous bulk that had straddled his sleeping form might be crouching there now within a few yards of them.

The thought chilled him. Then his brow puckered in the darkness. He was thinking: 'Goldarn It, why don't them hosses make a sound?'

He waited a second, holding his breath and peering towards that blackness. Then his keen eyes saw a movement – distinctly saw it. Something seemed to detach from the dim shape of the huddled bushes, something that was dark and shapeless in that night blackness – something that had bulk and looked big – bigger than any man could be!

Careless saw it move again, just a faint black shadow against a background of near-blackness. He realized that Crop Johnson was lying nearest to the intruder, that the thing was almost treading on his companion.

He shouted. His gun came out, but he held his fire; because to fire might alert more enemies in these hostile hills. Crop Johnson came rolling out of his blankets, his bandaged head showing white in the gloom.

The shadow vanished. It moved like lightning, faster than he could move. He heard a violent crashing as a massive body flattened the bushes, and that was all he heard.

The Texans gathered together, guns out, listening to the fading sounds as the intruder retreated at great speed.

'What was that?' – Smiler's voice, quick and anxious.

'I don't know.' Careless was more puzzled than he had ever been. 'It's that – thing.'

They knew what he meant. No one spoke, their ears straining to catch the last sounds from the mysterious intruder. Then they relaxed, sure now that no danger threatened – if it had ever threatened.

Careless said: 'We might as well git. C'mon, pards, let's get down an' rescue Marshal M'Clelland.'

An hour and a half of cautious riding brought them up against the barbed-wire fence that strung across the gap.

When they saw the sprawling ranch buildings they dismounted and went forward on foot, leaving Crop Johnson to guard their horses.

It was blood-tingling work, inching their way through the darkness and stacked timbers and skeletons of buildings. All around them men slept, about fifty picked desperados who would have little compunction in ending their lives if they were caught.

They caught a gleam of fire and guessed there were patrols around the buildings to protect the land-grabbers against a surprise attack. Somehow they had got in among the buildings without meeting a patrol.

They got down on their stomachs and crawled, one after the other, Careless leading, towards the group of men squatting round the cheerful, blazing fire. A coffee-pot was in the embers. That explained the lack of patrols – they'd come in for a drink of coffee.

Eight men were sitting there. They could hear their rough, growling voices quite plainly. One said: 'Aw, cawffee! That ain't no drink. I got a bottle of what's good in my blankets. Reckon a drop o' fire-water'll improve any cawffee ever made.'

There was a deep rumble of approval at the idea, and the gunnie rose and stalked across towards his blankets.

The gunnie came back carrying a bottle. He settled down by the fireside, and the bottle went from hand to hand, 'lacing' their pots of coffee. It made the men noisier, more talkative.

Then a *hombre* came drifting across from the darkness. He carried a rifle crotched under his right arm. 'Don' I get any o' that drink?' he growled complainingly.

Careless hissed to his companions: 'See that fellar. Reckon he's the guard.'

He began to slide round, aiming for the point where the lone guard had emerged from the darkness. When they had skirted the fire a good way, they began to make out the shape of the small hut that Careless had noticed earlier. The guard came back, carrying the coffee can itself. He settled into the doorway, and began to drink.

He never saw what grabbed him.

A hand neatly took the coffee can from his fingers so that it wouldn't clatter to the ground.

117

Another hand – a very big one – clapped across his mouth and lifted him by the head into a standing position. Two hands promptly gripped the guard's behind him. Two others held his ankles together.

He didn't have a chance.

These Texans knew how to hog-tie a man with the minimum of fuss and material.

There was a key in the lock. It was all too easy. They went inside. As the door swung open, the distant firelight illuminated the interior. Careless' big form entered, blocking out the light for a moment. Someone took a mighty swipe at his chin, then sucked in his breath because the blow had nearly broken his knuckles.

Careless shook his head, then said mildly, reprovingly: 'Now, Mack, there ain't no need for that! We're friends.'

M'Clelland was standing there. His fierce, blazing face changed at once. He was delighted to see them, and sorry he had hit out at the supposed guard. 'Reckon there's granite in that chin o' yourn, O'Connor,' he said shortly. 'Sorry I busted out at you.'

Careless said politely: 'That's all right, Mack. Mebbe I ought to have knocked. I'll remember next time.'

But his eyes were upon the right ankle of the marshal of Stampede, and they were bitter with disappointment.

For the prisoner had a loop of steel around his leg, and was chained to one of the corner posts of the hut.

9

FOOLED!

M'Clellend shrugged. 'They were holding me, not knowin' what King Grabber would do to a marshal. They were waitin' for instructions from him.'

Bandy Phelan said immediately: 'They killed your dep'ty, Regan.'

'They did?' They saw M'Clelland's lean young face go rigid with emotion. 'When they jumped us, I got in their way, shoutin' to Regan to break for it.' He paused. 'I heard him gallop off on his hoss. Someone fired, but we all reckoned he hadn't been hit. Seems he had been, and died.'

Careless told him: 'I figger it was Jones, who runs the hardware racket in Stampede, who fired them shots.'

M'Clelland looked at him. 'Thanks. I didn't know. I'll remember it when I meet Jones.'

'Mind you, I don't know for certain,' said Careless.

He'd been examining the manacle and chain.

Now he rose. The men around the fire were getting noisier.

Careless whispered: 'We could file through a chin link in less than an hour. You'd have to carry a bracelet round your ankle—'

'I was figurin' on cuttin' the chain from where it's plugged into the wall.'

Careless examined the place, then shook his head. Filing close to his ankle would be better. He'd never be able to escape carrying a couple of yards of heavy, clanging steel chain.

M'Clelland said that workman's tools were kept in a box on a wagon alongside the guards' fire. They sent Bandy off to look for a file because he was the smallest and lithest member of the party. He came back within a quarter of an hour. He'd found a file.

Holding their breaths, four men crouching outside, eyes focused malignantly upon the noisy guards around the fire, Careless began to use the file.

He worked in patches, stopping when the speakers stopped talking, restarting when they seemed involved in some noisy argument.

Once he thought they were discovered. Unexpectedly silence fell upon the drinkers, and that file screeched for a fraction of a second after the last spoken syllable. At once one of the gunmen at the fire reared round, peering towards the hut.

They heard him call sharply: 'What was that?

You all right, Eddie?' Two-gun promptly growled back: 'Sure'm all right. Why don't you let a fellar go to sleep, talkin'—'

He mumbled his words, like a man half-asleep, and it disguised his voice. The Texans listened, breath bated, their guns pointing.

Then they relaxed. The man at the fire returned to his drinking, satisfied.

Careless went on with his filing. He was nearly through. He whispered instructions to M'Clelland.

'Reckon we could jump their hosses an' ride off an' collect our own.' He thought that was safer than attempting to crawl away. If they were discovered, afoot and some distance from their mounts, they would be in a helpless position.

He paused in his filing. One voice only was holding out at that fire, not sufficient to cover the sound of his working.

'Sure I've killed an Injun. Not long ago, neether.'

The man was a bit drunk and boastful. Careless was listening. So was the marshal, and the four Texans in the shadows outside with their prisoner.

'We got paid to stir up trouble an' drive some Injuns off good land. That was the beginnin' o' this land-grabbin'. We figgered on some fightin' from them Injuns, but they didn't do much except talk with their tongues. We wanted a fight' – Careless got the note of cruelty in that boasting voice – 'an' we started to shove 'em around. That got some o' the young Injuns ready to hit out at us.

But there was one fellar there – a big, older Injun – who stood out an' told 'em not to be fools. He was a fellar who commanded respect in that village, though he wasn't a chief. They began to do as he said, an' I reckon we didn't like it. So-'

'So?' a companion prompted cynically.

'So I rode up behind him an' shot him.' The voice was hard with brutal satisfaction.

The Texans waited for the boaster's voice to become louder, or to be joined by others. Only a few minutes' more work with that file and M'Clelland would be free.

'I 'member I stuck the bar'l of my six-shooter on to his bare neck. He kinda lifted his hand in surprise, an' I saw that Injun's fist.' He paused, as if to think of it. 'It was the queerest goldarned hand I ever saw on mortal man. That Injun had got – two thumbs!'

'Two thumbs?'

Careless put down the file. Astonished, M'Clelland saw him brace both feet against the manacle that fettered his ankle; then those mighty hands gripped the chain, close to the near-severed link, and began to strain upon it.

The marshal exclaimed, 'You'll never bust it.' Then he saw the determination on that face, illuminated by the distant firelight only. He saw a glistening on it, and knew it to be from the sweat that was pouring from the herculean exertion. He saw the mighty shoulder muscles bunch and swell up under the torn shirt, saw the corded forearms, like the trunks of young trees, tearing at that chain.

The link came apart. He was free. O'Connor seemed to go down in a heap at that, exhausted by the mighty feat of strength required to break that filed chain link. M'Clelland rose and stretched, exulting.

He patted big Careless on the shoulder in a gesture of admiration and thanks. Then, almost as suddenly as he had collapsed, the big fellow was climbing to his feet again, nearly recovered. M'Clelland saw that big, battered face. It was without its customary expression of lazy good-humour.

M'Clelland saw the ridged muscles at the side of the jaw, saw that this big man was suddenly outraged, was evidently fighting mad. He exclaimed, 'What's bitten you, fellar? You look like you could kill somebody.'

Big O'Connor said tersely, 'Mebbe I could.'

Outside the braggart was explaining. 'Sure, he'd got two thumbs, both on the same hand. They kinda grew out like a forked twig. I ain't never seen a fellar with thumbs like that afore in all my born days.'

M'Clelland looked to O'Connor as the natural leader of this expedition. Careless said, 'You'n the boys creep round an' get them hosses. Ride off an' pick up Crop with his hosses.'

'An' you?'

'Don't worry. I'll be with you. Mebbe. Right now,' said O'Connor, 'I'm goin' to provide a distraction that'll sure keep their minds off their hosses.'

He walked out of the hut at that, leaving M'Clelland to stare after him. Then Mack called to the Texans, softly, and told what they had to do.

They stared after O'Connor. He was walking boldly, openly, towards the fire.

The gunmen sitting around the fire couldn't believe their eyes. They saw a man bearing down on them.

Open-mouthed, as if seeing a ghost, they watched his advance. He came with hands dangling at his sides. Some of the gunmen clapped hands on their six-shooters, then held their draw as they realized that the big *hombre* wasn't going for his gun.

Careless saw the men fall apart, sobered at the prospect of danger. He didn't say a word, didn't look at anybody in particular. He just reached the edge of the fire and then squatted down among the gunmen, as if among friends.

And yet they knew he wasn't friendly. No man could feel friendly with eyes as cold and bleak as those grey ones under that worn old hat. One of them growled, 'Where'n the tarnation have you sprung from? Lost your hoss?'

The big *hombre* ignored the question. He stared into the fire and said in that slow, Texan drawl, 'I once knew a fellar who had two thumbs like you said.'

He didn't know which of these firelit men had

been the braggart. They all looked tough and mean and bad enough for murder.

The braggart revealed himself. 'You bin listenin' – out there?' His head jerked.

Careless recognized the voice, harsh and biting. His eyes lifted. He saw the speaker.

'I was listenin'.'

The braggart knew he was being challenged from that moment. He snarled, 'What good does that do you? You ain't gonna live long, not after causin' that ruckus yest'day.'

Careless spoke as if he hadn't heard the threat. His own voice was as hard and biting as that file he had so recently been using.

'This fellar I knew with two thumbs on his right hand, he was an Injun, too.'

His Texan comrades could have walked upright to the horses then, for all the attention those fire-side gunmen gave to their surroundings. They slipped across, listening to that level, lazy drawl from their leader.

It was as they were silently mounting, holding their breath at the tiny creaking of saddle feather, that they realized that Careless was doing more than just provide a distraction for them. They heard him say, 'This Injun had a name, because of them two thumbs. They called him, Man-with-Thumb. That's the Kiowa way of sayin' things – it means he's got a thumb more than other men.'

Those gunmen knew that the big, torn-shirted

man from Texas was deliberately squaring up to them.

'Man-with-Thumb was a friend o' yourn?' Man-with-Thumb's killer asked the question. There was a sneer on his lips. In a moment he could satisfy yet again this lust that came upon him to kill.

'Man-with-Thumb was my blood brother. He was a fine man. He was brave an' the boldest of hunters, but he was also a friendly man who never lifted his hand against another. You, you scum, killed a man – took him from this earth – a man who was far and away better than you'll ever be.'

Those grey, slitted eyes were never leaving that stubble-bearded little face above the bandanna. Careless was rising with his words, because now, in this firelight, was the moment of showdown, and everyone there knew it. The gunman was rising, too, rising into a crouch, his right hand gripping his gun.

The big *hombre* went on talking, but he took a stride backwards, away from the fire. 'He was my friend, an' we went huntin' together in the old days. He had a wife – a young and pretty one. You left her a widow. He had two papooses – you made them orphans.'

The other gunmen were slowly rising. The atmosphere was electric. Something had to break.

Something did break. The rage of that mean-faced young gunman.

He snarled, 'You talk too much. I'm gonna stop that tongue o' yourn.'

He began to draw. It was easy. There was no difficulty in killing a man whose hand was a foot away from his gun butt, while your own was already wrapped round his six-shooter.

His gun was clearing leather when he realized that that big *hombre* could move fast.

Was going for his gun.

Was gripping the butt.

A flame was shooting out from the bottom of the holster.

It was a Mexican trick practised by some Texans. The over-confident gunman felt a shattering blow on his right shoulder, his arm was paralysed and he went reeling almost into the fire. His gun, almost levelled, fired with the convulsive jerk of his trigger-finger as the heavy Colt-lead knocked his arm back. The bullet flew within inches of the big *hombre* but only hurt the distant, unoffending prairie. Then the Colt dropped from a hand suddenly lost of all its strength.

All at once it seemed as if the night erupted action. Smoke was drifting from the exploding guns. The other gunmen shouted and jumped apart, tearing madly at their holstered guns, bringing them hip-high and triggering.

Big Careless fired – and smashed a wrist. Fired again – and chipped a collar bone. He was firing, even now, not to kill, but to protect himself. And as he fired he shouted out the reason for his restraint. 'I'm comin' back for you – all of you. You're gonna stand proper trial for your crimes!'

A horse reared out of the darkness, leaping madly over the fire. Other horsemen came pounding suddenly into the firelight. Startled gunmen found themselves being bowled over by their own mounts.

Little Bandy Phelan was on that first leaping horse. He was roaring, 'Hang on, big fellar!'

Careless leapt and grabbed stirrup leather. But the ground was too rough for running in the dark. He swung expertly and came sitting up behind Bandy. Behind him a shot rang out, then another.

He turned and had a fleeting glimpse of sprawling gunmen, recovering and getting their guns into action. He saw his comrades racing out of the firelight, disappearing almost as he looked at them, into the surrounding pool of blackness. The bullets weren't hitting anyone.

Beyond the fire men were shouting. The gunplay had roused the rest of the hired toughies, employed by the land-grabber. In a moment they would have fifty paid killers out searching for them.

They heard the rising crescendo of excitement, back among the new buildings. There was the sound of angry voices raised, shouting orders. The sound of horses milling around as saddles were hastily thrown on. Then the thunder of hoofs as men recklessly plunged into the darkness in pursuit of them.

They found Crop Johnson along the wire, holding their horses. Careless slid down and grabbed his own mighty black stallion, with its silver harness trappings glinting in the starlight. 'Git your own hosses,' he ordered swiftly. There was a commotion in the darkness as men swopped mounts.

A voice – probaby Ed's – asked, 'These hosses—'

For answer Careless slapped one on the haunch and sent it galloping off into the darkness. The other horses took fright and plunged after it. They heard the hoofs drumming away into the night.

'Keep quiet . . . keep still.'

Careless pinched the nostrils of his stallion to prevent a betraying snicker when other horses came by, though it was so well-trained that the action was hardly necessary. There was a shout from the darkness. 'There they go!' Flames lit up as guns spoke.

Then a party of vengeful gunmen tore past the silent, motionless group standing against the barbed wire fence. They went careering across the prairie – after a bunch of riderless horses.

10
BLACK CROW'S BID

Ed's voice came ironically from the darkness: 'They're gonna be pleased when they catch up with them hosses!'

Careless swung into his saddle. 'Let's go,' he ordered.

They moved off. Careless led the way through the sagebrush travelling by the stars. After only half an hour, Careless said, 'Oh, gosh, I'm tired. I'm gettin' down.'

He did, and the others followed, and they slept the night there among the sweet-scented sage brush. Before dawn they were moving again, however, not wanting to be seen so close to the land-grabbers' stronghold.

When the sun was hot upon them, a couple of hours later, they felt they were safe from pursuit by parties of gunmen out hunting for them, as undoubtedly they would be.

Careless rode out on to a small, bare prominence and again dismounted. He said, 'We're gonna have cawffee – light a fire.'

The others were still on their horses, and when he said that they didn't make an effort to dismount. M'Clelland, a cloth wrapped round the fetter on his ankle to prevent chafing of his flesh, asked, 'You kiddin'? This is Injun country. They'll be out for scalps after your war with 'em yest'day.'

Careless just gave that lazy grin but couldn't be bothered to explain. He went off afoot with his rifle. When he came back he was carrying a small, plump buck. They'd got a fire going when he returned – a small one – and the coffee was boiling merrily in the sooty can.

They pulled out the red embers and grilled some steaks, and then Careless piled logs on to the fire and tore up handfuls of green grass and roofed the lot with it. The fire started to throw off a dense white smoke.

Smiler, looking his usual unsmiling self, gnawed on a fleshy, succulent rib and said politely, 'That's makin' a kinda visitin' card. You figgerin' on entertainin' Injuns?'

Careless was fumbling in his saddle roll. 'Nope.' He shook his head. 'I'm figgerin' on callin' in on the Kiowas.'

They watched the big fellow return with his blanket. 'You talk sky lingo?' asked Two-gun.

'Some. Enough.'

Careless skilfully threw the blanket so that it completely obliterated the fire for the moment, checking the strong column of smoke. He held the blanket there until the damped-down smoke threatened to come swirling up around the blanket, and then, with one expert movement, he dragged it away. A new head of smoke began to go up in a dense white cloud. Almost at once Careless slung back the blanket and stopped the smoke. That round ball of whiteness went rising into the clear blue summer sky. It would be visible for miles around, and Careless knew that eyes would be watching for it, because of the attention caused by the straight spiral of white smoke that had been rising from the fire for the last five minutes. He withdrew the blanket – replaced it and a second ball of white smoke ascended into the sky.

He went slowly, patiently, through with his message, then repeated it twice. Crop, back from bathing his head in the clear mountain stream, asked what the sky talk said.

'It just says, "White man callin' on big red chief for peace talk".'

'Peace talk?' Crop grunted.

'Mebbe Black Crow an' his young warriors won't want us to go talkin' peace with the chief?' Bandy had his misgivings, too.

Careless shrugged. He was enjoying his meal now, the sky talk finished so far as he was concerned. His companions didn't ask why he wanted to parley with the big Indian chief. Instead, they watched the mountains all around them, and finally Crop nodded westwards and said: 'Here he comes, talkin' back to you.'

A fire had been started, many miles distant. They couldn't see the fire itself, because of the forests of pine trees on intervening mountain slopes, but they could see the strong, straight column of white smoke that went up into the distant blue sky.

The smoke stopped for half a minute, and then one by one, spaced at intervals of time and of different sizes, the clouds of smoke went rolling up after each other. Careless got the message first time. When they looked at him, they knew it wasn't good talk that came from that distant, Indian fire.

'Big Chief Fightin' B'ar says don't come, he is surrounded by tribesmen rebellin' agen his leadership.'

That was serious news. Bandy opined, 'Black Crow – he's the fellar back of the trouble. What's in your mind, pardner?'

Careless rose and went across to his horse, rolling his smoky blanket as he did so. 'We're goin' to help Fightin' B'ar put down them crazy young braves behind Black Crow.'

They all mounted and rode towards that distant signal. Five hours later they were in the middle of a savage Indian war.

From a bald, mountain peak, they were able to look down upon the fighting. Upon a hill that grew out of the rich, wide valley was an Indian camp – they saw the circles of tipis, and the lines of tethered ponies.

They also saw a ring of feathered defenders who crouched all around the perimeter of the plateau-like top to the hill, and they saw Indians, on horse-back as well as afoot, attacking the camp from two sides.

When they rode down about a mile, they heard the distant scream of war-whoops. Careless was standing in his stirrups, so intent upon catching the meaning of those sounds. After a time he was satisfied.

'Kiowa war cries,' he announced. This would be the rebellious Black Crow with his young braves attacking the older warriors of the tribe. To be able to besiege the tribe, as he was doing, meant that Black Crow must have secured most of the warriors of the tribe to his side.

They rode down in a compact bunch, hugging the wooded parts that covered their advance from the Indians below, or keeping behind the folds of rolling valley bottom where there were no trees to hide them.

In time they were near enough to the fighting to hear the crash of weapons upon war shields, and the cries of men injured by flying arrows and the occasional bullet from an old gun. Careless ordered his men to halt in a copse of elms, while he advanced cautiously to see the land before him.

What he saw instantly made up his mind for him as to his next course of action. Fighting Bear and his men were so hard-pressed that within minutes their defence position must be overrun.

Careless saw that a powerful force under Black Crow himself, all fighting on foot now, had broken through the line of defenders at a point where a tiny, wooded cleft ran into the hill on which the Kiowa camp was pitched. Some had stolen up through the underbrush while the defenders' attention was distracted by a feint attack at the rear of the camp.

They were screaming for the death of Chief Fighting Bear, the man who had been the hero of the tribe for a quarter of a century now. They had forgotten the great chief's bravery, had forgotten how he had saved the tribe time and again by his skill as a warleader and negotiator of peace treaties. Black Crow had distilled poison into their ears and now they cried: 'Fighting Bear wants us to be the slaves of the white men! Fighting Bear is a woman, content to sit in his tepee while the paleface steals our lands. Death to the paleface! Death to Fighting Bear!'

Careless saw the frenzied hand-to-hand fighting as the loyal Crazy Dogs battled to save their chief from an unmerited death. He also saw Fighting Bear himself preparing for the end. He had staked himself to the ground, Kiowa fashion, to show that he would die rather than yield an inch of ground to his enemies. He wore the loop of the Crazy Dogs on his left shoulder, and to this he had tied a long thong of tanned buffalo hide, which was fastened to a stake in the ground.

Fighting Bear was signifying his intention to die

rather than run away from Black Crow and his hot-headed young followers.

The Texans heard a whistle from the top of the slight slope; they saw Careless beckoning urgently, and they dug their heels into their horses and went over the brow at breakneck speed.

They saw Careless, crouching along the neck of his mighty black stallion, hurtling like an avenging fury towards that bitter fighting, and they came crowding in behind him, racing at top speed into the fight.

Black Crow's exultant warriors suddenly saw a gleaming black horse leaping apparently from out of the sky on to the plateau before them. Then they saw other horsemen, and their exultation died.

Then Careless wheeled his horse, right between the staked chief and the advancing rebels, and charged. The Texans came riding in behind him, boot to boot across the plateau. As they came, they gave their own war-cry – a devastating, 'Yip – yip – yippee – ee – ee!'

That charge of the mounted Texans was devastating. The loyal Crazy Dogs took heart at sight of the unexpected allies, and went plunging back into the fight with renewed encouragement and vigour. The rebels were dismayed – especially dismayed as they realized they were opposing one of the dreaded repeating rifles.

They broke before the charge and raced for the cover of the wooded cleft, where horsemen couldn't follow. But the Crazy Dogs weren't mounted, and they went in pursuit, determined to rout the young fools.

Careless came thundering back. As he passed the stake to which the chief was tied, he leant from the saddle and neatly uprooted it. That, he knew, was Kiowa etiquette. Until someone pulled that stake from the ground, the chief, in all honour, must stay tied where he was.

Black Crow was gathering his defeated warriors together, was mounting them on their ponies, and evidencing a determination not to leave the fight at that.

Big Chief Fighting Bear said gravely, 'My white brother came just in time.' Brother. The Texans all noticed the deliberate choice of the word. Careless had been blood brother to a Kiowa, and that made him brother to the tribe.

'I had need of your help, O Chief,' returned Careless O'Connor.

The chief shrugged and turned to look down where his enemies were gathering. 'You come at a bad time, O-Kon-Or. There is nothing I can do to help you.' It seemed that with those words a bitterness too great for the chief to contain overwhelmed him. He walked quickly away to his lodge, his head hanging, his shoulders drooping.

Careless didn't attempt to follow. He knew that the chief wanted to be alone in his sorrow.

'Now what do we do?' Ed demanded.

Their leader shrugged. 'Wait,' he said. 'That's

all we can do. An' sleep an' eat.'

Then they all looked into the valley end knew there wouldn't be much sleeping and eating. Though they were so far away, they could hear a voice haranguing the young warriors. It would be Black Crow, of course.

Black Crow was a clever leader. He sought to ensure victory for himself. When he was certain that his followers would ride with him, regardless of danger, he played a bold card.

He rode, with a few of his strongest supporters, to a point immediately below the steep hill upon which the camp was pitched. His hand was high and open to show that it was empty of weapons. It signified that he wished to have parley with his opponent.

But when Chief Fighting Bear and his chieftains came into the open to speak with him, he spoke not to the chief, whom he treated with contempt, but to Fighting Bear's supporters. Openly he urged them to cut down their chief.

'He is a traitor,' Black Crow shouted, sitting down there on his sturdy, well-fed pony, his body bare to his loin cloth, that black feather in his dark hair, his thin, angry face suffused with the temper he could hardly ever contain.

'Fighting Bear has made a pact with the white man to give them our hunting grounds.' He was a liar, that Black Crow, but men lie easily when they covet power and it is within their grasp.

Then his bare brown arm lifted and pointed at

the Texans, standing back among the tepees with their horses.

'When Fighting Bear was in trouble, who was it who came to his rescue? His paleface friends! He brought them here, and their guns have killed and injured Kiowas, rather than let Fighting Bear be removed from his position as chief of the mighty Kiowa tribe.'

He stood up in his stirrups at that, as if to make his voice carry farther; and now they heard him even to the farthest tepee.

'These men want to keep the lands they have stolen from us. They want to maintain those fences, and they seek to drive us from land which has been ours always. And they have bribed Fighting Bear to be their agent within the tribe. I say, death to all white men! Death to the traitor, Fighting Bear!'

'Black Crow has the tongue of a serpent,' Careless heard Fighting Bear call back, but he knew that the position had changed dramatically against the chief in the last minutes. The Texans had saved him from his bloodthirsty young followers, but now they were being used as the excuse to bring about his downfall.

He went forward, listening to the great chief of the Kiowas deride the arguments that had been put up by his vicious enemy. But he knew that Fighting Bear could no longer save himself.

Now, on top of the hill by the Kiowa chief, were no more than a couple of dozen faithful supporters. The men who had stood so loyally by him in the recent fighting were withdrawing into perplexed, unhappy groups, discussing the position. Some of them broke and ran down the hill to join Black Crow, and they were greeted with loud cries of triumph from his followers. But most of the braves retired to their lodges, like men who cannot make up their minds and withdraw from the fight.

The massed horsemen at the foot of the hill began to ride forward. They outnumbered Fighting Bear's forces many times, and resistance against them seemed hopeless. Careless came up to the group around the chief.

Black Crow saw him, and passion filled his mean young face. 'If you are not a friend of the paleface, O Fighting Bear, prove it. Give your white friends to our women, to be tortured and then killed!'

Fighting Bear was standing alone in front of his supporters. At that demand, he shook his bonneted head and called, 'That I cannot do. O-Kon-Or is blood brother to our tribe, and I will not let harm come to him in consequence.'

A shout went up from Black Crow's followers at that. To them it seemed confirmation of their leader's sneering slanders against their chief. 'Kill him,' they shouted. 'Kill Fighting Bear, the traitor!'

And then Careless O'Connor was there between them. He came plunging forward, down the hill just in front of Fighting Bear and his supporters.

It stopped the beginnings of that charge against Fighting Bear – or perhaps that menacing Sharps repeater, held aloft by the giant cowboy, stayed the rush. Careless lifted his voice, and it echoed down the valley and drowned Black Crow's furious bellow.

'Stay where you are, you young warriors of the Kiowa tribe,' Careless shouted in their tongue. 'Are you demented that you would destroy the saviour of your tribe, the greatest chief the Kiowa have ever known? I say, turn on Black Crow. He makes war within the Kiowa tribe, not against your enemies. I say, follow Fighting Bear, because he will lead you wisely and in your best interests.'

'Talk,' shouted Black Crow. 'Let us put an end to this talk.'

'It is not talk,' called Careless. 'Not talk alone. For I have a plan, and if you will follow me it will mean that before the sun is warm tomorrow that fence will be down, those buildings will be fired, and the paleface will be in retreat from your hunting grounds.'

Fighting Bear's head jerked up at that. M'Clelland translated quickly for his companions. The Texans and the marshal watched Careless, their hearts bumping because they had confidence in the man.

Big, lazy, untidy Careless O'Connor had a plan.

But though he had done well to secure their attention, Careless suddenly realized that he hadn't done well enough. These warriors were wavering; but then Black Crow went back among them with his angry, persuasive tongue, and in seconds he had them to his side again.

So Careless lifted his rifle and shot the young chief out of his saddle.

11

THE KING GRABBER!

As that sharp bark of the repeater went echoing down the valley, there was an instant commotion from the young braves who interpreted it as an act of war. Back on top of the hill, Fighting Bear shouted in anger against the man who had fired that shot, and he lifted his lance to hurl it with passion into O'Connor's broad back.

And then a roar of laughter went up from the braves at the foot of the hill – a roar that swelled as others saw the humour of the situation, so that their unexpected laughter spread across the valley and came reflecting back in echoing waves.

Careless had shot Black Crow from his saddle. He had fired at the moment when Black Crow was pulling savagely back on the single headrope that, Indian fashion, was his horse's bridle for war. That bullet, fired with the swiftest of sighting, had cut

through the tautened headrope like a sharp tomahawk into a stretched thong.

Black Crow, pulling back with all his weight, had
gone rolling over the haunches of his pony. Now
he was sitting in the dust, dazed by his fall, in his
hand the short end of the halter that had been so
neatly severed.

With that action, Careless decided the issue. He
had made braves laugh, and men who are laughing lose most thoughts of war. Much more important, he had made Black Crow look ridiculous, and
no man can survive ridicule with his followers
laughing uproariously at his discomfiture.

The Indian-wise Careless O'Connor rammed
home his advantage. He held aloft something that
sparkled. It was a piece of silver that he had torn
from the trappings of his Kiowa harness. He spoke,
and as he spoke enthusiasm grew and the young
braves came surging forward. But now they were
friends. Careless O'Connor was giving them a lead,
opening up an outlet for their fiery passions and
pent-up frustrations.

Black Crow did try to restrain them. Raging, he
jumped upon his horse and tried to ride between
his deserting followers and that big man on the
sloping hillside.

He lifted his lance to hurl it at his enemy – and
it snapped in half as a bullet clipped through the
ash wood. His tomahawk flashed above his head –
but when it was thrown it was without blade,
suddenly shot from the haft.

It was too much for the chief. That big, brown-faced cowboy was playing with him like a cat with a sick mouse, and humbling him, whilst he stayed there. He turned his horse and spurred madly across the plain; he knew it was death to stay with his tribe, anyway.

A bullet flicked the black crow's feather from his head. It was the crowning humiliation; it was something no man could survive. With that last bullet went all hopes of ever becoming chief of the Kiowas.

Black Crow rode into the hills, as solitary as the bird after which he had been named. He had schemed unscrupulously to gain power, but his wings had been shorn by a man wiser and greater than he.

All that day the skilled men of the tribe worked under the direction of the big, torn-shirted Texan. By darkness he was satisfied. Now he knew that he could defeat the land-grabbers.

M'Clelland said so.

When dawn came to bathe those rising new buildings in Cutthroat Gap, with the warm white sunshine of morning, it caught upon silver and it showed a grim, silent sight.

A neglectful guard around a camp fire looked, and then their cheeks blanched and their eyes widened with horror. They lifted their hands and said not a word.

Men came reluctantly from their blankets, yawning and reaching for their makings . . . they saw –

147

stood erect – and reached for the sunshine.

It was a victory in silence. Those over-confident gunmen were snapped up in bunches, before they knew what was happening, before they could use their superior weapons.

Last to be captured was the squat, long-armed Chimp Ayzed. He came from an improvised bed within a roofless building. His jaw dropped.

They were disarmed, then sent off under escort of a hundred braves across the border into New Mexico. Careless told his Indian friends they could help themselves to anything they valued in these buildings that were on their land. Then they dragged up the fence stakes and made mighty bonfires out of them, and then they fired the buildings which would have been a fortress against the red man whilst he stayed on that land.

Chimp Ayzed was shoved off with the rest.

But as he was leaving, he looked down from his horse at Careless and growled, 'You got friends in Stampede? You wanna go to 'em quick, big fellar. King Grabber's gonna be sore when Skippy Jones tells him – and he's gone to Stampede – you rescued the marshal yesterday, an' he'll sure take it outa your friends. That's in Skippy's mind, anyway.'

When the buildings were a roaring mass of flames, Careless called in his allies and told them their next destination. It was – Stampede. Now, he told them, because of the silver they wore against their bare chests, slung by thongs around their necks, they could go into this town which normally was outside their reservation.

M'Clelland nodded agreement, and he was the law. They took to their horses, and rode like furies into the mountains and through that long, sun-baked canyon.

That day, towards evening, they met again the printer and his daughter along the Wichita trail. And a few hours later Careless had his last encounter with this thing that haunted the trail between Stampede and the Kiowa country.

Careless, M'Clelland and the cheerful Texan punchers, their Indian allies behind them, met a few straggling folk along the Texas trail. They were riding with few possessions, like people who have quit in a hurry. When they saw M'Clelland they began to shout in anger, but it wasn't at the marshal.

'There ain't no danged law in this country,' they declared wrathfully. 'We was here first, settlin' nice an' peaceful where the law said we could settle. We was friendly with the Kiowas, an' things was fine. Then the land gets flooded with these grabbers.' The speaker, a middle-aged man who had his family riding behind him, grew grim. 'Yeah, it was deliberately flooded. Someone paid a lot o' fellars to come in an' make trouble – them's hired gunmen if ever I've seen any.'

Then they came upon the printer and his wagon slowly toiling up the winding valley road. When Pru saw them she came running up on foot, her face a picture of delight beyond description.

She hugged Careless, riding in and dismounting almost at full gallop. Then she hugged M'Clelland and would have hugged all the rest but that would have take her too long. She almost wept as she told her tale.

When they saw others leaving, the Sorensens had decided to play for safety and had fled before anything happened to them.

'But the town's full of gunmen,' Pru told them, her face anxious. 'Jones brought a lot in with him, and anyway the town's always full of that kind of man. Mack, you mustn't go in there. It will be death for you, and – and I don't want to lose either of you.'

She saw those Kiowas, coming two by two along the narrow trail. Her eyes widened. She looked at them, then looked at her companions, and she asked, 'Now, who thought that one up?' Her eyes were on those silver medallions on the chests of the warriors.

They camped there, where they had met the Sorensens. The town was only a few miles away, and Careless planned on reaching the place with dawn, as he had the building site in Cutthroat Gap.

In the night he came to wakefulness at some unusual sound. Immediately he knew that it was that strange animal intruder again. Something kept it to his trail, something about him or perhaps his companions was attracting it.

Careless came erect on an instant, his eyes

searching the darkness just faintly lit by a new-rising crescent of moon. He saw a massive bulk almost on top of him. Without realizing what he was doing, he lunged forward. His hand gripped long hair. A scream woke the camp.

They found big Careless O'Connor talking soothingly, like a father to a child. He was holding the head of a beautiful brown mare, who was trembling with fright and yet beginning to relax and feel reassured by this big man-creature's demonstrations of friendship.

'This is the ghost of the Wichita trail,' O'Connor told his companions. 'Look, she's got a bridle on, an' a saddle, too, though it's slipped round under her belly. Now I wonder whose hoss this is? She's a lovely, sensitive beast.'

Fighting Bear had come up in the darkness. He peered at the mare and then said, emphatically, 'This hoss belong Indian Agent.'

'Joe Ponder – the fellar that got killed an' scalped?'

'Him not scalped by Indian,' Fighting Bear told them and old Sorensen interrupted with, 'That's what I've bin sayin', chief.'

'Ponder him ambushed on way out to Kiowa camp after protest to Marshal M'Clelland about murder of Man-with-Thumb in Cool Creek.' The Indian's English wasn't good, and his next sentence had to be translated. 'Ponder's horse was frightened by the murder and ran away. We have seen her along the trail a few times since, but always she has bolted from any who tried to catch her. Her master was a good one, and she cannot forget that some man or men killed him before her eyes.'

'But she was lonely, she wanted to have friends again.' Careless was rubbing those silky ears and the mare was guzzling affectionately against his torn shirt. She had no doubts about this big, kind two-legged creature! He was like the man who had been her master.

They moved during the darkness. Again it was surprise which defeated their enemies.

In the early hours of that morning, just before dawn lifted the darkness off the land, there were men in Stampede who stirred in their sleep and imagined that horsemen were out riding even that early. Then their eyes flickered open and they listened more intently, for horsemen certainly were riding out there in the main street.

The citizens came to the doors.

All down the street silent men sat their horses, their guns covering the sleepers as they emerged. White men. Texans and settlers newly returned from flight away from Stampede town. And behind the grim, silent men, rode hundreds of near-naked Kiowas, proud men, not flinching for all that they carried only primitive weapons compared with the white man's deadly guns.

Some men ran back to get their guns, but most just stayed, dazed, their hands aloft before the menace of their compatriots' six-shooters. They were staring at those mounted braves as if they couldn't believe their eyes. Here was something that most wouldn't fight against.

Even so, there was desperate, savage fighting, behind the hardware store where Skippy Jones and his allies were caught trying to escape. It lasted a few minutes; and it ended in the capture of the most vicious of the land-grabbers. Careless shouted to herd the men together, down the main street. He had ridden in leading the mare. She was docile now, happy to have found a master after the loneliness of that trail upon which a murder had been committed.

The big fellow slid down and hitched his two animals to the rail. The Indians were bringing the white men in. They were a sullen apprehensive bunch; for they didn't expect mercy from these Indians.

'You've no right to bring Injuns here,' shouted Jake Ironside, of the Maverick saloon. 'Injuns shouldn't come on white territory. You're a rene- gade, you big ape.'

M'Clelland said, 'You fellars should have thought about rights before. You tried to grab Injun land, an' brought this upon yourselves. These Injuns have a right to be here – they've a right to go anywhere while they wear that badge.'

His hand was pointing to the glittering silver badges that all the Indians wore so proudly upon their chests. The badges of deputy peace officers.

M'Clelland shouted, 'These Kiowas have been

properly sworn in as my deputies. Any man who lifts a hand against them, does so against the law!'

Dazed men looked at those badges again and shook their heads in bewilderment. 'Where'n heck did he get all them badges so suddenly?' they asked each other.

If they had been in a noticing mood they would have seen that Careless O'Connor's horse was without its silver trappings. But Ed broke the secret to them.

He said contemptuously, 'Heck, you guys forget them Kiowas is the best silversmiths in all America. Give 'em some silver an' they c'n make anythin'. Marshals' badges was easy!'

M'Clelland came spurring across to Careless' side. He'd got Big Chief Fighting Bear to withdraw most of his men. 'Just in case they think to settle some old scores,' he explained. He had enough of his own kind now to cover the land-grabbers, whose numbers had dwindled, anyway, at sight of that massive display of law.

Careless agreed with the move. He added, 'Better run most o' the landgrabbers outa town, too. The sooner they get out of the county the better. But we've still got to find the king grabber, the fellar that started all this.'

'Okay,' M'Clelland shouted. 'You Clay Colbert – you, Ironside, Jones, Hobson, Scoll, Waite an' Tullet. Into the Maverick. We've got some questions we'd sure like to ask you.'

Big Careless followed him after putting his gleeful Texan pards to the job of running the rest of the rogues out of town. He went in and leaned against an open window, leaving the questioning to the tall young marshal.

M'Clelland was asking the sullen-faced men the same question in turn. 'Whose money has financed this plot to take the Kiowas' land from them?'

They wouldn't talk.

Careless pushed himself away from the window. As he moved he had an impression that outside came a queer, strangled little scream of a sound, but he paid no heed to it.

He stood by the marshal's side, an impressively big figure. His face was hard, and his words came out like bullets.

'All right, you *hombres*,' he rapped. 'You won't talk or you can't talk. Mebbe you don't know the King Grabber.' People were still coming in through the batswing doors behind him, but he didn't turn. 'But I figger there's one here who does, and unless he talks he sure will have his neck stretched.'

He seemed suddenly to jump at Skippy Jones. He didn't actually touch the fellow, but his action scared the heavy, middle-aged merchant. Skippy looked into grim grey eyes and licked dry lips.

Careless wheeled towards the marshal. 'Mack, I accuse this man of shooting Deputy-Marshal Regan. I want him to be held under arrest until he can be tried.' He bluffed. 'I'll produce witnesses.'

'No.' Jones hadn't guts. His voice rang out like a panic-stricken woman's – and it seemed to be echoed by an even shriller, higher-pitched scream from the street outside. Careless' head jerked up at the sound. The batswings opened and closed.

'I didn't murder Regan.' Jones' eyes were suddenly fixed upon the doorway. His face was desperate. He was a rat who would do anything to save his skin.

M'Clelland shouted. 'Then talk!'

'I'm not gonna suffer an' let the big boss get away with this,' Jones suddenly shouted. 'I'm goin' to talk—'

But Jones never spoke another word. A blast like the roar of a cannon reverberated in that saloon, and the heavy, ruthless business-man slumped, shot at point-blank range.

Massive, cold-eyed, unemotional Justin Foraiger, the straightest gambler in the West, who detested violence in his saloon, said gratingly, 'I've got another bar'l. Would anyone like it?'

M'Clelland came forward, his fists bunching, but that murderous weapon covered them all.

'So you're King Grabber?'

Justin Foraiger didn't say anything, but he didn't need to, now. He was backing towards the saloon door. Outside were horses. Now that his secret was out, he would try to find safety in flight.

All except one man came moving forward, as if they would stop the escape of the big villain in spite of that threatening gun. That one man was the mighty, ragged-shirted Texan. He knew that Foraiger wasn't going to escape.

Yet the gambler got right to those swing doors before retribution overtook him. He was going through. And then he came hurtling forward on his face, his body bouncing as it hit the floorboards with a crash.

A horse came in through those batswings. A mare. A lovely animal. but just now crazy with hatred. She came in, her intentions plain for them to see. Her forefeet were lifted to stamp the life out of this man whom she hated more than anything in the world. Her teeth were bared as that unearthly scream came from her throat.

Then Careless had her by the head, was soothing her, talking to her, and with his great strength keeping her down on all-fours. She wouldn't be pacified, though, until Careless shouted. 'Get that carrion outa the saloon. She won't be quiet till he's out of the way.'

They got him out of the room, and then the mare went quiet. Careless led her out through the throng of startled spectators on the broad-walk and took her round to the Sorensen stable. Marshal M'Clelland came out to the rail to look after him.

Careless jerked, 'You don't need to know now who killed poor Joe Ponder. She showed it plain enough.'

Bonny Pru Sorensen helped to tie up the horse. Careless rubbed the mare down, and then said,

'Wal, Pru, I reckon that's put an end to land-grab-bin' an' disturbances in Stampede County. You'll be able to run your noospaper without bother from now on.'

Her eyes were shining.

'With you to help us,' Pru was saying, 'we'll build up a fine business, Careless. You'll be the most respected man in town, and I can see our circulation growing with every week that passes.'

Then she saw he was shaking his head, and fear leapt into her eyes. She guessed the truth instantly, and it was like a stab to her heart. 'You mean . . . You're moving on?'

'Yeah. I'm a saddle tramp, a hobo on four legs,' he smiled. His big, brown, fighting face was gentle and kind and her heart went out to him. His hand waved to the little township. 'I don't belong,' he told her simply, and she understood.

When Careless rode out of town the following morning with his fighting Texan pards, the whole township stood out on their verandas to watch him go. He never knew he had so many friends!

M'Clelland was standing there with the Sorensens. Pru wept a little, and Careless saw M'Clelland's arm go round her to console her. He sighed, then turned his eyes to the winding red trail that led into Texas. M'Clelland was a good man; in time they would marry, and he, Careless, would become a dim memory.

He shrugged his shoulders and suddenly began to sing.

158

It was a song about a cattle drive and the companionship of the range. His Texans began to join in with him, and then as they climbed through land made safe for their Kiowa friends they forgot about Stampede.

Being saddle tramps was a life good enough for Texans.

M[uck]
But No
Money

Humorous Tales From a Cumbrian Farm
Joyce Wilson

Ellenbank
Press

Published by Ellenbank Press
The Lathes, Selby Terrace, Maryport,
Cumbria CA15 6LX

First published 1993

Designed by Pam Grant

Typeset in 10½/12 pt Meridien by
Deltatype Ltd, Ellesmere Port, Cheshire
Printed and bound in Great Britain by
Athenaeum Press Ltd., Gateshead, Tyne & Wear

British Library Cataloguing in Publication Data
A catalogue record for this book is available
from the British Library

ISBN 1 873551 07 X

CONTENTS

To my two grandchildren,
Sarah and David

PREFACE

This book describes a way of life which existed in rural Cumbria over many centuries, before it was swept into history by the numerous technological advances of the last fifty years.

The stories are based on events in the lives of a fictitious farming family – Jackson Strong, his wife Edith and their children Jane, Esther and Bill – whose smallholding nestled snugly in a tiny hamlet of five farms a few miles from the West Cumbrian market town of Egremont.

Jackson Strong had started his working life as a hired farmhand at Wasdale Head, and then spent twenty years in the coal pits and iron-ore mines of West Cumbria. Eventually he managed to buy a farm of his own. However, he moved on to the land at a time when even families who had spent many generations working the soil were finding it difficult to make ends meet.

Like all small farmers, Jackson was affected by falling prices and foreign competition in the years between the two World Wars. But the coming of the Second World War brought prosperity of a sort. Farmers who had hitherto had great difficulty in selling their crops were now called upon to 'feed the nation'.

Jackson Strong was already in his mid-fifties when war broke out for the second time, and his sharp Cumbrian wit proved to be a great asset in his battle for survival. Another was his ability to slaughter and butch livestock. This was a much sought-after skill in the war years, both for dealing with legal, and (much more lucrative) illegal, butching.

Our first tale begins one cold November afternoon.

Jackson had been busy the previous night butching several pigs that were to be sold on the black market . . .

1

The Tale of a Pig

'**D**on't fall asleep Jackson. I know you must be tired after butching all last night, but remember old Betty's due to have her young pigs tonight and maybe Bill can't manage on his own.'

Jackson stirred in his armchair by the kitchen fire as his wife gently prodded his shoulder. His two daughters, Jane and Esther, glanced up from their homework, the mellow glow from the paraffin lamp lighting their young faces.

'I'm not asleep, Mother. Bill will have to manage on his own one day so he might as well learn now. I'm not going to keep any idle buggers on this farm. You, Jane . . .' Jackson turned sharply towards his eldest daughter. 'Did you remember to feed them calves in the top hull?'

'Yes Dad, but the little black one didn't look so good. He didn't want to feed.'

'Aye, well, it'll be next Thursday's market for that 'un if he can't pay his way. There's a war on. Them that can't fight won't survive!'

'How many pigs did you get through last night, Dad?' asked Esther.

'Just six, lass. Biggest trouble was keeping the doors shut. Yon nosey policeman from Egremont can spot a chink of light from five miles! If he'd got in the way . . .'

Here Jackson chuckled at his own joke, his eyes sparkling gleefully. 'I'd have cut his throat and scraped him before anyone had noticed the difference between him and Harry Benn's black sow!'

'I hope they don't look for a grave for the poor old pig, Father.'

Edith looked up as she spoke; her pink, blue and mauve prodded mat drawn taut across its wooden frame, adding a splash of colour to the rather drab Cumbrian kitchen. Anxiously she continued. 'It's one thing putting "death from pneumonia" in the stock book, and quite another proving it.'

Her last few words were drowned by the noise of the back door being slammed shut and the sound of someone in clogs walking briskly into the house. Their owner, Bill, a young man of about twenty, came into the kitchen, a look of excitement on his face. He sat down quickly in the armchair facing his father's across the hearth.

'A fine litter, Dad! Eight pigs – all strong and well!'

'Mother! Just get the stock book and we'll fill in these births.'

Edith obediently left her work and reached for the stock book which was kept in a small drawer in the sturdy sideboard. Carefully she carried a bottle of black ink and a pen and placed them almost ceremoniously on the table. Then she sat near her two daughters to share the light from the paraffin lamp.

She turned expectantly towards her husband.

'Write in the sow's name first, Mother.'

Edith carefully filled in the particulars.

'Put down . . . five pigs born. That's five for Lord Woolton . . . and . . . three for me.'

Jackson chuckled at his ability to outwit the government minister.

'You should be careful, Father. One day you'll get caught doing this. All they have to do is come and count.'

'Don't be so bloody daft, woman! Yon policeman at Egremont wouldn't know a litter of pigs from a litter of pups! He didn't last time . . .'

Edith went back to her prodding, shaking her head.

Suddenly the girls, who had been stifling their giggles, burst out laughing.

'What are you two laughing at? You shouldn't be listening to this. Get on with your homework.'

He paused, then changed his tone. 'And that's a waste of time, if you ask me.'

Edith put down her prodder sharply, ready to defend her daughters.

'Now then Dad, the girls have to do their homework. The secondary school will give them a much better chance in life than we ever had.'

'Education, they call it?' retorted her husband. 'All they do is sit around writing a lot of rubbish about fellas who died centuries ago, long before my time. They've nivver done a day's work in their lives!'

Jackson was now warming to his theme, and his voice rose accordingly.

Indicating his eldest daughter, who looked unimpressed, he continued. 'Our Jane used to be some use; but now she can't help with the milking in the mornings because she has to catch the train to Whitehaven. You tell me,' he demanded, waving his arms in Jane's direction, 'who's going to pick the taties and do the harrowing next spring?'

Suddenly his glance fell on Esther who had been doing her homework throughout, oblivious of her father's familiar ranting.

'What are you doing, Esther?'

'Physics, Dad.'

'Physical! Physical! What's Physical? Sounds like taking off your jacket and rolling up your sleeves to me. Who do they pay to teach you that? I reckon you could do it at home for nowt!'

'No, Dad! Physics, not Physical! It's a science.'

Subdued laughter from Bill made his copy of the *Farmers Weekly* start to dance. Bill was a bit too frightened of his father to laugh out loud. Laughing with Jackson was one thing, but laughing at him was quite another!

9

'Science! Oh, aye!'continued the old farmer with an air of clarity. 'Them chaps from the Ministry know all about that. Tuberculin testing and suchlike.' Jackson was pleased with recent progress in this area. 'Is that what you're doing, lass? Now *that* might be of some use – maybe you could get a job testing cows or measuring the butter fat in milk. That would be a fine education.'

He leaned back in his armchair, comfortably, reflecting aloud. 'Fancy a daughter of mine being that clever! None of Tom Postlethwaite's lasses were ever any good at school. Aye! Education's a fine thing . . .'

'Oh, Dad! You've got it all wrong. We don't do anything about milk testing. We do harder things than that . . .'

'Like what? If education isn't about helping your father, then what is it about?'

'Well, Miss Jones says,' Esther explained defensively, 'that if the weather is right next Tuesday . . . we're going to measure the sun!'

At these words Jackson sat bolt upright on the edge of his chair looking in disbelief from one face to the other.

The *Farmers Weekly* struggled to keep its balance, while Jane smothered her giggles in her handkerchief.

The mat prodding too had stopped; the scientific bombshell had been too much for Edith Strong.

However, Jackson reacted with customary decisiveness.

'What a bloody waste! I think it's time you both left that school, stopped at home and did some proper work. We work like hell to keep you two like ladies – just so you can waste time measuring the sun! When it's measured all I want to know is if it'll bloody well rain. Can you tell me that then?'

'No, Dad.'

'What about Miss Jones then? Does she know whether the taties'll be frozen next spring?'

'Dad, will you please stop arguing? I'm trying to do my French,' pleaded Jane.

10

'French! French! What are they teaching you French for? When are we going to France? Don't they know at yon bloody secondary school that there's a war on? We're sorting that lot out. We had a go at them in the last war, but we're at it again.'

'Don't talk daft, Father. You know as well as I do that we're fighting the Germans,' said his wife.

Jackson was undaunted. 'Of course I know that, Mother, everyone knows that. But they're all foreigners – can't trust any of them. Didn't Gracie Fields marry one? Isn't he in prison?'

He glared questioningly at his wife.

'No Dad, he's Italian.'

'Italian! French! What's the difference?'

* * *

The welcoming smell of the noon meal and the slightly muggy warmth of the kitchen cum dining room contrasted pleasantly with the raw frostiness of the farmyard outside.

'A fine bit of spare rib, Mother. I didn't think Harry's old sow would cut up as nice and tender as this!'

Jackson reached for another piece as he spoke. It was common practice to offer the one who did the butching a choice cut from the carcass.

'It's lovely, Mam. And I'm ready for it!'

Edith turned sympathetically towards Esther. 'You must be worn out, pet. Cycling all round the countryside delivering butter is hard work. Did you put the money in the tin?'

'Yes, Mam. Everyone was in today. I was a bit worried when I passed the policeman on his bike. I thought he might look in my basket.'

'Yon silly bugger wouldn't think of looking in a tea packet for butter, lass!' interjected her father. 'I reckon you're safe enough.'

11

Bill leaned anxiously towards his father. 'I don't think anyone's safe these days. I was just talking to Tom Smith on the road to the army camp this morning. He says the police searched old Bill Kirk's house and buildings last night. He reckons they found some hams and sides hidden in the barn.'

'Silly old bugger! That's the first spot they'll search. Daft they might be, but stupid they're not!'

'Well, don't you boast,' warned his wife. 'Ours aren't even in the barn. They're sitting right there on the dairy sconces for all the world to see.'

Jackson looked thoughtful. 'I don't like to admit it but you're right. It would be a good idea to shift them. Daft as they might be, not even a policeman could be persuaded that a pig has six legs!'

He turned to his son. 'Bill, you take them this afternoon. You know where to put them. That reminds me – did you get the money at the officers' mess for those eggs and butter you left on your way through?'

'Yes, the money's in the tin.'

Edith Strong didn't like having the army camp so close. 'The noise from the target practice this morning was awful,' she said, as she cleared the table.

'Don't grumble, Mam,' replied Jane impatiently. 'Those cloth targets make nice skirts.' She turned to her sister. 'Won't it be smashing, Esther, when the war's finished and we can buy proper clothes?'

'Yes, if we have the money to buy them with.'

'We've got the money now, pet,' soothed Edith. 'War always brings prosperity. It's only a pity it's at the expense of so many young lives.'

'Never mind Mam. We'll win,' said Bill.

His mother continued. 'There are no winners in war, son. I feel for those German mothers who have lost sons too.'

Jackson laughed. 'Take no notice of your mother, Bill. She fought the last war on the Kaiser's side!'

The rest of the family were used to their father's teasing, but Esther sensed that her mother was often hurt by his remarks.

'Take no notice of him, Mam,'she said. 'Come on, I'll wash the dishes while you make some cakes.'

Suddenly she spotted a roasting tin filled with black pudding. 'That black pudding looks lovely. Can we have some for supper?'

'No, Esther, we'll have it tomorrow. Thank goodness we don't have to put it into skins nowadays – cleaning skins is hard work.'

'Yes, anything to avoid hard work! Black pudding in a tin looks nowt like proper black pudding,' retorted her husband. 'Come on Bill, get those sides and hams shifted!'

At the mention of pigs, Edith became agitated again. 'Oh, dear. It's all very worrying. If we only slaughtered the two pigs we are allowed, we wouldn't have all this trouble . . .'

'Stop fretting, Edith. The nation has to be fed. There's a war on, remember? I have enough to do fighting the Germans without fighting you as well. We've all got to make an effort.'

Suddenly they were startled by an unexpected knocking on the door, which was just as quickly opened by their neighbour, Tom Graham.

Tom was a frequent and welcome visitor, and Edith gave him a chair close to the fire.

Jackson greeted his friend warmly but Tom looked a bit anxious.

'Hello Jackson! I hear the police are getting active round here. You'd better look out. The government is doing its best to stamp out the black market.'

'I wish they'd just stick to fighting the Germans,' retorted Jackson indignantly. 'We never interfere with them. I bet Churchill and all that lot don't stick to their rations. Can you imagine Winston settling down to smoke his Havana cigar after a plateful of spam and dried eggs? Not bloody likely!'

Poor Edith couldn't stand this irreverence. 'Come now, Father. You shouldn't talk like that. We know what sacrifices they make. The poor King and Queen are still living in Buckingham Palace among all those bombs. We should be thankful.'

'We *are* thankful,'he answered stubbornly. 'And they should be thankful that there aren't any bombs falling here. It's us that feeds the nation. Don't worry, Mother,' he smiled. 'If Churchill lived near here he might find a dozen eggs and a tin of black pudding on his doorstep in the morning!'

Tom stood up to leave. 'I'm on my way to cut the thorns back on our ten acres near the camp.'

'About time!' snapped Jackson. 'Half your sheep are trailing around with thorn branches hanging from their wool.'

'Get yourselves off to work you two,' laughed Edith, shooing them out. 'The war won't get won at your speed.'

* * *

That evening, as Edith carried the supper dishes out to the scullery, the two girls began their homework as usual. Jackson was quietly dozing near the fire, his newspaper on his knee and his glasses perched precariously on his nose.

'Mam, did you finish cleaning up the salt in the dairy?' asked Jane, suddenly remembering the hastily transported portions of pig. Surplus salt on the stone slabs would be sure to raise suspicion if the farmhouse were searched.

'Yes, pet, all finished – only four sides and four hams to be seen. I hope the pork they took away has been salted down again properly.'

'It's always been OK before, so there's no reason to think it will be ruined this time. You worry too much, Mam.'

14

'Well, someone's got to worry. Your father doesn't. We could all end up in jail. I'd like to see him talk his way out of that! Illegal butching, falsifying documents and letters – I have to make sure I read them and sign them, otherwise he's likely to throw them on the fire. He seems to be able to lose bills and forms before he opens them.'

'I don't think we have anything to fear if the police raid us, Mam,' said Esther. 'We have the right number of pigs salted down. They won't know if they were killed yesterday or last month. All the butter has gone, so we have nothing to fear. No evidence, no arrest.'

'Rest! Rest!' Jackson woke up suddenly.

'No rest for anyone! How can anyone rest with you three talking non-stop? Where's our Bill?'

'Gone to the pictures.'

Did he finish feeding the calves, Esther?'

'Yes, Dad.'

'And did he check the young pigs? Are they all still alive? That sow's been guilty of overlaying her litters before now.' He laughed. 'We can't lose any of Lord Woolton's pigs . . . Sitting in the picture house won't win this war!'

'Just pass me that basket of woollen strips . . . Make yourself useful for a change,' said Edith.

Jackson obediently passed the basket to his wife so that she could continue prodding her mat.

Suddenly the sound of furious barking shattered the stillness of the night.

Edith was already on her feet. 'What's all that noise? It must be the police. I knew this would happen one day! What shall we do?'

'We'll just keep quiet, Mother. It's probably one of those soldiers trying to find his way back to the camp. You know as well as I do that these city folk have to have a number 39 trolley bus to get them home. Our horses find their way home better than they can.'

'That's true, Dad,' agreed Esther sardonically. 'Betty's brought you home from the pub often enough!'

The laughter came to a sudden halt as they heard a knock at the door.

'Go and answer the door, Jane. Most folk just knock and walk straight in. It must be something important.'

Jane opened the door to reveal two police officers each carrying a torch.

'Is your father in, Miss?'

'Yes. Please come in.'

They walked into the farm kitchen, taking off their caps and nodding politely to Edith and her daughters.

Jackson beamed at the policemen, full of benevolence.

'Good evening, gentlemen. What can I do for you? Are we showing too much light?' He turned to his wife accusingly. 'I've told you before, Mother, to make sure that the blinds are properly shut.'

'No, no. It's not that, Mr Strong,' explained one of the policemen hastily. 'We have received information abut an illegal butching session. We know that six pigs were butched last night, and we have reason to believe that you know something about it and may have the meat on your premises. We are authorised to search your house and farm buildings.'

'Go ahead, Officer,' breezed the old farmer. 'Let me know if you find anything . . . we may be a bit short this winter!'

Jackson chuckled to himself, but stole a glance at his anxious, white-faced wife.

'Search the buildings, Frank!' ordered the first policeman. 'I'll check everything here.' He turned to Edith who was fast gathering her wits. 'Now Mrs Strong. Would you please show me your bedrooms and the dairy?'

As they left the warm kitchen Jackson picked up his newspaper, nodded to his daughters, and began to read very studiously. Jane and Esther continued with their home-work.

Ten minutes later Edith and the first policeman returned to the kitchen, closely followed by the policeman who had searched the farm buildings. The latter spoke first.

'Nothing to be found, Sergeant. I've searched very thoroughly.'

'Yes,' interrupted Jackson, lowering his newspaper. 'You've both wasted your time. This country's at war and you spend your time chasing a few rats in our barn. And you Bill . . .' Jackson said, turning to the sergeant who was raking about under the sofa, 'the only think you're likely to find under there is cat shit. Hitler needn't worry too much . . .'

'I haven't finished yet, Mr Strong,' the sergeant cut in sharply. 'I'll just take a look around this kitchen before I go – if you don't mind?' He was clearly frustrated at failing to incriminate the self-assured, wily old farmer.

'Go ahead, Sergeant.' Jackson waved his hand expansively towards his daughters and the table which still displayed the remains of their recent supper. He smiled mischievously to himself as the policeman began to search the room meticulously.

Edith's eyes followed him nervously as he moved towards the sideboard. Then her heart missed a beat as she spotted the edge of the tin of fresh black pudding peeping out from under a clean towel. Would the policeman see it? Would he look beneath the towel? Her anxiety rose to fever pitch as the policeman's eyes moved slowly across the cluttered shelves. He lowered his glance to assess the possible contents of the boxes and tins placed haphazardly on the broad sideboard.

Edith glanced anxiously at her husband. He was already on his feet, making his way casually towards the sideboard.

'You will need some help, Sergeant, to find your way amongst that collection of tins. I don't think our Edith has much idea of what she has in them. I keep telling her it's time we had a good clean out, but you know what women are . . .'

By now Jackson was close to the tin of black pudding, but at that moment the policeman's eagle eye reached the same spot. One corner of the tea towel had not completely covered the evidence.

'That's black pudding, unless I'm very much mistaken.'

He pointed triumphantly past Jackson's bulky form to the guilty, sponge-like substance peeping from beneath the cloth, lying just beyond his reach.

The two girls and their mother looked alarmed.

Jackson, however, was already exploding, his outraged voice rising as he pushed the tin of black pudding into his wife's astonished gasp.

'Black pudding! Black pudding!' he roared indignantly.

'Tell me,' he turned back to the policeman. 'Just you tell me, when you have ever seen a black pudding not in a skin?'

He then turned insistently towards the sergeant. 'What do you take us for, Sergeant? Twenty years in farming and you accuse us of not knowing how to make black pudding!'

'Mother,' he stormed, pointing a furious finger at the offending tin, 'go and cut two pieces of that gingerbread for these fellas!'

'Jane,' he called in the same tone of outrage. 'Put the kettle on and let these two have a taste of something they haven't had since 1939.'

The two women scuttled off to do the old man's bidding.

'No thank you, Mr Strong. We haven't time now. Sorry to have bothered you, ladies. Good evening, Sir.'

'Oh my God,' breathed Edith as they heard the two policemen closing the farm gate. 'That was close, Jackson. How did you know I had any gingerbread to give them?'

'I didn't,' laughed her husband. 'I just knew they'd get tired of waiting for that old kettle to boil – especially with that poor fire! Put some coal on, Esther. We'll all have a mug of tea.'

'I wouldn't like to go through that again, Jackson,' gasped Edith. 'By the way . . . where have you hidden the pork? I was sure it would be in the buildings somewhere.'

'Not a chance, lass. Those pigs are as safe as the rest of us, protected by the British Army!'

'Where? Where?' they all exclaimed.

'In the ammunition dump at the camp. One good turn deserves another, Edith!'

2

THE HORSE SALE

It was six o'clock on a dark winter's morning, and rain lashed the windows and sneaked under the doors of the farmhouse. Bill felt the hostile bite of the northern wind as he crossed the yard. At last he reached the byre on the other side – already his cap was wet and drops of rain were exploring the lower reaches of his spine. Bill pushed the byre door open with a muddy boot, both hands holding empty milking buckets. He was glad of the warmth from the animals which wrapped itself around him as he entered.

His father was already busy feeding and watering the waking beasts. A bucket of water had to be taken to each cow and placed in her trough. Luckily Jackson had recently had his best byre floor concreted and a large concrete trough constructed beneath the single tap.

Cows vary greatly in the ease with which they can be milked. Rose was Bill's favourite. She was a dark roan, a shorthorn, and he always hurried to start milking her before his father finished the early feeding session. Jackson was an expert hand milker, but like most farmers, he was not averse to leaving the temperamental beasts to a younger and less experienced man. The chance of an easy milking session was the main reason Bill got up so early.

As he milked, Bill could hear the cows' contented munching and easy shuffling. A casual visitor would only have seen two rows of milking cows of various colours and mixed breeds. But within these outwardly placid animals existed a variety of personalities and neuroses which would have confounded any psychoanalyst.

Rose was the natural mother of the group – a Sunday

20

School teacher of a cow. She never kicked, she never strayed, and she could anticipate all the farmer's needs. True, like all her sisters, she was secured to the pole in her stall by a neck chain. But if by chance Rose was left unfastened, then little disturbance would be caused. She would remain obediently in her place without need of restriction or correction.

Many calves she had borne. They had been placed in the small pen at the warmest end of the milking byre, but like all these bovine matrons, Rose had soon lost interest in her offspring and had accepted Bill and his father as welcome substitutes. All in all, she was a dream of a cow.

Now, as Bill speedily milked her she politely eased forward to nuzzle her cow cake from the far corner of her trough. Neither cow nor milker were inconvenienced as she stretched gently forward to reach her titbit. As he drew the last drops from Rose, Bill knew the easiest part of this early morning job was over. Soon Rose would settle herself down in the warm straw to have a comfortable doze while the rest of the herd was being attended to. Having taken Rose's milk to the dairy for his mother to separate into cream and skimmed milk, Bill had to decide on his next cow. Mollie in the next stall turned her large inviting eyes in Bill's direction as he returned. Mollie was friendly . . . to a fault. Contact with human beings was the highlight of her existence! While standing in the farmyard, walking to pasture, or even grazing in the field, she always had an eye open for people.

Mollie's first port of call when she left the byre in warmer weather was the farmhouse. She loved to push her large wet nose against the kitchen window pane, even trying to sniff the air inside the back kitchen door. Hens, ducks and carelessly placed buckets were all scattered as her curiosity led her into places where a cow ought not to go!

The walk to her pasture offered an opportunity to sample the delights of humans on the move. Motor cars could be investigated and even be stopped quite still if she placed herself in the very centre of the road. Noisy children, noisy dogs and strange bicycles could all be inspected at very close quarters. Her favourite grazing areas were always the hedges which bordered her field.

Bill settled himself hopefully against Mollie's flank. The cow had willingly moved her hindquarters to the middle of the stall to allow him to place his stool between her and the wooden partition to which she was chained. As soon as this position had been reached, Mollie swung her head over her chain to gaze lovingly in Bill's direction.

'She's on form this morning,' Bill thought to himself.

Mollie's devotion took two forms. Firstly, like many cows, she had learnt the trick of holding her milk back, making milking an arm-aching job, and secondly the minute she felt the farmer's head lean against her flank, she felt inspired to lean back very firmly! To Mollie this was simply an expression of wholehearted affection. The fact that she weighed several hundredweight more than her luckless milker was well beyond her comprehension.

Eventually Bill was able to leave the friendly animal and wearily carry her two buckets of milk to the dairy.

'Why does she always give so much milk?' he asked as he deposited the brimming pails beside his mother.

Who would be next? Jackson had already milked several of the easier and almost dry cows whilst he had been busy with Mollie.

Nancy? She had been given the name when she was a cute little calf. It had suited her then. But if Bill had been asked to name her in adulthood he would have had no hesitation in calling her simply 'Tail'.

A tail is a very useful appendage for most animals, particularly large farm animals plagued by summer flies. However, in Nancy's case, it was an extension of her rather malicious personality, and using it fulfilled a deep psychological need.

Nancy's intelligence was beyond question. She knew that Bill would have both hands occupied while he milked. She also knew that both his legs were required to cradle the milking pail beneath her ample belly. Consequently placing his head firmly against her flank was his only means of pinning her against the stall partition in order to accomplish his task. Wearing a milking cap made it easier for Bill to exert the necessary pressure against her flank. To Nancy this whole procedure was a battle of wits!

She anticipated Bill's every move with the precision of a general on the battlefield, and her swishing tail was the perfect weapon. The slight bend to place his stool near her waiting udder resulted in the flight of his favourite milking cap. Bill glanced foolishly about him – where had it landed? Sometimes it spun crazily around on a neighbouring startled horn. Less appetisingly, it was wont to land in the freshly dropped and steaming cow muck behind the herd's feet. Such an event meant a new cap. Ah! There it was, stuck just out of reach between a beam and the floorboards of the barn above. No use wasting time retrieving his lost property now. Round one had gone to 'The Tail'.

'How much longer is it going to take you to get started on that cow?' growled his father from the depths of the byre. Jackson's voice came from the other side of a pleasant black heifer who had only had one calf as yet, and produced very little milk, her breed not being noted for their dairy qualities.

Angrily Bill attacked!

Sweetly and deftly Nancy whipped her tail around his neck.

She pulled. She wanted her tail back.

He choked. He wanted his breath back.

Both hands were needed to undo the wicked tangle, while the resentful cow shuffled uneasily about in her stall. Often Bill had cut off the long hairs on Nancy's tail, hoping to avoid the daily strangulation. But this had met with little success.

The malicious tail had managed to thump him just below his left ear with its reinforced stump! Some progress had been achieved by tying the tail to Nancy's hind leg with a piece of string. However, she then considered the two appendages to be as one and tended to raise and lower both of them together. Furthermore, Bill's father viewed such stringy aids as an admission of defeat.

Summer was always the time Bill dreaded having to milk Nancy. Her calves were born in June, thus increasing her yield and the delicacy of her temperament at the hottest time of the year. Flies were enemy number one and the searching tail flicked endlessly in spite of sprays and lotions. However the deadliest weapon in Nancy's armoury was diarrhoea. Summer grazing made most cows loose-bowelled. But Nancy religiously retained her share until milking time.

It never spurted or flowed. It just trickled slowly – down her tail. The tail became a brown slithery whip. Bill left her side during these steamy months evenly striped from his curly head to the tops of his sturdy clogs.

Neither flies nor diarrhoea were there to inspire Nancy on this cold winter's morning but she did her best!

Only one cow remained unmilked. Bill glanced round, hoping to see his father. But no, the old man must have left. After all, only one cow remained. This was Maud, a pure-bred Ayrshire, a Scottish breed renowned for their high milk production.

Bill stood for a moment looking at Maud, her long spike-like horns reaching well above those of her sisters. The milk was released through very tiny button-like teats which scarcely protruded from her distended udder. Did Scotsmen have smaller fingers than Englishmen, Bill wondered. He had to resort to milking with only one finger and thumb until the pressure had been substantially reduced.

Clumsy milking had made Maud the most neurotic of all Jackson's cows. She had built up a formidable wall of resentment and hostility over her four short years of life, and she was an expert kicker! The only solution was to bribe her with food.

Bill always piled her trough with cow cake, meal and finely chopped turnip before he began his assault. The speed at which she ate was only matched by the speed at which he milked. At no point could Bill relax and feel he was on the home straight. Leaving her, even for a moment, to empty a pail was courting disaster. And disaster could strike in the shape of a cloven hoof like that of the devil himself.

Maud often made her move just as Bill thankfully finished. The milk would be almost level with the rim of the milking bucket, and first she would stretch her hind leg as far back as she could, enjoying a lovely long stretch! Milk, bucket, stool and milker would be picked up *not* on the return journey towards their rightful position beneath her belly, but on the second, outward journey!

Maud's mixed up frame of mind meant that she could sometimes appear friendly and co-operative for days at a time. This was a trap, giving her owners enough time to relax and become complacent. After all one wouldn't expect a mere cow to harbour grudges or to plan revenge but Maud was no ordinary cow.

Her repertoire of tricks included another deeply antisocial practice. Again she would wait until milking was almost over. Then she would decide to empty her bladder. Bulls can perform this function with the minimum of adjustment; not so the female of the species. She is obliged to arrange herself in such a way that the force of gravity will speedily remove the contents of her bladder in a downward direction.

This is a major event for the milker. Legs apart, spine arching upwards, the resultant cascade gushes forth, endangering both milk and man. (After all, urine-flavoured milk has never been acceptable in the tea rooms of our genteel middle-class!)

Maud's dripping tail would remain a threat until Bill had finished, a clear challenge to the supposed superiority of man over beast. Bill was often tempted not to finish milking this enemy; but he knew that a bout of mastitis would probably betray his laziness to his father.

This morning Maud was kind.

'Hurry up,' called Jackson as Bill paused to fix the raincoat snugly round his wet trousers.

'Just give me a minute, Dad. I'm getting soaked through carrying these buckets of milk across the yard.'

'At the speed you carry them you'll end up with more water than milk. Coats slow a fella down. You never see me dithering about like you do. A drop of rain never harmed anybody yet!' he called to the closing door.

Edith was busy in the farm kitchen when Bill and Jackson came in from milking. The small fire was burning under the ancient boiling copper, and the first wash was already bubbling, the steam rising across the ceiling and finally slipping down the inside of the windows and walls. The smell of ham frying slowly over the kitchen fire wandered through the open doorway to tempt the family to breakfast.

Edith blew out the paraffin lamp as they sat down at the table. 'We can manage to see now,' she said, handing the bread around.

'Did you remember to put the lamps out in the byre before you came across, Bill?'

'Yes, Dad.'

'The amount of paraffin we use on this farm is ridiculous,' observed Jackson as he tackled his breakfast.

'Well we've got to be able to see where we're going, Dad. It gets dark so early at night now.'

'See? See? There's more lights in our buildings at milking time than there is in St Bees lighthouse! There's a lamp hanging up in every bloody building in the place – and you can only be in one spot at once you know.'

26

'But Dad, I carry buckets and hay across the yard and I can't manage a lamp as well. You've told me never to do that in case I set the hay on fire.'

'Or yourself,' said his mother.

'Who's bothered about him? He has enough sense to move out of the way – but the hay costs good money, and might start a fire which could burn the whole barn down! No lad, it's a question of having a good memory . . .'

'What on earth has a good memory to do with it, Jackson? You're talking some sort of rubbish again.'

'Rubbish! I never talk rubbish. Now just tell me, how does a blind man get around his house without falling all over the place? Tell me that . . .' he challenged his wife.

'I suppose he knows where all the furniture is.'

'That's right. Isn't that just what I've been telling you? He memorises it! It doesn't cost a blind man a penny for paraffin. He doesn't need a candle at all – only matches to light a fire. Isn't that true?'

Bill nodded. 'I suppose so but we're not blind – what has a blind man got to do with me feeding the calves?'

'Memory, lad, memory. You don't see me wandering about the place with a lamp, then going back for a forkful of hay, then carrying the lamp somewhere else . . . Oh no, I remember where everything is, then I can walk in the dark, just making one journey.'

Edith left the table to stir her washing in the back kitchen.

'Well Dad, I wouldn't like to go into that pigsty with two buckets of hot food in the dark. I wouldn't be able to see them. They'd knock me over.'

'That's because the pigs are used to the dark. If you didn't take a lamp everywhere you'd be able to see as well as them. It's just a question of use, lad. Anyway you could leave the door open, that'll let a bit of light in.'

'But the pigs'll run out!'

'They won't run far if their dinner's inside. You young

fellas like everything easy – you live a soft life these days.'

'Will you give me a hand to mangle these big sheets, Bill,' asked Edith as she came back into the kitchen. 'The mangle is heavy and the sheets are awkward.'

'They're not the only awkward things in this house,' muttered Bill as he went to help his mother.

'Lower the clothes rack please, Dad!' Edith called above the sound of the huge rollers as they squeezed the water from the sheets into the bucket beneath. 'I'll have to dry them above the fireplace today.'

'Not only do I have to work outside, but I've got to keep things going in here as well,' Jackson grumbled. 'Short-handed we are. Nobody would guess we had two daughters educating themselves out of having to work. I hope to God they can find husbands with enough money to keep them in idleness. Mind you, I don't know anybody who'll be able to afford them – they'll have to go a long way from here if they expect to get fixed up with a house with no work in it.'

'What are you muttering about Jackson? Aren't you going somewhere today? I don't fancy having you under my feet all day as well as the washing.'

'Don't worry, Edith. Tom Graham is calling for me at ten o'clock. There's a special horse sale at Wigton. A wet day like this is a grand day for a sale.'

'What are you going to a horse sale for? We can't afford a new horse and we don't need one, Jackson.'

'After all these years, Edith, you still think sales are just about buying and selling. That's not all the story. I like to see who is selling what, and besides I enjoy looking at good young horses. A day like today will be a real treat.'

'Oh I know the story all right, Jackson. You'll enjoy looking at the horses, but meeting friends in pubs comes an awfully close second . . . In any case I must get on, my next lot of washing is nearly ready.'

At the horse sale ponies and cobs trotted round the ring, their new rope or canvas halters making them look like little polished presents carefully wrapped for prospective buyers. Tails had been brushed and combed, and manes billowed gently as they trotted by.

Jackson and Tom assessed each animal as it circled below the auctioneer.

'Some bonny ponies,' observed Tom. 'It's grand coming to a sale when you have no money. You can just sit here and enjoy watching other folk part with theirs.'

'Yes, you're quite right, Tom. It's too wet to do anything useful in the fields so we might as well support this sale. We'll buy a few drinks and have a bite to eat before we go.'

Tom glanced at the sale catalogue. 'I see there's some young pedigree Clydesdales from Lockerbie coming through the ring now. Number fifteen, a two-year-old filly, a light bay, is the first one. Let's see what sort of quality they can bring down from Scotland, Jackson.'

The filly was led into the ring – a lovely light bay with four white socks and a white blaze down her face.

'She's a pure-bred Clydesdale all right,' enthused Jackson. 'You don't have to look in the pedigree book. It's there in front of your eyes. Walk her round!' he called out to the auctioneer's assistant.

'Certainly, Mr Strong.'

The filly moved gently and obediently round the ring, her long tail swishing gently against her young legs. Her unshod feet made little sound as she turned, stopped and backed.

'Who'll start the bidding? Will you bid twenty pounds, Mr Strong?'

'You haven't come to buy a horse, Jackson,' warned Tom as his friend nodded to the auctioneer.

'I'm only just starting her off, Tom. She's the finest filly I've seen here . . . She's too good to go to a bad home for nothing.'

'Be careful. There doesn't seem to be a lot of interest in unbroken stock today.'

'I'll just make sure she doesn't go for nothing', said Jackson nodding.

The price rose. 'Forty pounds, I'm bid. Forty pounds,' called the auctioneer invitingly.

'Forty-five pounds,' called Jackson. 'That's my lot . . . It's pushed the little lady on a bit.'

'Going at forty-five pounds . . . Any more bids, gentlemen? This fine pedigree filly going at forty-five pounds . . . Going! . . . Going! . . . Gone! Gone to Mr Jackson Strong.'

The hammer struck the bench sharply, as the mare was led from the ring.

'Good God! She's been knocked down to you, Jackson. What on earth will you say to your Edith? Go round and put her back through the ring. You'll probably sell her. Even if you lose a few pounds it's better than taking a horse home you never intended to buy.'

'I'll go round and have a close look at her,' said Jackson.

The two friends made their way to the long ropes where the horses that had been through the ring were tethered. Jackson ran his hands over the filly and she calmly nuzzled his jacket pocket.

'I've never owned anything as well-bred as this filly,' said the old farmer. 'She's coming home, even if we're a bit short of money.'

* * *

'You've bought a horse!' said Edith, amazed, as she handed Jackson and Tom mugs of tea to accompany the sandwiches and cakes on the table.

'I thought it was strange when you both came in for tea. You've brought Tom for moral support.' She turned to Tom. 'I thought he was safe with you, Tom. You know what a weakness he has for horses. I expect it was cheap. So what does it do? Bite? Kick? Bolt? Or what does it not do? Like work!'

'No, Edith, she has a pedigree as long as your arm,' said Tom.

'When is she coming home, Dad?' asked Jane, full of excitement at the prospect of a new horse.

'Any minute, lass. We thought we'd better hurry home before she got here.'

'Otherwise you would have toured the pubs. But at least that would have been cheaper than buying a pedigree mare,' complained Edith.

'She's just an unbroken two-year-old, Mother,' said Jackson.

* * *

31

As Edith began washing up she tried to analyse why she felt uneasy. Many years of penny-pinching had made her suspicious of all expenditure. But the war had brought a degree of prosperity and now that it was over perhaps she should be less wary and encourage Jackson to build up his stock. A sense of guilt nagged at her. Did she throw cold water over his plans too readily?

After all this was a new England. Surely her eldest son's death and other mothers' sacrifices would only be justified if ordinary people could build a new and better Britain? Poverty and want had to be things of the past. A new life . . . and a new young mare, the mother of generations of foals for the future.

'Ah well!' she said aloud, as she dried her hands on the roller towel hanging on the back door. 'We'll get by somehow. We've had worse setbacks than this.' As she made her way across the back kitchen she could hear a distant engine approaching the farm.

The huge cattle truck drew to a halt beside the farm gate and the whole family rushed out to welcome the newcomer. As the tailgates were lowered the young horse was led slowly down towards her new family.

The girls stepped forward to pat her.

'Be careful,' warned Jackson. 'We don't know her yet. She may kick or bite.'

The mare pricked her ears, then stretched her neck forward to nuzzle Esther's hand. Soon she was being stroked and patted, even by Edith. She was obviously used to kindness and attention.

'What are you going to call her, Dad?' Edith asked. 'She's a lovely mare and you bought her when no one else wanted her, so *you* give her a name.'

'I think Peggy is a good name for her,' Jackson said decisively as he watched his newest horse walking happily into the stable with his two daughters.

3

THE TALE OF A COW

There can be few times more delicious to a farmer than that half hour or so at the end of the working day. This is particularly true in winter, when all the milking and feeding is done and the cows are settling for the night. Huge lumbering bodies are gratefully slumping down in the stalls, one by one, and the sound of leisurely chewing spreads a feeling of contentment throughout the buildings. However raw and frosty it might be outside, the byre is always welcoming and snug. The smell of milk and warm cows gives a sense of comfort and security unknown in the town.

Jackson Strong, putting the finishing touches to his byre for the night, heard the click of the latch as the door quietly opened.

'How are you Jackson?' Tom Graham asked as he came in.

'Not bad, not bad,' Jackson answered his neighbour and friend of many years' standing. 'Just yon shorthorn cow over there.' He pointed towards a poor-looking cow. 'She's not giving as much milk as she should.'

'Well, what do you expect? She's had at least ten calves that I can think of, and I bet she's hardly any teeth left. She's not a machine you know and you bred her yourself . . . If I were talking to someone else I'd say you were bloody greedy.'

'Bloody greedy!' Jackson exclaimed, pointing to another cow. 'See yon good-looking cow standing at the top end of the byre?'

'That 'un with the good-looking head?'

'Aye, that's right. Well, she's the mother of that dry bugger we've been talking about!'

'That takes a lot of believing, Jackson. You've got your dates and calvings muddled.'

'Me get muddled? Never! It's only folks who rely on stock books that get muddled. Just come down to this doorway and see for yourself.'

Jackson led Tom through into an adjoining barn and indicated a long list of names, servings and calving dates written roughly on the whitewashed wall just near the byre door.

'There you are!' he pointed triumphantly. 'There's Mabel, that's Katie's mother, clear for all to see. Born September 1933.' He pointed again. 'And look. Here's Katie. Born December 1936!'

'Good God. Some of these cows must have been in the Ark!' laughed Tom.

'It's just a question of good breeding and kindness, that's all. You'll notice, Tom, that the Bible says they went in two by two – no mention of how many came out! It takes good farming to keep a few generations going.' He smiled gleefully at his own expertise. 'If my cows had false teeth they'd last half a century!'

Edith came in from the yard, having heard the laughter. 'Is that you boasting again, Father? Take no notice of him Tom. He didn't tell you he killed one of my ducks this morning, did he? Went over it with a wheel of his cart.'

'I've told you before, Mother,' her husband retorted tartly, 'you over-feed them ducks. A good duck'll soon duck out of the way! Reckon it had eaten too much of her bread, Tom . . . She always did have a heavy hand with bread.' He chortled happily at his little joke. Not so Edith . . .

'What cheek! I've never seen you or anyone else saying no to my bread. I came out here to see if you're going to the auction tomorrow. If you are, Bill says he'd like to go with you.'

Edith turned to Tom Graham. 'This newfangled Milk

Marketing Board has gone to his head, Tom . . . She's been a good cow to us. It's a shame to cast her off now.'

'Don't talk so bloody daft, woman. Farming's moving into a new era. The war's over but we've still got to feed the country.'

'It's just as well, you know him Tom,' she smiled. 'I haven't had a chance to say how nice it is to see you. Are you coming across to the kitchen for a mug of tea and a talk?'

'Of course he is,' broke in Jackson. 'He doesn't need to be asked. He can find his way to a drink as fast as that lazy horse I've got in the back field.' Turning to walk down the byre, he continued, 'I'll have a quick look at Katie before we go in. I didn't milk her tonight – with a bit of luck she'll milk out in the auction tomorrow.'

Tom and Edith left the byre while Jackson went off to check his stock.

'Hello Mr Graham!' Esther and Jane greeted their neighbour as he reached his usual armchair by the kitchen fire.

Bill gave a friendly nod before returning to his crossword, and Edith went off to make tea in the back kitchen using her new electric kettle.

'What have you been doing today, Mr Graham?' asked Jane as her father came in and settled himself comfortably opposite his visitor.

'Just the usual potato round at Cleator Moor, Jane. Nothing special.'

Her father, giving the fire a brisk poke, launched into a pointed appreciation of Tom's potato round. 'Good spot for selling potatoes, Cleator Moor. But you grammar-school-educated girls wouldn't know anything about history and potatoes.'

'What has selling potatoes at Cleator Moor got to do with history, Dad?' exclaimed Esther indignantly. 'Surely it's just the same as selling them in Whitehaven, Carlisle or London!'

'Well, that's just where you are wrong, my clever lassies! They're all Irish in Cleator Moor or hadn't you noticed?'

'Everyone knows that, Dad.'

'That's only half the story. Ever heard of the Irish potato famine?'

'Poor things,' said Edith, handing round mugs of tea. 'It must have been terrible. All those people dying of hunger, and England didn't do much to help them or so I've read.'

'Books! Books!' roared Jackson. 'You can't believe all they say.' He turned towards an amused Tom. 'Edith reads a lot of books, Tom, but she can't tell me why Katie doesn't give as much milk as she used to.'

'She's maybe sick, Dad.'

'Sick, our Jane? Sick? Bloody lazy if you ask me.' He turned to Tom. 'Just like all women, contrary and idle!'

Edith handed round pieces of cake as Tom pursued the Irish potato famine.

'What were you saying Jackson? I didn't know you'd read anything about the Irish potato famine.'

'Oh no,' answered his friend in a self-satisfied tone. 'No need to read about it. It's just a question of observation and common sense. The Irish can't farm like us – they never could. You just have to see them Irish chaps that's building that new atom bomb factory at Sellafield. The train fetches them back to the old army camp at six o'clock, mind you. Them Irish fellas first came over here in my grandfather's time because they knew we could grow good potatoes.' Jackson stirred the fire, looking as if he had proved his case beyond any doubt.

Esther had been boiling at this demonstration of her father's ignorance. 'That's daft, Dad. They came because the famine drove them here.'

'Daft is it? Well just tell me how many have gone back to Ireland? Just tell me that then.'

'I don't know, Dad. They've settled down here now. They

have no connection with Ireland any more.'

'You bet they haven't. They can't get potatoes like Tom's in Ireland.'

Here Tom nodded enthusiastically.

'And another thing, my girl. They gave them electricity in Cleator Moor too, just the same as us.'

Jackson settled back in his chair as though the matter was settled once and for all.

'Why shouldn't they have electricity like us?' asked his confused wife. 'They're English just like you and me.'

'English? English?' stormed her husband, sitting bolt upright in his chair. 'Since when were the Irish in Cleator Moor English? Foreigners they are and foreigners they'll stay.'

'If you are going to Whitehaven, Dad, I'd like to come with you,' said Bill, hastily changing the subject.

'Yes, son. I'm taking that useless Katie to sell.'

'Who'll buy her if she's nearly dry?' asked Esther innocently.

'She'll go to the butcher probably. It's a while since I've seen a decent bit of beef hanging in Reggie Watson's shop window and I know he'll be there.'

'He'll not waste his time buying that bag of bones, Jackson,' said Tom, knocking his pipe out against the grate. 'You'll be lucky if you get enough to pay your bus fare home, especially if the two of you are going.'

At this remark the three youngsters broke into peals of delighted laughter.

'Now girls, get on with your homework.' Their mother turned quickly on Esther and Jane, knowing her husband wouldn't appreciate merriment at his expense. 'And you Bill. Go and polish your boots and your dad's boots if both of you are going tomorrow.'

'What do you want us to clean our shoes for, Edith?' protested Jackson. 'We have to walk through cow muck at

Whitehaven auction just the same as we do here. There's nothing special about Whitehaven you know. It might have a grammar school but cows shite there just the same as anywhere else!'

'I'll do the boots, Dad.' Bill left the room, stifling his laughter.

'How's your Mary, Tom?' asked Edith. 'She'll be going to Whitehaven tomorrow, I expect. Has she plenty of eggs to take?'

'Yes, Edith. The hens seem to do much better now that they're kept in deep litter.'

'Oh yes, she read about it in the *Farmers Weekly*, I remember her telling me. Modern farming methods do seem to pay.' She turned to Jackson. 'If you get a good price for Katie tomorrow, it would be money well spent if we bought a new hen house . . .'

Jackson wasn't pleased by the direction of the conversation. 'All you think about is money. The minute it comes into the house you want to spend it again.'

'But egg production is increased this way, Dad,' reasoned his wife.

'The number of eggs makes no difference, Mother. Take no notice of what they tell you in the *Farmers Weekly*. If they could make money from eggs, they wouldn't be writing in the newspapers.

'Well, our Mary collects more eggs than she did before,' ventured Tom.

'But what about taste and flavour, Tom? That's the important thing, flavour. Last time I was in Whitehaven I had a fried egg as white as our Esther's face.'

'There's nothing wrong with our Esther's face, Father,' said Edith indignantly. Turning to their neighbour, she explained. 'It's all the studying she does, Tom.'

Tom nodded politely, not being familiar with the effects of studying.

'Hens aren't the same unless they can run around the farmyard,' continued Jackson. 'But you have a point, Mother. We could do with fastening our hens in for a month or two. I've never had a decent egg since John Hodgson bought those bloody stupid bantams. Bantie cocks roam this countryside like Martin Scott's Herdwicks.'

'That's enough, Father,' cautioned Edith, who didn't like to hear the neighbours criticised. 'Everyone does their best. Hedges are always difficult to repair.'

'Maybe for some. It would be a good idea if the *Farmers Weekly* wrote a few articles on how to fill a few gaps in a fence. But I suppose it's too much like hard work for young farmers these days!'

'Now, now, Jackson. Wasn't it our bull that strayed into Henry Casson's good Friesian herd?'

Jackson looked uneasy for a second and decided to play for time. 'When was that?' he retorted.

'Nearly two years ago.'

'Get on with your homework,' Jackson snapped at his giggling daughters, but recovered his composure almost immediately. 'Henry Casson has never done so well until this last year or so. His father bred shorthorns like us but of course he had to change over to Friesians. Good milkers maybe, but not a decent cow to look at in his fields. You can get sick of looking at just black and white in the byre.' He chuckled to himself. 'I reckon t'old bull did him a favour.'

'Maybe he could do us a favour,' said Edith. 'It's time you got rid of him. He's so old he'll need propping up with crutches to do his duty soon.'

The laughter roared round the farm kitchen.

'That's a good 'un,' spluttered Tom as Bill came back from polishing the boots.

'Have I missed something good?'

'For once your mother has outwitted your father. I always thought she could get the better of him if she really tried!'

'It's just a question of education, Bill,' giggled Esther.

'That's just the sort of daft remark you can expect from someone brought up in Whitehaven,' retorted Jackson, ignoring the laughter.

'Well,' continued his wife, 'I think it's time we sold him and took advantage of the new artificial insemination service that's been set up by the Milk Marketing Board.'

'Now that's a bloody stupid remark. A good bull knows what he's doing. A vet wouldn't get there on time. He didn't get there on time when that white Ayrshire died last June.'

'Be fair, Dad. That Ayrshire had been slowly dying for weeks. What did you expect? A miracle?' asked Jane.

'No, my girl, I didn't. I just expect an educated man to earn his money as well as I do. It's no use paying them to cure a healthy animal. I can do that myself. What do you say, Tom?'

'Yes, Jackson. They say some damned queer things these vets. My young cows had ringworm and yon vet from Calderbridge said I should clean the hull walls.'

'Yes, that's the sort of daft thing they say. They think the stock should live in more comfort than we do.'

'That's right, Jackson. We wouldn't make any profit at all if we did that.'

'Good farming means good profits,' insisted Edith. 'Things have changed since the war. We must move with the times, Tom.'

'Yes, Mother, you're right,' agreed Bill. 'We should start getting rid of unproductive cows like Katie. We shouldn't stop progress.'

'Progress?' snorted his father. 'What about the atom bomb? Yon President Truman set it off in Japan or China or somewhere. Call that progress!'

'Japan, Dad,' volunteered Jane.

'Well, wherever it was, they're making a lot more of them down the road at Sellafield . . .'

'They're very clever,' interrupted Edith. 'People say Seascale is going to be one of the biggest places in the district – full of scientists.'

'Bloody foreigners, all of them,' protested her husband. 'They wouldn't know a decent cow if they saw one.'

'Neither do you, Dad, when you hang on to old grand-mothers like Katie,' Bill pointed out quietly.

'Now then, lad. With the money we get from Katie at Whitehaven tomorrow I'm going to buy your mother a new hen hull. I've seen some decent ones in Mitchell's yard.'

'While you're there, Dad, you could look for some new gates.'

'Gates, Bill? What do you want new gates for? The gates were new when we came to this farm.'

'Twenty-five years ago,' exclaimed Edith.

'How much do you expect to get for Katie then?' enquired Tom, tactfully changing the subject as he emptied his pipe into the fading fire.

'Twenty pounds if we get a penny.'

41

Hoots of laughter met this optimistic evaluation.

Slightly nonplussed, Jackson continued. 'I'll tidy her up in the morning – her coat comes up a treat when it's brushed.'

'We'll help you, Dad,' offered Jane. 'We'll shampoo her and make her look lovely. But we'll miss her, she's nearly as old as me.'

'She's older than me!' laughed her younger sister.

Bill stood up. 'I'd better go and phone Frank Bates tonight, Dad, and ask him to call in the morning about eight o'clock with his cattle truck.'

'Yes, son. Go quickly and wrap yourself up well, it's a cold night,' warned Edith.

'Wrap yourself up son, it's a cold night,' said Jackson mimicking his wife. Then, turning to his friend, he continued, 'Listen to that, Tom. He'll never be any good if he's mollycoddled like that . . . He even has an expensive oilskin to pick potatoes and snag turnips in, while his poor old father has to make do with a tatie bag across his shoulders.'

'Aah, what a shame!' mocked Esther.

'Now, now, don't speak to your father like that, Esther.'

Then, turning to Tom, Edith explained, 'The truth is, Tom, he can't be bothered coming in to get a decent coat. He just takes whatever is handiest.'

'Aye, well, we're all used to the old ways,' said Tom, supporting his friend.

'It's cold enough to catch pneumonia I'm sure,' fussed Edith.

Jane looked up from her book. 'Martin Armstrong has had pneumonia these last three winters.'

'That's because of his tractor,' retorted Jackson. 'He never ailed a thing when he followed a pair of horses.'

'It's the fumes,' agreed Tom. 'Like that atom place they're building down the road at Sellafield. We never know what we're breathing in these days.'

'Quite right, Tom. These educated, modern folk don't know all the answers. Now just look at that byre full of cows. We'll never see the likes again. In another ten years you won't get beef and milk like ours.'

'Like Katie, Dad?' laughed Esther.

'Your father has bred some very fine stock in his day, my girl,' said Edith. She didn't encourage her daughters to laugh at their father in spite of his faults.

Her husband nodded his approval. 'That's the most sensible thing you've said tonight, Mother.'

'You've always bred fine stock, Jackson. Never a weak one among them,' Tom observed, contentedly puffing his newly lit pipe.

'Aye!' pronounced Jackson, encouraged by all this support. 'You can read the *Farmers Weekly* as long as you like, but the only way you'll learn how to breed good cattle is here on farms like this, with farmers who have listened to what's been passed down from generation to generation. Listening and looking, that's what's important.'

'Yes, Jackson. Listening and looking,' echoed Tom. Then, turning in the girls' direction, their father's friend advised them. 'I hope you appreciate that, you young lassies. Your father is known the length and breadth of Cumberland. Nobody knows stock like him, an education in himself he is.'

'You're right, Tom. He has his faults. I know that. But breeding weak cows isn't one of them,' agreed Edith proudly.

'Yes,' said Tom. 'Whitehaven auction has seen many fine beasts in its time, but it takes a good cow to beat Jackson Strong's.'

Pleased with such recognition of his abilities, Jackson addressed his two daughters with an air of authority. 'You hear that, my girls? They can't tell you how to breed fine cows in Whitehaven Grammar School. Clever as they might be! Oh no! It takes generations of education – proper

43

education. Listening and learning! Just you see, tomorrow Katie will fetch her price. I've never been wrong yet.'

The noise of hurrying footsteps brought the conversation to a sudden halt and Mrs Strong glanced through the curtains.

'It's Bill. He must have been checking the byre and the hull.'

'Good, he's learning at last. I usually have to remind him to check the stock.'

'These young fellas are all the same,' said Tom. 'It takes time to educate them.'

'I hope he reminded Frank Bates to call here last tomorrow. I don't want my good stock crammed in the top end of his lorry with Henry Casson's sickly black and white bullocks pushed up against her.'

'Don't worry, Jackson. Frank Bates recognises a fine beast when he sees one.'

At this point Bill hurried into the kitchen looking very agitated.

'Oh, Dad!' he stammered. 'I don't know how to tell you.'

'Tell me what? Come on, lad. Has Frank Bates not got a decent truck for tomorrow?'

'It's not that, Dad. It's Katie.'

'What's wrong with Katie?'

'She's dead!'

'What of? Has she choked?'

'No, she died peacefully in her sleep. It looks like Old Age!'

4

THE TALE OF A HORSE

'What on earth made you bring that dirty old thing out into the light of day. I thought you'd thrown it away years ago,' Edith asked her husband as he busily polished what looked like a piece of well-worn leather.

His daughter Jane looked up from her book. 'What is it, Dad?' she innocently enquired.

'What is it?' snapped Jackson indignantly. Then suddenly he stopped polishing and continued in a more tolerant tone. 'Come to think of it, you might well ask . . . You don't see riding saddles of this quality nowadays . . .'

'A riding saddle?' exclaimed Esther, his youngest daughter. 'It doesn't look like the one Miss Fitzherbert uses when she rides through on her hunter.'

'Not the same quality at all. You young folk are easily misled by a bit of polish and a pair of fancy breeches . . . Bareback . . . Now that's the way to ride!'

'Well, why are you polishing a saddle then, Dad? When are you going riding?'

'Tomorrow, first thing in the morning. After milking I'm off to Appleby to sell that bloody useless thing that's eating its head off in yon far field.'

'Ginger? Appleby Fair?' Edith was astounded. 'That's the daftest thing I've heard you say since we got married. It's all of fifty miles.'

Jane looked alarmed. 'Poor Ginger, she won't be able to make it that far, Dad. She'll drop under you.'

Esther chipped in. 'Why do you think you'll sell her there? You've never been able to get rid of her in this district . . .'

Edith agreed. 'That's right. There's no call for a light horse around here – she hasn't enough class for the gentry, or enough strength to work on a farm. You've always been too easily taken in by a horse that looked good, Jackson. She's never earned her keep.'

Jackson was indignant. 'Best-looking horse around here, our Ginger! It's a shame to waste her. There'll be plenty who'll fancy her at Appleby. Mark my words, them gypsies know a decent piece of horseflesh when they see it.'

Bill, who had been filling in his crossword, stopped to listen to his father. 'What decent piece of horseflesh, Dad? She might look decent now, but by the time she's staggered over fifty miles it'll look as if she's led the Charge of the Light Brigade!'

'Besides,' broke in their mother, 'if you can't sell her, Jackson, the poor thing will have to carry you all the way back home. She's not used to being ridden like that. She's only done a bit of harrowing in the last year or so. Her feet won't last out.'

'What a lot of rubbish! Do you think I can't judge a fine horse when I see one? Don't you worry, Mother. You'll see me back in a couple of days. I'll have enough money from the sale to come back on the bus. A grand ride it'll be – you can't beat a ride upstairs on a double-decker coming through Keswick and Cockermouth. It's time I had a bit of a holiday. Can you look after things at home, Bill?'

'Yes, Dad.'

'Good, it's about time you learnt to take a bit of responsibility, lad. I won't always be here to look after you all.'

'We'll manage, Dad,' laughed Esther. 'Just you concentrate on getting ready for this great ride . . . I bet you don't get beyond Cockermouth!'

'Now, now, young lady,' warned Edith. 'Don't speak to your dad like that. He may be a bit foolish but there's no need to make him out to be stupid. Besides, I don't like the sound of betting.'

'I bet he makes Penrith by tomorrow night,' challenged Bill.

'That's enough, both of you.' Their mother turned back to Jackson. 'I'll make sure you have a few sandwiches and a bottle of cold tea to take with you.'

'Cold tea!' exploded her husband. 'You'd think I was an invalid – what's wrong with a glass of pale ale? There's plenty of good pubs between here and Appleby.'

'Wait until the neighbours hear about this!' exclaimed Esther. 'They'll set up a betting board in the Grey Mare.'

'Now you know why I've said nothing. It's a right to do when a fella can't sell a horse in peace.'

The amused children ganged up on their father.

'The odds would have been against you getting there at all,' mocked Bill.

'And longer odds on him selling Ginger to the likes of them that buy and sell at Appleby Fair,' said Jane.

'And remember, Dad,' added Esther,'you have to trot them up and down to show that they're fresh and sound in wind and limb.'

'Are you trying to tell me how horses are bought and sold, my girl?'

'You know she's not, Jackson,' soothed their mother. 'We're all trying to help you. Don't you think you should forget about riding such a long way? I've never heard of anyone riding so far before – in just one day. Besides, where are you going to sleep tomorrow night?'

'Poor Dad,' sympathised Esther. 'You'll have to sleep in a field. You won't half feel cold the next day!'

'Stop fussing, Esther. Why do you think we were called Strong in the first place? Your Uncle Fred used to sleep in a trench in the Great War – nobody asked him if he was comfortable or needed a pillow. It would have been just the same for me if I'd gone to the war but unfortunately I was married then.'

Edith nodded. 'Yes, it was all those "Your Country Needs You" posters. He would have gone, but I talked sense into him. I needed him much more than the country did. It was all right for the unmarried men. They could throw their lives away, but your father had too many responsibilities here.'

'But Mam,' interrupted Esther, 'think of the glory of fighting for your country – and maybe giving your life to save England from foreign oppression.'

'Patriotism it's called, Mam,' added Jane.

'You can give it any fancy name you like,' insisted Edith, 'but just remember, my girls, there's no glorious dead, only the glorious living.'

'Politics! Politics!' Jackson broke in. 'How about some supper, Mother? I need a good sleep tonight.'

* * *

As it grew dark Clare Tyson placed her sewing carefully to one side and left her seat by the fire to close the heavy curtains. Very little happened in the evenings in the small village of Temple Sowerby. Clare smiled across at her mother who was still sewing diligently.

'We'll have our supper soon, Mother. I'll just finish this blue flower.'

Suddenly she stopped her work and glanced towards the window. 'Did you hear a noise outside? I thought I heard the gate being closed at the bottom of the yard.'

'No dear, I didn't,' replied her mother, looking up at the clock on the mantelpiece. 'It's rather late for anyone to call. It's eleven o'clock!'

Suddenly they heard a loud knock on the door.

'Oh dear, you're right, Clare. Who on earth can it be? I hope it isn't a tramp.'

'Don't worry, Mother. I won't open the door. I'll ask who it is from inside.'

Clare went nervously to the door. 'Who's there?' she called out.

'My name is Jackson Strong. I'm a farmer from over on the west coast, Whitehaven way. I'm on my way to Appleby Fair but my horse is too tired to go on. Yours is the only light I can see in the village. Could your husband let me sleep in your shed for the night?'

'He sounds genuine, Mother. Should I let him in?'

'It's a good West Cumberland accent. Open the door Clare.'

The broad-shouldered farmer stood diffidently in the cottage doorway, his cap held politely in his hands.

'Good evening, Mr Strong. I am Helen Tyson and this is my daughter, Clare. Please come in and take a seat by the fire. You must be cold and tired.' She turned to Clare. 'Go and put the kettle on. Mr Strong has come a long way and must be ready for some supper. There's plenty of bread and cold meat in the kitchen.'

Clare disappeared to do her mother's bidding. She felt excited – visitors were a rarity in Temple Sowerby.

'Now Mr Strong, tell me, where is your horse?'

'I've tied her to your gate. She's tired out and isn't likely to stray. I walked around the village for a good while before I spotted your kitchen light. I didn't want to get people out of bed at this time of night. I took a chance by knocking at your door, hoping that you would be kind enough to help me, or suggest where I could get a bite to eat and a night's rest for Ginger and me.'

He glanced enquiringly round the cosy kitchen. 'If there is no man in your house, Mrs Tyson, I'll accept a cup of tea, then bid you good evening. Perhaps you can suggest someone else who could put me up?'

'Don't be silly, Mr Strong. True, there is no man in the

49

house – my husband was killed during the war – but we'll make you up a bed here on the sofa. It may not be as comfortable as the one you're used to at home, but you will be most welcome. As for Ginger,' she continued, not giving her visitor time to accept or refuse, 'the village green is just round the corner – you can tether her there. There's always two or three goats grazing there. She'll be all right until the morning.'

'You are both very kind,' said Jackson, getting up from his chair. 'I'll just go and see to Ginger and bring her saddle inside, if you will allow me to leave it in your kitchen.'

'Of course, you must bring it inside. Do see to your mare, then come and have a bite of supper with us. We haven't a lot to offer but you are very welcome to what we have.'

Jackson soon returned to spend the evening with the two rather lonely but very hospitable ladies.

This small cottage in what for him was a distant village was a far cry from the pubs in which he usually spent his evenings. Tea was a mild substitute for beer and his attentive audience lacked the ribaldry and roughness of his usual companions. Nevertheless the time he spent with Mrs Tyson and her daughter was just as delightful to Jackson as any of his regular evenings. Appreciation was all he asked for. He enjoyed nothing better than telling tales of his youth, the time he'd spent down the pits, and what the local farmers got up to. After a good few hours of entertainment, the three of them eventually went to bed at an unheard of hour, the ladies having plied the old farmer with numerous blankets and two hot water bottles just in case he should feel the cold.

* * *

The small kitchen in Temple Sowerby was full of activity the following morning.

'Now make a good breakfast for Mr Strong, Mother. I

heard him go out to the green this morning to see to Ginger.'

A knock on the door announced that Jackson Strong was ready to leave.

'Morning ladies! Thank you kindly for the night's lodging,' he said, entering the kitchen. He had obviously been up early. 'I must be off to Appleby now. I still have a good ride ahead of me . . . How much do I owe you?'

'Come and sit down. Here's a good breakfast for you,' invited Mrs Tyson. 'We see few visitors and we certainly enjoyed your company last night. How's Ginger?'

'Thank you. A good breakfast is very welcome. Poor Ginger's in a bad way this morning. She had a job to stand up first thing. Never mind – I've given her a good rub down . . . I'll have to walk to Appleby with her.'

'How will you sell her if you can't ride on her Mr Strong?' asked Clare.

'Don't worry. I'll have to ride her the last half mile or so.'

After eating a hearty breakfast Jackson bade a reluctant farewell to the two ladies who were equally reluctant to see their unexpected visitor depart.

* * *

Edith fussed around her kitchen, glancing anxiously at the clock. Her husband had been gone two days now.

'God knows where your father is,' she remarked in the general direction of Esther and Jane. 'Half past ten and no sign of him. I should never have let him go.'

'Stop fussing, Mother. There was little you could have done to stop him. He'll be all right.'

At this point Bill returned from the farm buildings.

'Is everything settled for the night, Bill?' asked his mother. 'If your father comes home and everything isn't done properly there'll be trouble.' She spoke uneasily. 'I wonder where he is.'

'Probably halfway between here and Cockermouth . . . unless he's found a good pub before that,' replied her son.

'I bet he had a job to get Ginger past the Grey Mare yesterday – all our horses know that's their first stop!'

The three children burst into roars of laughter at Jane's remark.

Edith, however, jumped to her husband's defence. 'I've never heard so many lies. You'd think your father was one of these pub crawlers!'

'He isn't – doesn't touch a drop,' stated Bill, his tone heavily ironic. 'But it's a funny thing that none of our horses can walk past any pub door between here and Wasdale Head. They know where he likes to stop.'

'They can find their own way home even if he falls asleep in the trap,' laughed Esther.

'Yes,' agreed Jane, 'if Dad ever buys a motor car he'll have to stay sober!'

The sound of laughter was interrupted by the rattling of the chain on the yard gate and the excited barking of the farm dogs.

'Is that Dad?' asked Jane. 'I can't hear Ginger's shoes on the cobbles. He must have caught the last bus from Whitehaven. Mam, do you think he could have sold Ginger?'

'More likely she dropped dead somewhere and he had to bury her,' said Bill.

Jackson entered the farm kitchen just in time to catch his son's remark.

'Who dropped dead, my lad? No faith . . . None of you had any faith in me or my horse.'

'Did you sell Ginger, Dad? Honestly?' Esther was excited. 'Did you ever get to Appleby?'

Bill was still sceptical. 'I bet you let her loose in someone's field, then walked home!'

'Be quiet, all of you, and let your father speak.' Edith

52

began to prepare the supper. 'Come and sit down, Jackson, and have a bite to eat. It doesn't matter if you sold the horse or not – just so long as you're all right.'

Jackson ignored all their questions and took off his jacket in a leisurely way, followed by his boots. He then carefully positioned his comfortable armchair close to the table, where he could benefit from the warmth of the kitchen fire.

'Come on, Jackson. A few slices of this brawn and a mug of tea will make you feel better,' his wife soothed.

Bill could hardly contain his curiosity. 'Never mind the brawn, Dad. Where's Ginger? Who did you trick into buying her?'

The old farmer wasn't going to be hurried by anyone. He was enjoying keeping them in suspense. Slowly and deliberately he cut the brawn and began to butter his bread. This was a task he very rarely did, but tonight he waved his wife aside. The urge to play his family like a river salmon was irresistible.

As his daughters and son pulled their chairs expectantly towards his end of the table Jackson turned confidentially to his wife. 'I told you, Mother, it would be a lovely bus ride back through the Lakes. It's years since we've been on that run . . . I think it was the year the war ended. Didn't we go to see your Lizzie in Ambleside?'

'That's right, Jackson. She'd just had our Ben. A fine baby – the image of his father. But none of hers looked like our side . . .'

'For goodness sake, Mother, will you stop distracting him?' Jane turned desperately towards her father. 'You must have sold Ginger if you came back on the bus, Dad?'

'Wasn't that the idea, lass? I said I would sell her – and so I did. Here's the money to prove it.'

Jackson threw a bundle of shabby notes on to the table. As the family stared at the money, he turned to his wife. 'Go on, Mother, count it.'

Edith picked the money up and carefully counted it back on to the table. 'Thirty-nine pounds ten shillings,' she finally announced.

'I spent ten shillings on my way home – the bus fare is highway robbery these days.'

'Dad, you're marvellous. Who bought the horse?' questioned Jane.

'I know. You stopped at Cockermouth and sold Ginger there,' suggested Bill.

'Quiet now and let your father speak.'

But Jackson didn't satisfy his questioners. Instead he picked up his mug of tea in one hand and a large piece of cake in the other, then gently pushed his armchair towards the fire. He was obviously planning to enjoy himself telling the tale . . . in his own time. They all crept forward, placing their chairs in a ring round their father, who turned casually to his wife.

'That was a lovely bit of bread, Mother. Last night I had a good supper in a village called Temple Sowerby. Mrs Tyson was the lady who let me sleep on the sofa in her house. Mind you, Mother, her bread was "bought bread" – not a patch on yours.'

'Where did Ginger sleep?' asked Esther impatiently.

'On the village green, lass. What a fine village green they have.' Her father turned to Bill. 'That's what made her so bad this morning. I had no cover for her – she had to sleep in the open after walking all day.'

'Poor Ginger,' Jane interjected. 'Was she stiff?'

'Yes, lass, and at first she limped like hell.'

'You didn't ride the poor thing, Jackson?' asked a shocked Edith. 'Lucky the local policeman didn't see you and charge you with cruelty . . . How on earth did you get all that money for her?'

'Mam, stop thinking the worst and let Dad go on,' said Esther.

Jackson nodded and continued his story. 'Like I said, she was very stiff and I thought if I got on her back she might collapse under me and that would be that. So . . . I started to walk. I reckoned I had about ten miles to go, but what sort of shape she'd be in when we reached Appleby, God only knew.'

'You should have turned right round and brought the poor animal home, Jackson. What a disgrace! Fancy forcing a poor beast to walk like that. I'm glad there was no one to recognise you so far from home.'

'Go on, Dad, finish your story. We can see you sold her, so how did you do it?' urged Jane.

'Well, as I was telling you, we wandered towards Appleby. Ginger straightened up a bit and the limp disappeared – but I knew she wouldn't sell very well as she was.'

'Yes,' agreed Bill. 'They're all fine horsemen who go to Appleby Fair. No one can fob them off with an unsound horse.'

'True enough, lad, true enough. But you see, none of them reckoned with Jackson Strong!' Here the wily old farmer chuckled delightedly. 'Just as I was getting very near Appleby I spotted a pub by the side of the road.'

'I might have guessed it,' burst in Esther. 'I wonder what made you spot a pub!'

'I bet he could smell one a mile away!' laughed Bill.

'You can laugh if you like . . . but it was the pub that saved me. I looked up at the sign and it said "The Drunken Duck"! That gave me an idea . . . If you can have a drunken duck, why not a Drunken Horse?'

'Oh Jackson, you didn't?' gasped Edith. Her husband ignored her question and continued his story.

'I went in and had a fine glass of ale – nearly as good as the beer at the Grey Mare. Then, before I left, I bought a bottle of whisky.' He turned to Edith. 'It was a good thing you made me take that extra money, Mother. If those two ladies at

Temple Sowerby had charged me for supper, bed and breakfast, I would have been finished.'

'Go on, Dad,' urged Jane impatiently.

'Well,' continued her father slowly, 'when I got near the horse fair, I climbed up on to a low wall and poured the lot down Ginger's throat.' Jackson turned to Bill. 'Not so easy, lad. You try doing that sometime.'

'Go on, Dad,' implored Esther.

'Well, lass, it must have been good whisky . . . because she gave a toss of her head, a loud snort and down we went into the Fair, straight between the rows of caravans. Her feet hardly touched the ground.'

Esther interrupted. 'Did you have any trouble selling her, Dad?'

'No, not a bit. This half-drunk gypsy spotted her right away.'

'Are you saying, Jackson, that the gypsy was too drunk to know what he was buying?'

56

'No, Mother, don't be daft. A gypsy can judge horseflesh drunk or sober . . . No, no, you miss the point. I knew that when he looked into its mouth to check its age, he wouldn't be able to smell the horse's breath – because he had too much drink on his own!'

When the laughter had subsided, Jackson continued. 'No, Mother, I reckon he noticed the lively look in Ginger's eye. That's what sold her.'

Esther nodded. 'A good price, Dad – forty pounds. You did well.'

'I have only one regret.'

'What's that, Dad?'

'My saddle. It was worth more than the nag!'

'Why didn't you keep it?' Bill looked puzzled. 'You could have brought it back on the bus.'

'Not on your life! The minute I'd shaken hands with Gypsy Joe, I went hell for leather for the bus station before Ginger sobered up. I couldn't have disappeared so easily with a saddle over my shoulder!'

5

HEDGING AND THE LAW

The chain on the farm gate rattled briskly.

'Who on earth can that be at this time in the morning?' Edith said, placing a third rasher of bacon on her husband's plate.

'Probably just the dog jumping between the bars and making it rattle,'suggested Bill as he tucked into his own breakfast.

A knock on the outside door, accompanied by noisy barking, was enough to inform the family that it was not one of their regular visitors. Country people rarely knock at a farm door and wait for someone to come and open it.

'I didn't hear any clogs,' said Edith, smoothing her apron and glancing quickly at the small mirror hanging on a nail above Jackson's armchair. 'It must be someone to look tidy for then,' snapped Jackson as she went to the door. 'I never see you smartening yourself up when you hear a pair of clogs clattering across the yard.'

Edith soon returned to the warm kitchen, closely followed by a young policeman.

'Good morning, Mr Strong. How are you today?'

'Very well – so far! I thought I didn't recognise your step. It's a while since we've seen a policeman. What can I do for you?'

'Now just let P.C. Williams enjoy this mug of tea and a piece of the gingerbread I made yesterday. It's a little chilly this morning, don't you think?'

'It certainly is, Mrs Strong,' he said, munching away. 'This is a lovely piece of cake. I always enjoy a bit of really good gingerbread.'

Jackson continued to eat his breakfast while his wife attended to the policeman.

Edith was finding it very difficult to hide her unease. Knowing her husband as she did, she was busy worrying about unmended fences, straying stock and broken gates, any of which could prompt a visit from the local policeman.

She glanced at her husband, who, as usual, had shown not the slightest sign of concern. He held the police, the local bye-laws, and indeed any form of bureaucracy in complete disdain. She was the one who filled in all the forms and stock books. She it was who stood sentinel between her husband and the fireplace when he took exception to a letter he had just opened. His only filing system consisted of either the fire or her outstretched hand.

Now Edith wondered, as she made her visitor comfortable, what she might have overlooked. Had the odd overdue bill reached the flames in spite of her vigilance?

'If you'd come ten minutes sooner, you could have had some of this bacon and black pudding,' said Jackson amiably. 'You can't buy anything like it in Egremont . . . There's nothing to beat home-cured bacon.'

'This will do fine, Mr Strong . . . though I must admit, that bacon looks lovely. But my wife doesn't like so much fat on her bacon.'

'Well, young women these days don't know what a decent bit of bacon tastes like. It's that rubbish they sell in the shops makes them think lean bacon is best . . . But unless it has a good bit of fat on it, it won't fry decently.' He pointed his fork at the policeman for emphasis. 'Just like a crumpled leaf . . . just like a crumpled leaf . . . Hardly worth switching the electricity on for.' Waving his hand in his anxious wife's direction, he continued airily. 'Just you cut this young fella a few slices from that side hanging up there, Mother . . . and put some black pudding in the bag along with it. Let his wife have a taste of some decent food.'

Edith obediently sliced the bacon as her husband turned his chair from the breakfast table, placed his fresh mug of tea on the hob beside the fire, and addressed his visitor warmly. 'Well now what can I do for you today? It must be a slack time in Egremont if you're forced to ride this far first thing in the morning. When I was a young lad . . .' He chuckled as he remembered. 'I got many a clout round the ear for being in places I shouldn't.'

'Oh Mr Strong, we aren't allowed to deal with young people like that any more. That would be an "assault".'

'What do you do with them then?'

'We have to charge them.'

'What! Take them to court?'

'Yes, I'm afraid so.'

'Well, that's a bigger crime than anything a youngster . . .'

'Mr Williams hasn't time to waste discussing what happened years ago,' Edith interrupted her husband, afraid of what he might say next.

Not so Bill and Esther, who were listening keenly and exchanging looks, plainly wondering whether their garrulous father was talking himself into trouble, or out of it . . .

Their mother, however, realised that her husband was following his usual policy – attack as the best form of defence.

The young policeman smiled a little uneasily. He wasn't used to dealing with noisy, elderly farmers. And he was beginning to understand why the station sergeant had explained that a visit to Mr Strong's farm would be a useful experience for him, now that he had been in the district a full year.

'My visit this morning is only about a small matter, Mr Strong. The sergeant has noticed that your hedgerows are rather overgrown. You know that hedgerows on the main roads have to be kept trimmed. It's a hazard to pedestrians.'

Edith sat down relieved. This was just a routine warning, usually delivered by Sergeant Johnston when he met Jackson as he made his rounds by bicycle.

'Well, lad!' The brown stream of tobacco juice streaked into the red flames and the hot coals spat angrily as Jackson turned his sharp eyes on John Williams. 'It's taken Bill Johnston a long time to notice the length of grass on my hedges. Last year he stopped me and mentioned it at least three weeks earlier than this. I was beginning to wonder if he was getting a bit absent-minded . . . You know, lad, he's not as young as he used to be . . .'

He leaned towards the young man and continued, his manner warm and confidential. 'Bill can always be relied on to remind us of all these bye-laws. He knows a busy man like me hasn't time for reading the law.'

He turned to his younger daughter who was straining every muscle to keep a straight face. 'Esther, what is that modern expression you mentioned the other day that means the police warn you well before you might do it?'

'Crime prevention, Dad.'

'That's right, Esther. I read about that in the *Daily Herald* just a week or two ago.' He turned back to the puzzled policeman. 'Both my daughters went to the grammar school – they're good with difficult words. It's a good thing, young man, to have up-to-date information.'

'Yes, Mr Strong. Crime prevention is the latest in police work. We certainly try to keep farmers informed of possible hazards. Lengthy thorn hedges do make it difficult for cars and carts to pass.'

'Yes, that's true,' agreed Jackson. 'Last year John Steel's corn was hanging on my thorns for days. Mind you . . . it was so poor that when the cows went past they never even reached up to pull a mouthful down.'

'Now then, Jackson, you said yourself it was a poor year for everyone,' Edith said hastily, not wishing her husband to speak so unkindly to the policeman about a neighbour and friend.

'Poor or not, it hung there until it was brushed off by Joe Watson's van.'

'How do you know?' asked his wife. 'He drives past here most days. Why should he have suddenly brushed against the thorns on that particular day?'

'I know which day it was, Mother. It was that Saturday that Joe's niece was married. Tom Graham was telling me he was so drunk they had to lift him into the cab. His van was wandering all over the road before it got out of their sight . . . Sure enough the corn that had hung there for the last three weeks was strewn along the road on the Sunday morning! I remember it clearly . . .'

'Take no notice of what he says, Mr Williams. It's all his imagination, he likes to tell a story.' Edith was wishing the young policeman would go, but he seemed to have settled himself firmly by the fire. Her two children, meanwhile, were totally fascinated by their father's dissertation, their expressions reflecting their curiosity as to the direction in which he was leading his visitor.

'Oh no, Mother, don't you mislead this young policeman. Anything I tell him has a firm base.' He leaned warmly towards his new friend. 'I can see that you are a young man who is willing to learn – even from an uneducated farmer like me.'

'Certainly, Mr Strong. I think we can all learn from older people. Policemen these days are more concerned with people; that is, getting to know people in our district rather than just catching criminals and making sure that they are punished. We were taught in police college that a good understanding of people is worth much more than a good knowledge of criminal law.'

'Quite right,' applauded Jackson. 'My daughters think they can learn everything that's worth learning at

Whitehaven Grammar School . . . but *you* realise that all worthwhile knowledge isn't to be found in books.'

'Come now, Jackson,' scolded his wife. 'Education is the future of this country. I don't want my children to be unable to appreciate books.' She turned towards the policeman, hoping to bring the conversation to a rapid end. 'You know, Mr Williams, I often read my daughters' books . . . Modern books are most interesting.'

'Now then, Mother,' interrupted her husband. 'Don't let this young man think I never read anything.'

At this, his two children could scarcely stifle their laughter which threatened to bubble and burst out at any moment. They had immediately recognised the genuine-sounding, friendly tone their father adopted whenever he wanted to trick or mislead a visitor. This always resulted in the stranger having total confidence in the truth of whatever tale he was telling. Truth for their father was always his current opinion. On another occasion the reverse point of view could be equally truthful!

'I'm sure you read, Mr Strong.'

'Certainly,' agreed the old farmer. 'My family . . .' Here he nodded towards Esther and Jane, '. . . seem to think they are the only ones who can learn from books. You see that pile of *Farmers Weekly*s on that sideboard over there?' He pointed beyond his daughter's astonished head.

The young man nodded.

'Well I was reading a good article in one of those. It was about nature and rare wild flowers. Mind you, they used big words . . . Now, what was it? . . . Nature conservatory . . . I think that was it.'

'Nature conservancy, Dad,' volunteered Esther, as her brother struggled valiantly to hide his mirth.

'That's right. Why they can't just say – don't cut down rare wild flowers, I don't know!' He leaned confidentially towards his listener. 'They were saying that in the south of the country all these wealthy farmers are destroying their hedgerows to make bigger fields. All for profit, young man.' He paused for effect. 'No conscience! No thought for the rare plants that are being destroyed! Just gentleman farmers wanting to make a few more hundred pounds – and many of them are millionaires already. Have you read about all this, young man?'

'No, I'm afraid I haven't read about that, Mr Strong.'

'Well, a country policeman should be aware of the changes that are taking place in the countryside.'

The young man nodded in assent. 'Yes I realise that, Mr Strong. Perhaps a glance in the *Farmers Weekly* would prove of interest.'

'Certainly it would,' smiled Jackson. 'You should realise that we aren't just a bunch of illiterate country yokels with straws in our mouths . . .'

'Oh I never thought you were . . .' the young man interrupted apologetically.

'Oh I know *you* didn't,' soothed Jackson. 'But you can't expect fellas like Bill Johnston to move with the times . . . *they* still wait for the crime to be committed before they wake up to the damage! He doesn't realise that our wildlife heritage as a nation may very well rest upon the "conservatory" we have managed to build up here in Cumberland.'

The young man stood up as Jackson finished speaking. 'Well I must be going, Mr Strong. I have enjoyed our conversation.'

'Good,' nodded Jackson. 'You'll enjoy the ride back to Egremont.' He paused for a moment, then continued. 'And just take a close look at those wild flowers in my hedges as you go by. There'll be very few for anyone to see tomorrow . . .'

Edith handed a large paper bag to their visitor as he made his way to the farmhouse door. 'I've put in half a dozen nice, fresh brown eggs for your wife.' She smiled kindly as the young man thanked her and left the kitchen.

'I've put in half a dozen nice, fresh brown eggs for your wife,' mimicked Jackson as soon as the policeman had crossed the yard. 'God knows what you'll be handing over if he comes here to discuss a serious matter!'

'What a pack of lies you told that poor chap,' laughed Bill.

'And he believed every word of it,' added Esther.

'Your father has always been a convincing tale-teller.' Edith tended to avoid calling her husband a downright liar.

'Very clever, all of you,' snarled Jackson tetchily. 'Esther just you go over to that pile of *Farmers Weekly*'s and look at last May's edition. I think it is the second week.'

'Oh go on, Dad, you never read the *Farmers Weekly*. You're always criticising all the modern methods they write about.

'The trouble with you, Bill,' answered his father, 'is that you don't know the difference between useful, interesting information and the sort of rubbish that is just selling new calf feed or a fancy-priced roll of fencing wire. You young folk can't look far enough into the future. It's no good living for just today and tomorrow. Oh no, the real experts in the world know what they're talking about.'

'Look, Bill, here it is!' exclaimed Esther incredulously. 'An article on the disappearance of the country hedgerow.'

'There you are. Didn't I tell you? You two think I'm just an illiterate old farmer.'

'No they don't,' interrupted their mother. 'It's just a rare thing for you to read such an article. The *Daily Herald* is about as much as you manage most evenings.'

'And then you fall asleep,' laughed his daughter. 'It's a fine thing when it takes a visit from a policeman to convince you all that I know about something more than the current state of the Labour Party.'

Jackson had risen to his feet as he spoke. He reached for his cap and stick which were always conveniently placed on a nail just inside the door. 'Well, I suppose I'd better go and dispose of the professor's rare specimens. Bill, fetch Peggy and the cart and in a couple of hours come to collect the heaps of thorns and grass from the roadway, otherwise the police will be back complaining that I'm obstructing the highway for pedestrians!'

* * *

'You're making a good job of that hedge, Jackson. I thought you'd be starting cutting your hay today!' Tom Graham brought his horse to a halt alongside his friend.

'This is the nearest I'm getting to haytiming today. Yon silly Bill Johnston sent a young policeman to sort me out this morning, so I thought I'd better tidy my hedges up. Our Edith nearly has a heart attack if she sees a policeman stopping at the gate. She never got over the black market during the war . . . It's a terrible thing to be brought up with a conscience.'

'She's a good woman, Jackson – probably too good for you. She has a religious turn of mind!'

'Maybe,' agreed Jackson as he settled down in a convenient hollow to have a crack with his friend. It was warm and comfortable in the afternoon sun, and the old farmer carefully sliced a black twist of tobacco before placing it ceremoniously on his tongue. 'Maybe . . . the only thing wrong with religious folk is their idea of sin. They automatically think that anything you enjoy is a sin; that breaking a useless law is a sin. You know, Tom, it's a hard life for anyone burdened with a conscience. I keep telling our Edith to stop worrying about things that might never happen – but she never takes any notice. You should have seen her this morning when that policeman knocked on our door. You'd think someone had committed murder!' The old man chuckled.

'Why didn't Bill Johnston come himself?' wondered Tom.

'I reckon that young fella needed a bit of "educating".'
Jackson stressed the last word. 'He seemed to have plenty to
say . . . They probably wanted a bit of peace in the station for
an hour or two! Bill reckoned that half an hour in our kitchen
would help the young man complete his local education!'

'What on earth did you say to him, Jackson?'

'Very little . . . He was explaining the law to me . . . He
seemed to know it well enough.'

'But you weren't going to be told to dress your hedges by a
young man still wet behind the ears . . . eh, Jackson?'

Tom laughed, knowing that any young policeman who
had started being pompous under Jackson's roof would have
had a rough ride.

'I just informed him about wildlife "conservatory". I was
reading a load of rubbish about it in a copy of the *Farmers
Weekly* the other week . . . Lucky I'd read it. Anything
sensible wouldn't have impressed him – poor lad was
completely out of his depth!'

'That's right, Jackson, there's nothing like a bit of education for fooling folks.'

'Just look at that black nag of yours, it's nearly eaten its way back home!'

'Well it'll save you cutting some of that grass. Anyway I can hear your Peggy coming this way. Bill must be loading the piles of grass you've left down the road. You'd better get cracking or he'll catch you up!'

* * *

A few weeks later Jackson pulled his horse to a halt outside the Midland Bank in Main Street. Egremont was always busy at this time of the morning, and Peggy was more than willing to stop.

'Please, Mister, can I hold your horse?' A boy of about ten quickly reached for the horse's bridle, as the farmer tied his rope reins to the side bracket of his cart. Young lads in the small Cumbrian market town were always on the lookout for such opportunities, hoping to get sixpence or so for holding a farmer's horse while he visited the bank or pub.

'Yes, lad.' Jackson climbed down, placing his foot on the hub of the large iron-clad wheel.

Peggy rested gratefully at the side of the busy street, allowing her minder and a small crowd of his admiring friends to stroke her nose and pat her neck. This had been a tiring morning for her. Early on, her cart had been loaded with corn to pull to the mill in Egremont. Then her load had been wheeled bag by bag into the noisy, rattling building, while she had waited in the yard, listening to the sound of Jackson's voice shouting above the vibration of floorboards and noisy hoppers. She was always glad when he returned. She knew then that her cart would be reloaded and she would be soon making her way home. Why she should have to carry a load all this way, just to carry the same load home again, was a tedious affair – but no doubt there was a good reason. She glanced impatiently at the door of the bank. Jackson should soon be out . . . She heard his voice and her head lifted . . .

'A long time since I've seen you, Jackson!' Peggy's heart sank. She knew her master would be good for at least another half-hour's chat.

It was Sergeant Johnston who spoke.

'Aye well. I don't have much time to spare, you know,' replied Jackson. 'The time it takes to get to Egremont and back could be better spent in the fields. You don't see busy farmers sitting around like some of these shopkeepers.'

'It's time you bought a lorry. A lot of farmers have them now, Jackson.'

'And where would I get the sort of money you need to buy one of those? Besides, what would Frank Bates do for a living if we all bought our own trucks? You've got to live and let live, you know. It's no good taking the bread out of someone else's mouth.'

'But you've also got to move with the times, Jackson . . . Remember what you said to my young constable the other week?' Bill smiled as he spoke.

'Oh yes – I remember him – a nice young lad. I think that young fella will go far, Bill.'

'Not far enough,' muttered the sergeant almost under his breath.

Seemingly unaware of the policeman's observation, Jackson spat carefully and deliberately over the edge of the pavement. 'Intelligent young man. I like to see young folks who are willing to listen to new ideas . . .'

'What on earth were you telling him about "nature conservancy"? He's babbled on about nothing else for the last three weeks . . . He's even stuck some posters up on our Wanted board!'

'Quite right too,' nodded Jackson. 'Fancy sitting at your

desk looking at a row of murderers and escaped prisoners all day long! Thank God I don't have to be faced with my failures all the time. No wonder you sent that young lad out to see me. I said to our Edith afterwards ''I know Bill had a good reason for not coming himself . . .'' The lad needed a good crack. We were very pleased to see him, Bill. Send him again next year – that lad will go far!'

6

AUNT MAY

'What are we doing tomorrow, Jackson?'
Edith paused, rested her darning on her knee and glanced at her husband.

Jackson was seated in his deep armchair, chewing his black twist contentedly.

'Tomorrow . . . Now let me see . . . What day is it tomorrow?'

'Friday.'

'What's special about Friday? No market . . . I'll maybe go to the bank. It's about time I reminded them that I'm still alive.'

'Oh, so you are going to Egremont with the horse and cart?'

'Either that, or maybe Tom'll give me a lift in his motor car.' He looked at his wife suspiciously. 'Why do you want me to stay at home? You usually like to see the back of me.'

'No, I was just thinking that if you were taking the horse and cart to Egremont, you might like to take that load of manure to our May. She asked you weeks ago, and I've stopped calling at her house when I go shopping because she keeps asking when you're bringing her muck.'

'It's a wonder she knows what muck is. She makes sure it's a warm dry day before she decides to visit us. She's very careful about where she puts her feet . . . How she ever gets round to putting muck on her garden I'll never know.'

'She never does it herself. She's paid old Harold Thompson to dig her garden over for years. It's always a picture in the summer,' Edith said a little wistfully. 'It would be nice to have a garden here.'

71

'A garden? What on earth do you want the trouble of a garden for? There's enough work here growing potatoes and corn without frittering time and energy on a few flowers that can't bring any cash into the house.'

'Well, it would be nice,' said Edith, picking up her darning. She was used to her husband's attitude towards anything unprofitable. She knew it was the result of many years of hard work and little money.

Jackson had now warmed to his theme. 'We can't afford to pay a gardener. I don't know where your May gets her money from. I should think George left her without a penny when he died.'

'Our May has worked – off and on – ever since he died, Jackson . . . She has earned her own money and I'm quite sure she has the right to spend it any way she likes – she doesn't have to ask you first.' Edith was indignant.

'It doesn't stop her asking me to take her a load of muck. She likely thinks that's all I'm good for! Next time she wants some, ask her to come and load it, then lead the horse and cart the three miles to Egremont . . . And don't forget, she'd have to lead the horse right through the main street – seeing she lives at the far end of town.'

Here Jackson burst out laughing. The idea of his snobbish sister-in-law leading a cart of farm manure through the main street, in front of the whole town, gave him the greatest pleasure.

'She'd have to wait until after dark . . . and make it quick in case the horse's hooves wakened anyone she knew.' Then another idea struck him. 'She could muffle Peggy's feet . . . like they used to do during the war in case the enemy heard them! Or better still, she could put on a disguise – Wellington boots and my old cap. No one would recognise her in old clothes. She always looks like mutton dressed as lamb when she goes out . . . She gets up at six in case the milkman sees her in her curlers!'

'And how do you know so much about her habits?' Edith asked coolly.

'You think I never listen to a thing she says. But she always shouts, so I can't avoid hearing what she says, whether she's talking to me or not. Besides, when I took her load of muck last year, she said I should come as early as possible next time. The truth is, she doesn't want the neighbours to see me and my cart. She sticks a mug of tea and a small piece of fancy cake on the wall the minute I arrive and then disappears. I have to fork the muck over the wall into her garden as fast as an Irish navvy if I'm to get a reasonably warm drink. Snobby old bugger!'

'Now, now, don't swear like that about our May. She's good-hearted really. It's you who doesn't know how to talk to her . . .'

'Talk to her!' exploded Jackson. 'Nobody can talk to her . . . She never listens . . . She makes no difference between me and the muck I fork on to the garden. It's a wonder she doesn't sprinkle scent all over the heap as soon as I've gone!'

Edith shook her head and went back to her sock, ignoring her irate husband.

Jackson poked the fire reflectively, then thought better of it. 'Oh, I'll take the silly old bugger her load of muck tomorrow. If I don't, she'll only have more to grumble about next time she comes here for her eggs, bacon and black pudding.'

'It's good of you, Jackson,' said his wife. 'You know how difficult it is for her – being a widow.' She lowered her darning. 'I'll just go and make a bite of supper. You'll be ready for something tasty.' She left the warm fireside, thankful that the yearly load of manure had once again been successfully negotiated.

* * *

73

Peggy felt the shafts lift as Jackson balanced on the rear of the cart and began to fork the load over the low sandstone wall. She didn't like to be so far from home and she was looking forward to getting back to her grazing. Small hands patted her nose and offered her titbits – town children liked to gather round country horses when they paid their rather infrequent visits. Peggy was friendly and patient by nature. She began to doze, one hind leg resting on the toe of her hoof, both ears gently moving in opposite directions to monitor her master's voice, along with the laughter of passing children and Aunt May's shriller tones.

'Just be careful, Jackson,' she admonished. 'That wall has never stood straight since you backed into it last year. If it falls down when you've gone, I'll have great trouble finding a good man to repair it for me . . . You don't know what it's like, Jackson, to be left alone to fend for yourself, with the best man in the world lying six feet down in the cemetery over there.' She pointed significantly in the direction Jackson would take as he left.

'Yes,' she continued, 'God removes the good and leaves the wicked to be a trial to us all. That reminds me, I must go and bring you a mug of tea and a piece of cake. I know you don't want to bring your smelly clothes into my house . . . I'll just put it on the wall for you. Then you can go as soon as you're ready. I know you farmers are always busy.'

While his sister-in-law was gone Jackson surreptitiously ran his hands over the irregular sandstone blocks which formed the old garden wall. One or two of the flat coping stones were loosening with general wear and tear . . . May returned with tea and cake.

The old farmer wiped his brown, muck-stained hands on his corduroy trousers before reaching for the large slice of fruit cake.

'Your wall's like us, May. It's getting old and a bit worn,' he remarked.

'You speak for yourself,' snapped his sister-in-law. 'It's just a question of not letting yourself go . . . You never hear me complaining about getting old. Just you ask any of my neighbours – none of them think I look old and worn.'

Jackson's eyes ran along the row of closed front doors as he finished his mug of tea. 'No,' he nodded, 'I'm sure they've all noticed how well you're wearing!'

'Women who have to fend for themselves never look as old as those who are pampered by their husbands. You mark my words, Jackson. I'll follow many a coffin to that cemetery before they shovel the soil on to my poor George and me.'

Jackson looked down at May from his position in the empty cart, then picked up the reins, allowing Peggy to move off without a word of command. 'Thanks for the tea and cake, May. We'll be off now.'

'I'll be coming to see Edith in the next few days,' called May as the horse moved off eagerly. 'Tell her the brown eggs she brought last week were lovely!'

The cart disappeared, and May held the dirty mug and plate well away from her spotless apron as she carefully stepped over the scattered heaps of manure. Her front path had been rubbed with a large piece of soft red stone early that morning. Such stones from the iron ore mines were frequently used to redden the steps and paths in front of these terraced houses, for their redness was a clear indication of the owner's cleanliness and industry. May rose well before six each morning to be certain that no puddle, stray leaf, or invading footprint could declare her negligence to neighbours or passers-by. Even a careless postman or milkman could be met at the gate by a beslippered May determined to prevent him leaving marks on her pristine flagstones.

'I must make sure that Harold Thompson can come today,' she thought as she hurried indoors. 'The sooner that offensive manure is dug well into my garden the better . . . I can't understand how our Edith can live all year round with that smell coming in through her windows! Goodness only knows why she married a man like Jackson Strong when she could be living in a nice clean house like mine. Still, she was always different from the rest of the family. She never had any sense of what was proper . . .'

As May closed the door on the obnoxious smell left by her brother-in-law she imagined the sharp clang of Peggy's metal shoes and the rattle of the big iron-clad wheels as Jackson – standing up in his cart, and waving and shouting to his friends on the pavement – drove along the main street. Fortunately, the nameplate on the side of the cart, which read 'J. Strong. Farmer', had been partly obscured by the leaking contents of the load. Even so, she thought, 'I won't need to go into town to shop today.'

* * *

'Hurry up, Jackson, and finish your breakfast. I'm in a hurry this morning.'

'What for? Can't a working man finish his breakfast in peace? I don't know what all the rush is about. You have an electric cooker to do your cooking, and no butter to make. You lead a life of leisure these days. Can't a chap have a quiet sit? The milking finished, milk tins on the stand, calves fed, byre swilled, cows in the big pasture – I've done a day's work already. What are you fussing about for?'

'You never remember a thing I say, Jackson. I told you our May was coming today, if it's fine, that is. Well it's a lovely day so she'll be coming on the eleven o'clock bus. And if you'll just hurry up and finish your tea, then I can clean up before she comes.

'What do you want to dash around for? If she doesn't like the way the house looks, she can always set to work and clean it herself.'

'Oh come on, Jackson. How can she clean my house? She'll be wearing her best clothes! Besides, I don't want anyone to clean my house for me. I can do it myself, thank you.'

'Oh aye! She *will* be dressed up. Fancy a woman of her age wearing lipstick and scent! Them dogs of ours never recognise her like they would anyone else. When Tom Graham or John Hodgson come, they always know who it is. But they sniff round her as if she's a complete stranger. She's been coming here for nigh on twenty-five years and she's outwitted every dog we've had.'

'Well maybe you're right, Jackson,' said Edith impatiently. 'But you just let me get on now. You know our May. She can spot a layer of dust the minute she comes through the door. Her house is as clean as a palace, and I don't want to give her anything to nag me about.'

'Right enough. She's not content with just covering herself in scent to outwit the dogs, but she doesn't seem to be able to keep her tongue still when she comes here.'

'Have some pity, Jackson. She must have been very lonely since her George died.'

'I've never known a fella more ready to die than poor George,' interrupted Jackson. 'My God, I couldn't have stood living with that tongue. It was a happy release if you ask me.'

'Well I'm *not* asking you. Now just you behave yourself when she comes. And keep your own tongue quiet.'

'Me quiet? I can't ever remember upsetting her – or anyone. I don't know where you get that idea. No, Edith, it'll take a better man than me to sort her out. Poor George died trying!'

Jackson reached for his stick as he spoke, and his dog Patch rushed happily from under his master's chair, anticipating the pleasures ahead. He would race ahead of farmer and horses as they worked in the fields. And if they worked in the one at the far end he might just catch an unwary rabbit or have a good paddle through the beck. Yes, it was going to be a very good morning. It was only a pity his master was setting off a bit late, but Patch had learnt over the years that humans didn't seem to follow a regular routine, and were easily diverted by unimportant events.

Being an old dog now, he had been snoozing under Jackson's chair, reliving his early days in Wasdale Head. Like his mother and brothers he had worked the sheep on the high fells above the lake. Then, as he'd slowed down, he'd been sent to live with his first master's friend who farmed in this low country. Cows were a big change from sheep. They were great lumbering animals that moved too slowly. And if you tried to make them run like sheep they could toss you with their sharp horns.

These days Patch often dreamed about his youth – racing up and over crags and leaping becks to bring distant sheep down to be dipped, clipped and sometimes sold. Nose, tail and toes would twitch at the memory. Responsible work it was, often out of sight and sound of the farmer. He knew his present master understood sheep and their ways just as well as he did. But perhaps he too had grown too old to race across the hills.

* * *

'Well, Jackson, and how are you today?'

Aunt May was sitting at the kitchen table, her polished high-heeled shoes, permed hair and long gold earrings looking very much at odds with the homespun surroundings. Catching sight of her brother-in-law's clean clogs as he stepped into the farm kitchen, she turned sharply towards her sister, scarcely giving Jackson time to mutter a reply to her cursory greeting.

'Well, I see you still allow him to come in here wearing those filthy clogs, Edith. You work your fingers to the bone making those hookey mats. And look what happens – they get cut to ribbons in no time. I noticed the minute I came in that this was a new mat. No consideration . . . no consideration, at all. Now my George wouldn't have done that.'

Jackson looked uncharacteristically meek as he slid into the large chair at the opposite end of the table from his daunting sister-in-law.

'Mind you, he would have been just as bad,' she continued as Edith dished up the dinner. 'But I made it clear from the day we were married that he could forget his lazy ways. His mother had waited on him hand and foot – hand and foot Edith,' she emphasised, as she tucked into the hot meat pie and vegetables.

'Clogs and boots are for outside,' she began again, waving her knife across her sister's line of vision. 'But you have always been weak, our Edith. If I kept house here you wouldn't know what had hit you. And as for dogs, I wouldn't allow them in the house. Dirty things! You never know where they've been. Nor cats either,' she snapped as she pushed the begging cat forcefully away from her stockinged legs.

Edith quickly removed the offending animal, and Patch took the opportunity to escape as his mistress opened the kitchen door. Who was this alien creature who had suddenly invaded his territory, he wondered as he settled himself by the barn wall in the warm sun.

'You've certainly let your standards slip, Edith. Our father had much more respect for mother's things, but he was a gentleman.' She glared at Jackson, earrings swinging angrily.

By this time Jackson had taken refuge behind the unfamiliar pages of the *Farmers Weekly*.

'Do put your paper down, Jackson,' asked his wife timidly. 'May doesn't often find time to come and see us.'

The paper was lowered and with an attempt at a friendly smile Jackson Strong faced his sister-in-law across the table. 'Well now, May, and how's life treating you? Things never really change out here in the countryside. What's new in Egremont?'

'I'm glad you asked me that, Jackson. As you both know life has always treated me badly – my poor George having been taken from me – but they say the Lord always punishes the innocent.' Here she took a conveniently placed hankie from her capacious handbag to wipe her eyes.

'Yes, you may well ask how life is treating me. My Malcolm decided to live away from home as though Cumberland wasn't good enough for him.' She turned to her sister. 'As you know, Edith, I brought our Malcolm up properly even though I was on my own. He should know how much he owes his mother. Ungrateful he is. When I do get a letter from him, he's writing to tell me about his girlfriend . . . a southerner.'

'Oh how lovely. It would be nice if he got married, wouldn't it?'

'Married!' sniffed her sister. 'He's too young to be married. It's time he thought of his mother and came home. He has no sense of duty, Edith. That's what's wrong with him.'

'But he's thirty-five. It's time he was settled.'

Knowing his wife was treading on dangerous ground, Jackson cut in brightly. 'Well at least you're keeping well, May. I can see that just by looking at you.'

His sister-in-law shook her head gloomily. 'That's just where you're wrong, Jackson. You should never judge by appearances. Many's the healthy-looking person I've seen, fit and fine one day, but – mark my words – dead as a doornail by the end of the week. None of us know what we carry around inside us. Oh no, Jackson, never judge by what you see. I could be at death's door for all you know.'

'That's hardly likely, May,' her sister tried to comfort her. 'It's no good looking on the worst side of life. We could all be dead tomorrow, but the odds are against it happening.'

'Well, Edith, God must know what trials and tribulations I have faced.' Looking meaningfully at Jackson, she continued. 'And I have faced them with fortitude and patience. But you never know where God will strike next. A blameless life is no protection, Jackson.'

'I suppose not,' muttered her brother-in-law. 'If He's looking for perfection then He'll probably not look my way.'

'Don't be so ready to mock! He could strike you down, at any minute.'

Putting her cup down carefully, Aunt May leaned towards both Edith and Jackson, her voice dropping discreetly. 'Yesterday I went to see Alan Tyson.'

'Alan Tyson?' Edith asked, shocked. 'Why on earth should you go to see an undertaker?'

'Did the doctor reckon you should go?' Jackson was suddenly full of keen interest.

'No he didn't,' snapped May her earrings flashing with annoyance. 'I have no time for Them. When I last went to see my doctor he was most insulting . . .'

'Surely not . . .' Edith's voice was both soothing and questioning. 'He seems a very polite and pleasant young man . . .'

'They always do,' cut in May sharply. 'It's the nice quiet ones you have to watch, you never know what they're thinking . . .'

'For once I agree with you,' Jackson said firmly. 'It's the nice quiet chaps you have to watch. I reckon clogs is a good judge of character. You can always trust a chap who wears clogs.'

'As I was saying,' May's voice was icy. 'He's young enough to be my son and I was *shocked* at the way he spoke to me. A young man like him should be very careful when discussing anyone's . . .' Here her voice dropped almost to a whisper . . . 'Private parts.'

The *Farmers Weekly* had quickly regained its position and was drunkenly trying to hide Jackson's trembling glee. May continued, apparently oblivious of her brother-in-law's stifled merriment.

'Yes, Edith, after many years of suffering and discomfort I mentioned my . . .' She paused. 'My trouble underneath.'

'Dear, dear!' soothed her sister. 'I'm sure you were very wise to mention it. What did he say?'

'Believe it or not, he said he'd have to examine me – underneath.' Her tone had become angrier. 'As though he didn't believe me! I wouldn't let a young man like him poke around to learn his job at my expense. Young women seem to be ready to take their clothes off in front of anybody these days, but not me. Besides, he was insolent.'

'Surely not. Doctors are usually very polite. What did he say?'

'When I told him I wasn't prepared to allow him to make

such an embarrassing examination, do you know what his answer was . . .?'

By this time Jackson had managed to wipe his eyes and blow his nose and was peeping around the edge of his magazine.

Edith nodded expectantly.

'. . . He actually said that, to him, examining me was the same as lifting the bonnet of his car to look at the engine!'

The *Farmers Weekly* was by now dancing a lively jig.

'. . . Imagine that, Edith. Speaking to a sensitive woman that way. The engine of a car! How coarse can these young people be?'

'He'd be checking the mileage . . .' bubbled Jackson, his voice mercifully scarcely audible.

Edith glared in her husband's direction. With difficulty he controlled the rising laughter. As May continued her explanations only his trembling shoulders betrayed his suppressed hilarity.

'Anyway,' said May, 'I've been to see Alan Tyson to choose my coffin,'

'Your coffin? What on earth have you done that for, May? Do you feel ill?'

'Oh no, I've never felt better. But last week I went to Anne Jackson's funeral.'

'Oh yes, I know she didn't ail long. Was it a nice funeral?'

'As nice as you can expect from the Jacksons. They've never been ready for anything. Can't you remember their Alice? She had that little boy just a fortnight after her wedding – and he was properly overdue. All of ten pounds he weighed; you can't tell me that's a normal term baby.'

'Come now, May. It's not Christian to judge people like that.'

'I don't judge anyone – it's the whole town! Made a public scandal of herself, she did.'

'You went to Anne's funeral then?' prompted Edith,

pouring her sister another cup of tea.

'Oh yes, I always like to pay my respects when neighbours pass on. A lovely tea they put on in the King's Head; as good as the one we had when poor George left this world.'

'But what has Anne's death to do with you choosing your coffin?'

'Well it's obvious. There was only one thing wrong with the funeral.'

'What was that?'

'The coffin. It was one of those cheap pine things. I could smell the cheap wood before I saw it. Mary Jane Porter was there when I went to see her laid out. "She does look peaceful," she said. "But just look at that flimsy wood. I bet they're thankful she lost so much weight during that last week. I'm sure they would have had a job to lift her and her coffin together if she had died suddenly with all that weight on her." Of course I could see Mary Jane was right. And I thought to myself – what a disgrace it would be if my bearers got hold of the brass handles on my coffin and lifted the lot off me!'

By the time his sister-in-law reached this point in her account, Jackson's shoulders were performing a rapid tango and the *Farmers Weekly* was no longer responsible for its actions. His stifled giggles had not escaped Aunt May's indignant attention.

'Don't you tempt Providence,' she warned, shaking an irate finger at Jackson. 'I wouldn't want to follow *your* coffin with the bottom sagging down, and the whole congregation wondering if you were going to make the grave with the lid on.'

'What has all this to do with you going to see Alan Tyson, May?' urged Edith, her warning glances bombarding the unconcerned Jackson.

'It's obvious, isn't it? I don't want anyone following my coffin and then saying I don't know how to arrange a decent burial. I told Alan straight – "A good lid," I told him. "I don't want the first cobble that comes down to go straight through. I want a lead-lined lid." You know yourself what a wet cemetery it is in Egremont. I thought my poor George would float the day we buried him. No, I told him straight. "It doesn't matter what it costs," I said. "I want a decent coffin."'

'What did he say to that, May?' queried her sister.

'Oh very polite he was, and helpful – once he'd measured me up and down with his eyes, that is. He's had that nasty habit for the last fifteen years or so. But, as I always say, our Edith, everyone's got to earn a living – and he does everything so nicely. A lovely black hearse he has, with bearers in top hats. It's nice to go out properly. The church was packed the day I buried my poor George. It was a pleasure to go to such a well-organised funeral.'

'But why arrange your own? Surely Malcolm will see to everything?'

'Oh no, I'm not prepared to rely on him. He might end up marrying a wife from the south, and what chance will I have of getting a decent burial then? Our cousin John married a girl from London and he's never had a good meal since.'

'He looks all right to me,' volunteered Jackson. 'Not that I know what she says – can't understand a word – but she seems a nice enough little body.'

'You never notice anything,' snapped May, as Jackson retreated again behind his *Farmers Weekly*. 'Last time I saw him, his wedding suit was hanging on him; you would have thought he'd been on bread and butter for a couple of months. She's nice enough, but these southerners are all talk and no do. I'm not going to rely on her or anyone. It will all be done properly – I've seen to that. Which reminds me,' she said, turning to her sister. 'All the linen is ready to lay me out with, in the top drawer of the small chest of drawers in my small bedroom. I've got a beautiful nightdress – never worn.

There'll be no gossip when the neighbours pay their respects at my coffin. And if it's hot weather, Edith, make sure Alan Tyson nails the lid on after the first day of viewing. One day is quite enough to leave the lid off in warm weather.'

'We might turn our toes up before you do May,' ventured Jackson, who was deeply interested in the direction his sister-in-law's conversation had now taken.

'Not very likely,' retorted May. 'There is no justice in this world – some of us are born to suffer.' Her voice took on a self-righteous tone. 'Oh no, mark my words, I will be called to join my poor George – perhaps sooner than any of us thinks . . . Well, I must be going. It's a long walk to Egremont; pity there's no later bus.' She turned to her brother-in-law. 'If you had anything about you, Jackson, you would have had a car by now.'

'If I want to go anywhere I can get a lift – I still speak to the neighbours – or I can ride Peggy into Egremont.'

'It's been so nice to see you May,' Edith cut in quickly, fearing an exchange of open hostilities. 'It's a lovely day. I'll walk as far as Tom Graham's farm with you.'

'Thank you, Edith. He has a nasty-looking bull in that big field beside the road. It makes me nervous!'

'You haven't anything to fear from it,' muttered Jackson with a malicious twinkle in his eye.

'The rest of the way should be very pleasant for you on a day like this,' said Edith hastily. 'I'll just get you a few eggs and some cream.'

May followed her sister to the dairy door. 'Thank you, Edith – I'll enjoy the walk. It will give me time to think out what I'm going to say to Joe Dixon when I go to Whitehaven next week.'

'What on earth do you want to see a solicitor for?' asked Edith.

'I'm making a will.' Her voice was both dignified and determined.

'Surely you will leave everything you have to Malcolm – won't you May?'

'I shall have to think about it on the way home. If he marries a southerner what will happen to all my good china, linen and furniture? I won't rest easy in my grave if that lovely dinner service Aunt Hannah left me doesn't get dusted and cared for as it should.'

'All our stuff came from the sale room,' broke in Jackson. 'So we aren't troubled with problems like yours.'

'Yes, I've noticed that, Jackson. Our Edith's had quite a struggle considering the hand the Good Lord dealt her when she got married!'

'Here's your coat, May,' said Edith. 'And do keep that dog away from us, Jackson. May's coat is too good to have paw marks all over the front.'

* * *

Edith, Jackson, Bill, Esther and Jane sat round the supper table as Jackson mimicked his sister-in-law's imperious tone. 'I don't want the first cobble that comes down to go straight through the lid!'

The family roared, imagining exactly how their aunt would have delivered her speech. They had all found something to do well away from the farm the day they knew Aunt May was to call – the effort of stifling their giggles was always too much. An aunt with no sense of humour and, with such an over-developed sense of her own importance, had to be left to the diplomatic skills of their mother.

'She needn't worry,' snorted Jackson. 'It would take a mighty big cobble to mark that face – alive or dead!'

'She's not really so bad.' Edith rushed to her sister's defence, ignoring the peals of laughter from her children. 'She has lost her poor husband and is now faced with making a will – it is a problem!'

'She could leave her money to me,' suggested Bill.

'To you?' his father said with an air of exaggerated disbelief. 'Never! You've got dirty clogs, my lad. Oh no, you don't have the right qualifications at all . . .'

'What qualifications do we need, Dad?' asked Esther.

'Well, you must love, dust and polish her furniture and china. And, oh yes, you must marry someone from Egremont after she's dead!'

'Now, now, Jackson, you're as bad as she is. You twist everything to suit your story.' Edith turned to her daughters. 'Take no notice of your father. She has a heart of gold. She visits all her neighbours when they're ill – she feeds them, nurses them and lays them out beautifully.'

'Yes,' agreed her husband. 'Once May gets into their houses they're doomed. No one would dare to live once she'd made up her mind to lay them out . . . an angel of death with gold earrings!'

Jackson stopped to chuckle at his own wit. Then he turned to his family, looking more serious. 'If I'm suddenly taken ill and look like dying . . . don't tell her, for God's sake. As soon as I'm cold, get Alan Tyson here and ask him to nail the lid on right away. She's bad enough in life . . . but I'll have no defence against her in death!'

7

A New Tractor

The rain poured gently but steadily down the windows of the Grey Mare. It was a late evening in July. Jackson was sitting at his usual table playing dominoes, a pint of pale ale near his right hand and Patch dozing happily under his chair.

'That's it.' Alan Steel placed his last domino triumphantly on the table. 'Domino.'

'You're on form tonight, Alan. I don't know how you beat us three so regular like.'

Tom Graham pushed his chair back and made his way to the bar to buy another round. 'Same again, lads?' His friends nodded.

'Where's your John?' Bill Brown asked Alan as he reached for his new pint. 'I thought he would have been in here by now.'

'He's not bloody likely to be in here before eleven. When I saw him early on this afternoon he was just starting to lead in the hay from the big ten-acre field down by the station.' It was Jackson Strong who proffered this information.

'Have you finished leading your hay, Jackson?' asked Alan.

'Tom Graham and me finished before milking time today. Anyone with half an eye could see it was going to rain today.'

'It wasn't on the weather forecast. I listened early on this morning,' ventured Alan.

'Surely you can't expect them fellas in London to know what the weather's going to be like. Not one of them has ever put a clog in Cumberland. If your John's been listening to them it's no wonder he's making such a mess of his farming.'

'What sort of a mess is he making, Jackson?' asked Bill Brown. 'Anyone can get a bit behind with the hay.'

'Well, for a start, he has two mares just foaled. That's left him with two inexperienced young horses to do all the hard work. I watched him cut that field with that new mowing machine. Every time he started it up, both horses danced and snorted, and that young bay put her leg over the pole at least twice – she was terrified of the cutting blade. Remember Jos Thwaites? That's how he lost two of his fingers – inexperienced horses. They panicked when the wheel went into a rut, he was thrown across the knife bar, and he didn't know for a good two minutes that he'd lost his fingers. A dangerous thing to have only young horses to work with at hay and harvest time.'

'You're right,' agreed Tom Graham. 'Jackson and me have finished today. That big barn of mine and Jackson's top barn are both full.'

'We couldn't have done it as fast without that black gelding you brought at Cockermouth, Tom. He came with a pedigree as long as your arm, and it shows in every bone. He's a real mover – as soon as he feels the shafts he's ready to be off. We had a job to stop him trotting to Tom's seven acre this morning; he only settled when he could feel a load on his back.'

'Aye,' nodded Tom. 'He cost me all of a hundred pounds, but I reckon he's worth every penny. He didn't half shift some hay today. A few times he had to wait his turn to be unloaded – we couldn't keep the other two horses moving fast enough for him.'

'That's right,' Jackson said. 'Our Jane was leading the hay and driving the empty carts back and forwards all day – and there's no living with her tonight. Suddenly our two horses are too slow and old for her. She'll be pestering my life out to buy something new with a bit more speed. She thinks I'm made of money.'

'Well how about buying a tractor?' interrupted Alan. 'Horses are out of date now. Besides, a tractor isn't eating its head off when there's no work for it. They're no trouble to catch early in the morning either.'

'What about starting it off?' asked Jackson. 'I've heard they're often bad to start.'

Alan nodded. 'Aye, Abe Mossop has one and he says that it's bad to start on a cold morning.'

'I can't see that a tractor's made much difference to him then!' laughed Jackson. 'He never kept a decent horse; the ones he had were always coughing and staggering about first thing in the morning. Like a lot of us he hadn't much money to buy a decent horse so he bought anything that was offered cheap; plenty of work horses come through the sale ring with no guarantee of a good character.'

'A good many of your horses were bought cheap that way,' Bill pointed out as he placed his domino on the table.'

'Yes, you're right,' agreed Jackson. 'I've rarely had enough money to buy an expensive horse. So long as I can keep a decent mare for breeding, I'm not prepared to fork out money for an expensive general workhorse. Mind you . . .' He turned to his audience as the game finished. 'The first thing to spot in these sales is which animals are weak, worn and hungry; and which are in there because they are wicked. To my way of thinking it's a waste of money to buy a horse that's already been worked to death. A young horse is often chased to exhaustion by farmers' sons who think an animal of flesh and bone can work like a piece of machinery. Them's the folks that should buy a tractor; they don't know how to handle horses. No doubt they'll hammer the guts out of a tractor too. But at least a machine will just pack in if it's abused. It won't carry on until it can hardly pull a load like some of those poor beasts I've seen sold off for a few pounds. In countries like France and Belgium they wouldn't even have gone for butching. Come to think of it, our horses might be better treated if they ended up in a butcher's window instead of a knacker's yard.'

'You're getting soft in your old age, Jackson,' laughed Alan. 'To listen to you, a stranger might think you treated your horses like Arab hunters! I can remember last year when you were harrowing that big field by the camp. Our John and me stopped to talk and you had that big rangy gelding working alongside Peggy.'

'Well, what was wrong with the gelding?'

'Nothing that a good feed couldn't mend! I remember our John looking hard at it and saying "My God Jackson, just look at that horse's hook bone . . . I could hang my hat and coat on it!" '

The farmers leaning on the bar roared with laughter. They always appreciated Jackson's jokes, but they also liked to see him on the receiving end of a witty remark now and then.

'What did you say to that?' asked Bill, his shoulders shaking.

Jackson smiled to himself and carefully placed his pint of ale on the table. ' "Well lad," I said. "I've heard my horses called a lot of things . . . but never a bloody clothes horse!" '

The laughter round the bar was warm and relaxed.

As it died away, Jackson redirected the conversation. 'Them that can't handle horses will manage a lot better with tractors, but they needn't think a tractor won't have a belly to feed. Diesel will have to be paid for, and a lot of the pottering jobs an old horse can manage – like grubbing and general light carting – will cost far too much.'

'But it should even itself out, Jackson,' suggested Bill. 'The big jobs will pay for the small ones.'

'I suppose you're right,' nodded the old farmer.

Bill got in quickly while Jackson was off his guard. 'We're having one of those new Fergusons down for a day next week – just to try it out,' he began casually. 'I was telling your Bill about it a couple of days ago.'

'Oh, aye! And what did he have to say?'

'He reckoned that if the chap fetched it round to your place just after dinner next Tuesday, that you'd likely be keen to have a go on it . . .'

'Well, he needn't have said any such thing. No wonder he's said nowt to me about it. He knows it's a bloody daft idea.' He turned towards the pub door. 'I'll just bid you all a good night . . .'

'Not so fast,' called Bill. 'I seem to remember you telling us all how it takes a clever fella to work with horses but any fool can manage a piece of machinery . . .'

'All you have to do is pull a lever and press a button – nothing to it at all,' Alan chimed in.

'Come on Jackson! We'll come with the young chap who's demonstrating it.' Bill paused for effect, then delivered the final blow. 'After all, our John says any fool can manage one of those Fergusons.'

Jackson's eyes glinted, 'In that case,' he retorted tartly,

'make sure you arrive no later than one o'clock. I don't want to waste a whole afternoon playing with a toy.'

'Jackson struggling with a tractor is something I wouldn't miss for a gold sovereign!' laughed Bill, as the sound of disappearing clogs grew fainter.

* * *

'What on earth made you agree to try the tractor out, Jackson?' Edith cleared the empty dishes from the table as she spoke. 'It's a quarter to one already. They'll be here soon, and you know you have no experience of driving a tractor. You might kill yourself.'

'Don't be so silly, Edith. I never managed to kill myself when we had a motorbike and sidecar.'

'Goodness me, that was twenty years ago when you were much younger and there was little traffic on the roads.'

'I'm not foolish enough to try a new tractor out on the main road, Edith. I'm not so daft as you think . . . I've no intention of killing anybody.'

'Where are you going then?'

Jackson nodded towards the kitchen window. 'In that seven-acre pasture field out there, in front of the house. It's good and flat.'

'Oh, that's why you drove the milk cows down to the far meadow this morning. I wondered why . . .'

'It's a right state of affairs when a chap can't do anything without being watched. It's the electricity that's done it.'

'What do you mean?'

'You women have all the work done for you these days. You have too much time on your hands so you use it to spy on an old fella who's only getting on with his job.'

He paused, his eyes twinkling wickedly. 'I expect you noticed what time I went to the closet as well?' He chuckled gleefully, anticipating his wife's shocked reply.

'Now, now, Jackson. There's no need for such coarseness.'

An explosive sound reached her ears. 'Here they are.' Three men were perched on the shining tractor as it turned into the yard. 'Isn't that nice of Bill and Alan to give up their time to come and give you a hand for an hour or so? I'm sure no harm'll come to you if they're close by.'

'Bloody nosy parkers!' muttered her husband as he closed the door firmly behind him.

'A fine piece of modern equipment. It's a pity my son is at work today . . .' Edith could hear Jackson's friendly greeting as he walked towards the fresh-faced young salesman. Three minutes later she heard the seven-acre field gate being pushed open to allow the tractor to be driven through.

The young man jumped lightly from the tractor seat. 'Here you are, Mr Strong. Take this seat and I'll show you how it works.'

'It took me a week to learn how to harness a horse,' boasted Alan Steel, 'but only an hour to master one of these.'

'That's right,' added Bill. 'He had it going in no time at all. Provided you take notice when it's explained to you, you can manage a simple machine like this fine.'

'You are quite right, Sir,' the salesman agreed eagerly. 'Indeed, my firm designed this tractor specifically for those of you who find technical machinery rather complicated. After all, gentlemen like yourself, Mr Strong, who have grown used to relying upon horses to share the load, so to speak, cannot be expected to adapt to a complicated gearbox which relies upon a series of consecutive manoeuvres . . .'

'If you're trying to say that chaps like me are too bloody thick to drive a few bits of tin like this round a field, then you needn't bother!'

Jackson was by now firmly ensconced on the seat which bent slightly unhappily under his weight.

'Just show me where the starter and gear lever are, lad, and I'll show you who's boss in my field.'

'There's the starter, gear lever and throttle . . .'

The engine roared into life as Jackson's finger pressed the starter; the throttle action reminded him of his motorcycling days. The machine trembled impatiently beneath him.

'Right foot brake! Left foot clutch!' called the salesman to a fast-disappearing Jackson.

'He's getting the hang of it fast.' Alan remarked to Bill.

'Too bloody fast, if you ask me,' replied his friend. 'He took yon far corner a bit sharpish.'

'I think we'd better move back, nearer the gate. He's coming this way a bit uncertainly. I'm not sure whether he's going to make it back up the field again.'

All three watchers reached the safety of the gate a split second before Jackson flashed past.

'Look at that! He turned that corner on only two wheels! God help us if he doesn't make it next time!'

As Alan spoke, the tractor completed its drunken turn at the far end of the field, where a row of curious cows had gathered in the adjoining meadow to gaze over the hedge in amazement. One or two of the younger ones had begun to gallop alongside, quickly losing ground to the luckless Jackson who had long since lost his cap along with a great deal of his usual aplomb.

'Right foot brake!' yelled the young salesman who had run to the middle of the field, judging this to be the safest place.

'Whoa! Whoa!' replied Jackson as his rear regained the bucking seat. 'Right foot – what?'

'I must make him understand the next time round,' gasped the frantic salesman, his vision of a rapid sale completely overshadowed by the need to salvage as much as possible of his demonstration tractor.

'Right foot – brake.' At last Jackson grasped his meaning, as his mount roared through a low gap in the hedge to end up with its nose buried deep in a gently rocking stack of hay.

'Are you all right, Jackson?'

'Look at the hole you've made in that hedge.'

Jackson stepped slowly and as steadily as he could from the now sliding haystack. 'What hole are you talking about?'

'That one, where you've just driven through.'

Jackson walked away from the silent tractor. 'Just what I've wanted for a long time. A handy little gate on there will do fine when our Edith wants to take a short cut to Mary's house.'

'What on earth is all this noise?' said Edith as she emerged from the farmhouse. 'What's happened to the haystack?' she asked anxiously, the tractor having been totally submerged in hay.

'That fancy tractor is underneath,' replied her husband. 'I don't think it has the height to hold it upright.'

'At least it won't eat the bugger while you go in for your tea,' laughed Alan.

'How did it get there?' asked a puzzled Edith.

'You'd never believe it if we told you,' said Bill as he joined the salesman in his hunt for the tractor.

'I wonder how many'll believe it in the Grey Mare!' laughed Alan.

'I can't see as how there's anything to tell them,' snapped Jackson, rubbing his tender rear end. 'Some folks are bloody hard up for a decent story if they have to come spying on folks who might think of buying a new tractor.'

8

CATCHING RABBITS

The farmer is perhaps the only member of society who breeds and keeps animals, and can at the same time kill them for necessity and for sport. This is not true of all farmers. Many cannot kill the animals they have bred; they prefer someone else to do it. And some reject any form of hunting as barbaric.

Jackson Strong enjoyed caring for his stock. But he was also prepared to destroy them as painlessly as possible if they were ill or injured, and he would butch for a living. In addition he loved shooting and rabbiting.

Shortly after milking time one fine morning, just after the harvest had been brought in, Jackson lifted his double-barrelled shotgun from its place above the mantelpiece and began to polish it lovingly.

'I wish you would put that thing away, Jackson. I can't see the need to kill anything these days.' His wife cleared the breakfast dishes as she spoke.

'Ah! But I can remember a time – before the war – when you were glad to see as many rabbits as I could catch or shoot coming in through that door.'

'Yes but times were bad then, Father. I know we would have had a job to manage if it hadn't been for the few shillings the rabbits brought in. It's a great pity that it took a war to bring prosperity to the ordinary working people of this country.'

Jackson glanced at the clock. 'Bill Brown's late. He said he'd be here by now. He's bringing his nets and two of his best ferrets.'

'What about Spot? Is Spot not coming?'

'Well that goes without saying. We couldn't go rabbiting without a terrier, could we?'

'I suppose you couldn't, but you could go without that gun. Surely you don't need it if you're taking the ferrets with you?'

'What? Go without the gun? Impossible! You never know what I might see while I'm out – a pheasant or maybe a partridge – you never know your luck. Even a hare would make a change. We've never had a hare for a good bit now. I think we'll be lucky with the rabbits though. When we cut yon eight-acre cornfield the little buggers were running all over the spot. They live in those big hedges. It's a bit sandy up there, and there's nothing rabbits like better than sandy soil. It's easy for them to dig. I want them cleared out before the spring. We'll be ploughing that field and planting it with cabbages, carrots and potatoes – just right for young rabbits to feed on. You should have seen them last spring when I sowed that corn. They sat outside their holes watching us, just like big families in slum tenements. They let us get right up to them before they scuttled off down their tunnels. Mind you, I got two with the old gun, but it made such a racket poor Peggy did a tango as she pulled the roller.' He chuckled at the memory.

Bill Brown's Ford truck rattled into the yard and pulled up close to the back door. A barking trio jumped down in response to Flash's noisy greeting, and Bill's cheerful voice echoed from the outhouse walls as he lifted a neat wooden box from the passenger seat.

'Come in, Bill! Why are you bringing the ferret box in?' asked Edith.

'Just you look,' he replied as he carefully unstrapped the box. 'I've bought a new ferret from Alan Steel – she's a beauty. Alan says she's a great rabbiter.'

Bill lifted his prize from the box, making sure that her companion didn't escape from the snug little nest inside. As he held her up by the back of the neck the little animal opened her eyes and protested feebly. She was certainly pretty.

'Oh, isn't she sweet?' cooed Edith as she gently stroked the uncomplaining ferret.

'Yes,' agreed Jackson. 'She is bonny, but why did Alan Steel part with her? He knows a good ferret when he sees one.'

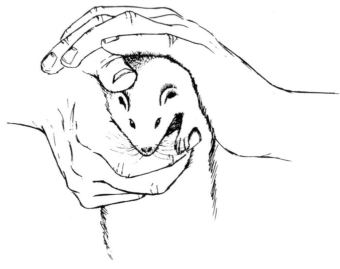

'Says he has too many. He does a lot of ratting now and doesn't want her bitten – she should make a good breeding animal if she's looked after.'

'We'll give her a try this morning then Bill. That is – if we get anywhere before dinner. I thought you were coming early this morning.'

'I had to go to the bank.'

'I've made some coffee and sandwiches for both of you,' said Edith, handing her husband a bag which he slung over one shoulder.

Jackson picked up his gun and made his way from the kitchen. 'Have you plenty of nets, Bill?'

'Enough, Jackson. Come on, let's be off.'

The sun shone down on the two friends as they made their way across the bare eight-acre field. The binder had cut the corn, leaving the sharp stubble to stick a good few inches out of the ground. Cutting, drying, loading, leading and stacking corn was long and laborious work for the farmer and for all his family in those days. Neighbours often helped each other to make sure of everyone's hay. Then, once the corn was gathered and housed for the winter, the farmer could relax for a few days before beginning his autumn work, sorting and selling his sheep.

Flash and her friends raced ahead of their masters, chasing, teasing, rolling and occasionally barking with the sheer delight of being dogs. By the time the two men reached the long hedge their quarry had disappeared. Young rabbits had been led by their mothers through the labyrinth of tunnels to the safest corners. Their ears had picked up the sound of dogs long before the hunters had come anywhere near them.

Now the excited dogs were ordered to keep close to the men. Spot, in particular, was straining to dive down a rabbit hole, but that couldn't be allowed. Both men knew the trouble terriers caused if they disappeared down an inviting hole and became trapped, unable either to turn or continue. They then had to be dug out – if they hadn't suffocated first. No. Spot's task was to catch any rabbits as they tried to struggle through the nets or to wriggle free from the men's hands as they expertly broke their necks.

'Get the nets out, Bill,' ordered Jackson eagerly.

The two men carefully pegged the rabbiting nets over the exit holes on both sides of the hedge, and the dogs lowered themselves obediently into the soft grass, silently awaiting the command to retrieve. Tails scarcely dared wag.

'Which ferret shall we start with, Bill?'

'Well, I don't want my new ferret overworked. I think I'll just send old Nip down there first.'

Carefully he opened the lid of his box and gently lifted the darker of the two ferrets out. Nip wriggled excitedly, his eyes wide and his nostrils turning towards the smell of rabbits.

Bill popped him into the end hole, replacing the net as soon as he disappeared. Squealing, scratching and vibration could be heard inside the hedge. Suddenly all hell seemed to break loose as rabbits rushed into waiting nets, dogs barked and men shouted.

Soon all was quiet, the nets were re-pegged and Nip was replaced in his box.

The rabbits were laid out on the grass to be examined and counted.

'Fourteen,'declared Bill. 'All fine rabbits. I'll tell you what, Jackson, let's have that drink of coffee and some of the gingerbread I saw Edith put in your bag. Then we'll see what the new ferret can do. Let them all settle down first.'

'That's fine with me, Bill. I'm ready for a sit down. I think I'm getting too old for this game'

The two men settled themselves down to enjoy their snack.

'Lovely gingerbread your Edith makes. I was in such a rush this morning, Elsie didn't have time to make anything up for me.'

'Aye, you said you went to the bank this morning. I thought you'd have enough sense to go to places like that on a wet day, instead of wasting good rabbiting time.'

'It was a waste of time going anyway. You see, I got this letter from the bank manager, asking me to call about the state of my bank balance. To be honest, I didn't know what state it was in. What with buying and selling every week, I'm not sure how things are.'

'That's true of all of us, Bill.'

' "Come on in, Mr Brown," says the manager. "Do take a seat." I wasn't too happy when he said that, Jackson. Bank managers are often polite when they feel superior. Anyway, if there's any problem here, I thought, I'll play the country yokel. Once they get dressed up in their pin-stripe suits, these fellas like us to think they're financial experts.'

'So what did he say?'

' "Now then, Mr Brown," he says. "I'm afraid you have an overdraft of one hundred and twenty pounds seventeen shillings and sixpence. I've asked you to come today to see if we can sort something out.'

' "Can you explain that in ordinary words?" I asked.'

'Just what I would have asked,' chuckled Jackson. 'Go on, Bill.'

' "Well it means," says he very slowly and clearly, "that you owe the bank one hundred and twenty pounds, seventeen shillings and sixpence."

"Now I understand," I said. "I owe the bank one hundred and twenty pounds, seventeen shillings and sixpence."

"Yes," he says.'

"Would you check my account for this time last year," I asked him with a puzzled look on my face. He looked surprised but asked the cashier to go and fetch my file. When it came he looked carefully through it. "Ah yes, here it is – Mr William Brown. You were in credit then. You had a total of two hundred and seventeen pounds, ten shillings in your account." '

'What did you say to that?' asked Jackson. 'I said just what I said the first time. "Can you explain that to me in ordinary words?"

"Well it means," said he very patiently, "last year we owed you two hundred and seventeen pounds, ten shillings."

"Now I understand," I said, getting to my feet and putting my cap back on my head. "I don't remember writing and asking *you* for it then, so I can't see why you should be bothering me now. Good day, Mr Smith,'' and I walked out!'

The two farmers chuckled heartily over the joke.

'You did right,' laughed Jackson. 'Education is a fine thing for them that's got few brains. It teaches them things they can't think out for themselves!'

'But the likes of you and me, Jackson, have to survive by our wits.'

'Talking about using our wits reminds me of how my father told me they used to scare the rabbits out of their holes years ago when they hadn't a ferret.'

'What was that, Jackson?'

'They used a crab.'

'A crab? Go on, Jackson! I can't imagine a crab racing down a rabbit hole . . .'

'Now just you stop and think, Bill. You know as well as I do that crabs like darkness and will scuttle into a dark corner if they get the chance?'

'Yes, we all know that.'

'Well, what they used to do was put a lit candle on the crab's back, put it inside the entrance to the rabbit hole, then off it would go as fast as it could into the darkness, rushing to get away from the light.'

'And the rabbits?'

'Well you can just imagine the panic when they saw the strange light coming towards them.'

'Fancy that! We think we've invented everything but our fathers before us certainly knew a thing or two.'

'True enough. Now let's give this little ferret a try. There's plenty of rabbits still down there.'

Bill quickly opened his box, then popped the little animal into the rabbit hole. Soon the sound of scuffling and squeaking could be heard. The men ran to the exit holes and the dogs danced in anticipation. Two, three rabbits were caught, then – nothing. The noises quietened down.

'Where's my ferret?'

They peeped through the netting over all the burrows – no ferret.

'It shouldn't be long,' said Jackson.

'It's a lovely day. We can sit for a few minutes. Three fine rabbits she's chased out.'

'Maybe – but I'd rather she got on with the job and came out herself.'

'Give her time, a few more minutes.'

No sound came from the burrow. Bill sat down and smoked a cigarette, while Jackson took a piece of black twist from his pocket and sliced the tobacco with his penknife.

The hedge remained silent.

'Do you think she's dead, Jackson?'

'Dead? No. Asleep? Yes! I thought she was a bit reluctant to open her eyes when you lifted her out on to our kitchen table. She's bonny, but she's a lazy little bugger. Just you shove Nip in there, he'll waken the lot up. The rabbits daren't move, they know she's in with them.'

'OK. In he goes.'

Soon the scrambling and squealing began, and men and dogs shot into action.

'I'm glad she came out. She's certainly not worth digging for. She'd have had to live on the rabbits, then maybe turned wild,' said Jackson.

They collected the rabbits, stringing them by their hind legs along their walking sticks. Both the ferret box and bait bag were slung from one shoulder and Jackson carried his shotgun 'broken' over his left arm as they made their way across the eight-acre field towards the road and Bill's waiting truck, rabbits swinging in time to their strides. The dogs were well ahead, occasionally circling back to make sure the two men were still following.

'A good catch eh, Jackson! Twenty-four rabbits. How will we share them? Twelve and twelve?'

'No, two will do us, Bill. Take the others to Whitehaven tomorrow. Hang them on the side of your truck and you'll soon sell them. Fresh rabbits will be a treat for town folk.'

'Yes, you're right. I think I'll put a few more potatoes, cabbages and carrots on the truck. The rabbits should attract a few extra customers. Sure you won't take more, Jackson?'

'No, no. Two will be grand. A rabbit pie is one of the tastiest meals you can eat. No fancy feeding stuff, like you get in beef and pork. Artificial animal foods change the taste of the flesh – that's why the gentry live on game. You never hear of the King and Queen eating shepherd's pie or tatie pot. They've been better advised. Pheasant and venison are what they eat.'

'I suppose that's why they go shooting in Scotland at this time of year.'

'You're right, Bill. Good sport and good food. But you don't have to be a king to live like one. Come on, let's get home. After a few days' hanging in the back kitchen these rabbits'll be really worth eating.'

The truck bumped along the narrow road, dogs leaning out at all angles with their tongues flapping and tails waving as they struggled to keep their balance.

'Good God, Bill, slow down. It's harder work sitting on this seat than riding that wicked chestnut I used to have. I've picked that ferret box up five times already. That new ferret'll have a nervous breakdown if it gets rattled round in the box like this!'

Bill slowed down. 'I think I've been taken in over that ferret, Jackson,' he admitted.

'You didn't buy it though, did you?'

'Yes I did. Two pounds I paid. He said it was one of his best ferrets.'

'It certainly is, especially when it's in your box! I think Alan owes you a pint or two. You would have been better off with a crab. At least you could have eaten it,' smiled Jackson.

'A good idea,' chuckled Bill as the truck turned into his friend's yard.

9

THE AUCTION

To farm children, who lived in comparative isolation, a visit to the local auction mart was a rare treat. It was always busy and noisy. However, whilst selling fatstock of any kind was a necessity for the farmer, his children would often be sad to see bullocks they had fed from calfhood disappearing through the gateway to the butchers' ring.

Such emotional considerations had never disturbed Jackson Strong. Used to butching his own pigs, as well as those of his neighbours, he saw the butching of his stock as the happy culmination of his breeding prowess.

His enemies were disease and accident which could result in the total loss of his investment. To save additional expense, a vet was only called for difficult calvings, lambings and farrowings where there was a possibility of saving one or more of the participants.

Any animal that contracted any sort of wasting condition was likely to die anyway, in the farmer's eyes, so the additional cost of treatment was a foolish expense. Such animals were left in a field near the house to die in their own time, or were shot by the farmer; in both cases the carcass was either buried or sold for animal food, depending on the cause of death or the amount of flesh on the bones.

'It's a long time since I've seen you here, Jackson. Are you buying or selling?' Abe Telford shook Jackson's hand as he spoke.

'Well I've just put five bullocks through the store ring. They weighed out fine . . . I have room to tie up another milk cow this winter so I thought I'd come and see how a few of these young cows are milking out. I might just buy one.'

'The very thing is standing third in from the far door. That black Friesian. She's only had two calves – calved last Monday – and she's easy to milk.'

'I might have guessed you were selling something, with such a big smile on your face!'

'I'm always pleased to see you, Jackson,' laughed Abe as the two friends walked into the auction milking byre to watch the hand milker working his way slowly down the row of cows so that the prospective buyers could see each cow's yield.

It was usual not to milk the cow on the morning of the sale so that the udder and milk yield were as heavy as possible. Many of the cows shuffled uneasily as the surplus milk dripped and trickled from their distended teats.

'But that Friesian is a fine young cow,' continued Abe. 'I've too many to winter properly and I have two of her older sisters tied up in the byre so I reckon that's enough of one family. Besides, she's a nice quiet little cow. Look! She wasn't a bit of bother when John Burns sat down there to milk her. Young Esther could manage her fine.

'You know as well as I do that no kickers ever get in here now, since that white Ayrshire kicked poor old Alec Parker round this byre!'

They both laughed at the memory.

'They had to stop selling in the fatstock ring,' Jackson reminded him. 'There was too much entertainment in here. The bucket, stool and poor old Alec were kicked all over the place.'

'He didn't give in easy, Jackson. He came back a few times for more – but the Ayrshire won in the end.'

'That's right. They looked all over the auction for Gordon Scott to come and milk his own cow. But he couldn't be found anywhere, not even in the Fox and Hounds across the street.'

'A sure sign he didn't want to be there when it was milked!'

Abe paused to reflect. 'You must have been coming to this auction for a good many years, Jackson?'

'Oh yes . . . I remember very clearly the first time I bought a cow in here. We'd just taken up the tenancy of our first farm and I had twenty pounds in my pocket. I was building up a reasonable milk round and needed a good milk cow.' Jackson's eyes lit up at the memory.

'I had been here a Thursday or two before, just to watch the farmers bidding. None of them knew me. I knew one or two by sight but not to speak to. They wore polished boots and leggings, carried smart sticks and were all known personally by Graham Smith, the father of this auctioneer. I watched them buying cattle – they raised their sticks or nodded and the price went higher. "Going, going, gone . . . to Mr Kenneth Allen at fifteen pounds. Thank you, Sir" he would say.'

Jackson brought his hand down smartly on the top of his walking stick as he imitated the auctioneer's hammer.

'Did you go back then?' asked Abe, who always enjoyed his friend's conversation.

'You bet I bloody well did,' retorted Jackson. 'A bonny little roan shorthorn heifer came into the ring. She'd only had one calf – I knew she'd do me fine. Nelson Bragg had put her up for sale. One or two farmers put in a low bid or two, then there was a pause. "Eleven pounds ten shillings," I shouted up to the auctioneer. I was standing opposite him on the other side of the ring so he was bound to see me. The bids rose. I could see that old Graham Smith was bothered about knocking a cow down to an unknown young chap rather than one of the local farmers and dealers whose bid was their bond.'

'Did you buy the cow?' Abe couldn't wait to hear the end of the story.

'Oh yes! Nineteen pounds ten shillings he asked and I nodded. "Going, going . . . gone," he said unwillingly. Then there was a silence round the ringside, because no one there knew me, and he said "Would the gentleman who called the highest bid for this animal please go to the auction office and give his name and money to the clerk?".'

'You couldn't blame him Jackson,' Abe interrupted. 'They never did trust outsiders in those days . . . So you went and paid?'

'No, not before I'd stood up on the bench, turned to the crowd of farmers and shouted, "My name is Jackson Strong. You might as well all listen because you're all going to hear a lot more of it – and here's my money for all of you to see . . . I never buy anything I can't bloody well pay for!" Then I walked the long way round the ring to the office, paid my money, asked the nearest farmer to point out Nelson Bragg, and went up to him for one pound back for luck money.'

'What a bloody cheek! Did he give you it?'

'Yes he did. He bought me a pint of ale as well. Not bad for a cheeky miner, eh?'

'That takes a bit of face to do, Jackson.'

'Maybe, but not as much face as some of these farmers' sons who buy cows in the open market and take their time about paying for them. Their names are good, however bad their bank balances might be. I'll tell you what! Everybody in this auction knows who Jackson Strong is these days.'

'The two friends made their way to the dairy ring and settled down in their usual places where they had a good view of the auctioneer, the stock and the local farmers.

'I'll bid for your cow, Abe,' said Jackson as he cut into his chewing tobacco. 'Even if she passes my price you'll get a tidy sum for her; she's a classy beast.'

A short time later Jackson had bought the Friesian and the two farmers wandered over to the pig area, to see what their neighbours were selling.

Anyone entering a small auction mart would have no difficulty finding their way to the pig ring. The cacophony of squeals and grunts can be heard at a fair distance. Consequently it takes a special sort of auctioneer to sell pigs, one whose voice can reach a frequency outside the range of his squealing merchandise.

The skilled auctioneer discovers this note early on in his career and learns never to deviate from it. His distinctive 'bur' of rising prices can be picked up above the whole orchestral range, from the tiniest pigs' squeaks, through to the boars' deep-throated objections. The breeders, for their part, have long since learned to ignore the din, and are quite able to continue talking, listening and bidding despite the deafening racket.

Unlike cows, pigs enjoy coming to market. They are very

gregarious and seem to like sniffing and nuzzling the sawdust and straw. Railings are for chewing, while other pigs are for pushing, biting and shouting at. Sows will doze happily as their litter feed, climb over and roll about happily in the straw.

Very tiny piglets are perhaps the most lovable and entertaining of all baby animals. Throw an armful of straw into their newly cleaned hull, and they will entertain you for a good hour or so – making tunnels through their fresh bedding, then racing excitedly through the maze of passage-ways, chasing, waylaying and surprising each other.

By nature the cleanest of animals, pigs will never sleep in their own dirt out of choice. They will clean themselves carefully, always in the same corner of their hull. There are no dirty pigs, only lazy pig owners!

It's said that pigs are physically the nearest animals to humans. Being bare-skinned, they feel temperature just as we do. They get painfully sunburnt if they sleep in the sun, but unlike us they instinctively search for shade!

Their diet is as varied as ours, and they eat with gusto. However, any food which has been prepared for human consumption and is then thrown out for pigs must first be boiled to make it safe. Unsterilised food would result in all kinds of worms breeding in the pig's gut, making their meat a potential health hazard for humans.

At farrowing time young sows can become over-protective, resenting the farmer's care and assistance. A sow's powerful jaws can break an arm with ease, and they have even been known to eat their own piglets if they feel threatened.

'A couple of fine shotts in that pen, Jackson,' remarked Abe as the two farmers strolled round.

Jackson leant forward to read the name chalked on the metal plate set into the small gate. 'No wonder – they're Harry Jepson's. Fine long pigs, a bit on the skinny side.'

'That's the fashion now. Long lean pigs cut up as lean bacon. The housewife won't buy fat bacon any more, Jackson.'

'That's what they all tell me. If it's not a Large White, it's not worth keeping.'

'That's the way it goes now. I've never seen our local Cumberland breed for years. And you are the only one I know who breeds Saddlebacks. Alan Steel keeps a few Landraces as a hobby, but the fatty breeds are rare now.'

'Well, all I can say,' said Jackson sadly, 'is that few people recognise a decent slice of bacon when they see it these days. A bit of fat gives all the taste to the bacon. There's nothing nicer than slicing a strip from one of the sides hanging from our kitchen ceiling and frying it up with a couple of duck eggs. Now that's a real treat, Abe.'

'You try telling the housewife that, Jackson. As for duck eggs; they're hard to sell. Folk don't realise a good duck egg's twice the size of a hen's egg – and a darned sight tastier. But that fatty bacon you cut off your Saddlebacks wouldn't sell in a shop. Mind you, the little pigs are bonny . . . black-and-white pigs make a change from all whites.'

'Yes, they are bonny,' replied Jackson, poking his stick into the pen. 'A bit lean, that's all. Somebody couldn't keep them any longer. I might just put a bid or two in for them. There'll be plenty of room in the wagon beside your Friesian cow; they'll fatten up nicely before Christmas. See anything you fancy Abe?'

'I looked through those calves over there.' Abe pointed in the direction of a cluster of small pens which housed a number of calves, some standing gazing around at their new world; others lying in the straw dozing. Some of them had only been born that morning, and would be sold for veal in the afternoon.

'There are four bonny little shorthorn heifers in the bottom pen. I might make a bid for them, but I haven't a field to take any bull calves. I have enough of my own at home.'

'Aye, a milking cow adds to the milk cheque every week, but bullocks need feeding for a few years before they give you any return.'

Jackson's last remark was partly drowned out by the entrance of the auctioneer, his clerk and a crowd of farmers who had been waiting for the eleven o'clock start of the pig and calf sales.

The sale was soon underway, Graham Smith deftly weaving his way across the top rails of the pens, his clerk balancing equally well as he recorded the lots that were sold.

The auction yard was busy again in the afternoon, and cattle trucks were loaded again as stock was bought. Farmers hurried here and there to find haulage contractors who had room for their new stock. Wagons made as many journeys as possible to fill and then clear the market.

* * *

There was always an air of suppressed excitement at Jackson Strong's farm if he had gone to the auction with even the slightest intention of buying a new animal. The bullocks had been herded into the truck very early that morning and Jackson had been talking for a few days about buying another milk cow.

Esther and Jane both knew that any stock their father might buy would reach the farm long before its new owner who would be obliged to make a tour of the various farmers' bars in Whitehaven, renewing and cementing friendships – an essential activity for a man like Jackson Strong.

A stall in the large byre was ready for any new cow that might appear, with tasty cow cake and chopped turnip in the trough and a bucket of water placed nearby. Most cows are thirsty after such a hectic day, especially heavy milkers. Any other stock could be put in an empty hull immediately.

As the family were finishing their tea, Frank Bates' cattle truck drew up at the farm gate.

'Look Bill!' called Esther excitedly.

'Dad must have bought something.'

It was difficult to see what he'd bought, as the truck was half full of stock. Frank's itinerary included a number of farms further on.

They all dashed outside to see the new arrival, even Edith.

'One black milk cow,' Frank announced loudly as he unlocked the huge rear doors and gently ushered the weary and nervous little cow down the ramp and into the yard, the sticky label positioned near her tail proclaiming her new-ness. The whole family accompanied her into her stall.

'Thank you for bringing her, Frank. She's a real bonny cow,' said Bill as they tied the stranger up and watched her drink her water.

'That's OK,' replied Frank. 'She needs a good night's sleep and she'll be as right as rain in the morning. But I've got something more for you in the lorry.'

'What else have you brought?' asked Jane, always delighted by this sort of surprise.

'Have you an empty hull?' he asked.

'Yes, of course,' said Esther.

Frank had locked the huge tailgates to stop the remaining cows escaping, so they knew their father must have bought a small animal which could be lifted out from the front section of the lorry.

Frank reached in through a small door immediately behind the cab door and grabbed one of the squealing, protesting pigs. 'This is yours,' he said, passing Bill a small wriggling body with the letters J.S. marked across its back. 'Five more to come.'

*　*　*

A few hours later Jane and Esther leaned over the pigsty door watching the six new arrivals. A long low trough had been filled with warm milky pig food, and a large bottle of fresh straw had been shaken into one corner.

'Aren't they thin!' exclaimed Esther.

'Dad must have taken pity on them,' agreed Jane. 'They must have come from a hungry home – perhaps they had too many. But they're all healthy little pigs. Just look at them!'

The sisters laughed as they watched the youngsters racing from trough to straw, tossing the bedding over their backs, rolling, disappearing through their new tunnels – racing back to steal a few more mouthfuls of food – squeaking, grunting and exploring their new home.

'Let's shut this door tight to keep them warm,' said Esther as the piglets began to snuggle up together, ready for sleep.

'We could go and see our new cow,' suggested Jane. 'I wonder what her name is. If Dad hasn't asked her previous owner we'll have to give her one.'

'How about Patience?' She came in so calmly and quietly . . .'

'Why not?'

'You know,' said Esther, 'if I went to the auction with money in my pocket, I would spend every penny and bring back a truckful of all the thin, sad, sorry animals that I had taken pity on.'

'So would I,' agreed her sister. 'But farming isn't for the soft-hearted. It's a business, just like any other.'

10

MODERN METHODS

It was 8.30 am one fine Thursday morning. Jackson Strong put the chain on his farm gate and watched the cattle truck drive slowly off towards Whitehaven.

'Come back inside,' called Edith from the scullery doorway. 'I've made a mug of tea and there's a fresh piece of cake for you. Hurry up! Tom Graham will be calling soon to take you to the auction.'

'I'm coming, Mother,' replied Jackson slowly walking back to the farmhouse. He reluctantly hung his cap on a peg on the outside door as he made his way to the kitchen.

'That's been hard work for you, Father, getting the old bull into Frank Bates's cattle wagon. He was suspicious. Maybe he guessed it was the end of the road,' she said sadly.

'Maybe, but you can keep a bull far too long – it causes inbreeding . . . Still, he was a good-natured old thing. Friesians often are. Remember that wicked shorthorn we used to have?'

'Oh, yes I do. It was a nuisance. It always had an angry look in its eye, and if we went near it, it would shake its head and make an awful rumbling noise in its throat. If you were away from home, none of us dared walk it to the water trough.'

'It was a good bull, though, Mother. It bred some fine calves – real bonny they were. Not like these black and white things; you have to look twice at them to know which is which. As a matter of fact Tom Graham's new farm lad got himself in a right muddle with their cows.' He chuckled at the thought. 'He was tying them up in the byre as they were coming in to be milked. All the cows were making for their own stalls to tuck into their cowcake, but young Ben was sure that two of them were in the wrong stalls so he tried to change them round! Of course the cows knew better than he did. It was soon chaos in there as they all changed places, rightful owners pushing intruders away from their troughs!'

'He'd just left school, Jackson. What do you expect?'

'They stop at school till they're fourteen now. When I was fourteen I'd been working up in Wasdale for a couple of years. If that's education I'm glad I got so little. The bloody cows knew better than he did!'

'When you've seen the old bull sold, will you buy a new young one?'

'No, mother, I think I've had enough of fighting with bulls. I'm getting too old. I think we'll use the new Artificial Insemination service . . . it's just a question of ringing up and they come right away.'

'Well, you'll have to learn to use the telephone in the new kiosk down the road. You've never tried to use it yet!'

'I'm not going to use a telephone. Why do you think I sent two daughters to the grammar school? And if they're not here I can walk over to Tom's farm – he'll be glad to do it for me.'

'Well, just so long as you know what you're doing. Oh, here's Tom. For goodness sake get a move on and don't keep him waiting.'

*   *   *

A few weeks after the old bull had gone, Jackson came into the farm kitchen for his breakfast. Edith and both the girls were busy.

'That good-looking roan cow, third stall in, is ready for the bull this morning.' Jackson was addressing his daughter Jane. 'Would you ring the AI centre and ask them to send one of their county vets along to serve it?'

He sat down to his breakfast a little uneasily.

'You look worried, Jackson. Something wrong?'

'No, not really, Mother. It's just that I don't altogether trust these modern methods. Cows are only ready to be served for a short time. Any bull knows all about it – but I'm not so sure about these vets. He maybe won't make it in time.'

'Stop worrying, Dad,' interjected Jane as she put her coat on. 'What breed of bull do you want? I believe they'll want to know that.'

'An Aberdeen Angus, Jane. We might as well have a change. I reckon the price of a good steak will go up before long; anyway that roan's a bit heavy to produce a heifer calf that would milk out well.'

'OK, I won't be long.'

*   *   *

Jane left the farmyard and made her way to the phone box. What would her father do when she left home, she wondered, smiling. He seemed almost afraid of newfangled things like telephones, as if they possessed some sort of magical power.

A neighbour was phoning; she'd have to wait. Her gaze travelled from the small village towards the distant fells. How she would miss them when she left the district. They had always been there, in their different shades of blue, brown and green . . . brooding over the coastal plains. She could make out the clear outline of Scafell as it gazed out to sea. Could it be watching the changing faces of its fellow mountains, Scottish Criffel and Manx Snaefell?

These three giants had stood sentinel over men's comings and goings in these sea lanes since the dawn of civilisation. Had they watched the Vikings sneak along the coast to raid the local villages? Had they witnessed the Romans stepping ashore at Ravenglass? Or watched a diminutive St Bega take possession of the land she had won? And had they held their breath as Paul Jones attacked the merchant fleet in Whitehaven Harbour? If they could only speak, what tales could they tell? Good heavens, Jane thought I'm treating mountains like people! Ah, at last the phone was free.

*   *   *

'I rather like the idea of this AI,' mused Jackson. 'I suppose I can experiment with different breeds.'

'Yes, Jackson. They say the bulls they use are of the highest quality, better than those that most of us can breed.'

'Well, I'll soon know,' smiled Jackson. 'It'll cost money, so if I'm not satisfied I can always buy another bull . . . Yes, Edith, it's a chance for the experts to show that they can breed better stock than me.'

'The vet will be here very soon,' said Jane as she came back in. 'You have to have a bucket of hot water, soap and a towel ready for him.'

'I'll get it ready,' said Edith, bustling into the kitchen.

'It's more work already,' remarked Jackson tartly. 'I never had to wash t'old bull.'

'Don't be silly, Dad. The poor vet can't drive away with wet dirty hands,' laughed Esther who was busy reading the morning paper.

'That's because he'll be wearing good trousers – he can't wipe his hands on his corduroys like I do. Once you've bought a car you've got to be clean to ride in it. A pony and trap used to be good enough for vets. They're like a lot of folks who decide to work with animals – they soon start replacing them with motorcars, medical syringes and the like. Before long they'll invent a machine which takes grass, hay and cowcake in at one end and delivers bottles of milk at the other – probably ready pasteurised!'

'That'll be the day,' quipped Jane. 'Fancy you with no cow muck on you! None of us would recognise you. I bet you'd have a totally different smell if you were away from cows!'

'Now don't you be cheeky with your father, girls. He was a good-looking young man when I first met him.'

The sound of a car pulling into the yard brought Jackson to his feet.

A short time later he and the young vet were standing in the byre, looking at the roan.

'A nice-looking cow, Mr Strong. How many calves has she had?' asked the vet.

'Four, and fine calves they were. Let's hope she produces as good a calf this time. After years of using a bull I'm not so sure about these modern methods.'

'Don't worry, Mr Strong, our service has produced many fine calves in this area. The stock bulls we use are of a superior quality to most of those that small farmers like yourself are capable of breeding. Farmers must become much more forward-looking; modern science should be used to raise the level of milk and meat production in this country. Mark my words, there will be a revolution in farming, many farmers will go to the wall, old-fashioned methods and inefficiency will not be tolerated.'

As he spoke, the vet turned towards the roan cow who was none too pleased to find a well-dressed stranger approaching her at an angle that was just out of her line of vision. She moved to get a better view of her attacker, and the young man found his left hand reaching for a rounded cobble which protruded a few inches from the whitewashed byre wall.

As the cow deftly swung her rear end to the right, the vet smartly took her place in the stall. The roan cow was now placed across the feeding end.

Jackson was in the neighbouring stall, resting his elbows on the wooden partition, watching this demonstration of modern science in action.

'You'd better get her turned round, lad,' he advised. 'You'll have a job to do owt, with her arse in that trough!'

The roan, feeling safer now, quickly lifted her head over her neck chain, cocked her ears forward and gazed expectantly at the young man as if to say 'Your move next.'

'Please hold my syringe, Mr Strong.'

'Gladly,' replied the old farmer as the vet wedged himself between the cow and the partition. He needed both hands free to push the unwilling animal back to its original position.

He pushed.

Most heavy cows and horses react in a similar way to this situation. The more a man pushes, the more the animal pushes back!

Now the cow had her new friend neatly pinned to the wall.

'She won't move . . . I can't get out,' gasped the vet as the cow's ribs pressed against his own.

By this time Jackson had placed the medical instrument on a nearby milking stool. He reached for his cow's tail, gave it a sharp twist, and returned the wayward animal to its proper position.

'Now, lad,' he said pleasantly, still holding the cow firmly by its tail, 'get on with your job.'

Smoothing his suit and gratefully reaching for his plunger, the vet quickly inseminated the cow. One minute later the embarrassed young man carefully washed his hands. 'I can't understand why I've had such trouble with your animal, Mr Strong. I've never had any difficulty with Mr Steel's herd. Two years I've been working here now, and I know I've become very experienced.'

'But *your* experience isn't the problem, Mr Smith. The problem is *hers*,' said Jackson, pointing at the cow. 'She's never been served by a bull with a bowler hat on before!'

11

HARVEST TIME

'Half the bloody field left on the road and the rest hanging from the thorns on the hedges,' grumbled Jackson as he reached his harvest field. Jane ignored the remark which was aimed in her direction every year. 'Well, Dad, if you reminded some of our neighbours to trim their hedges more frequently then our corn wouldn't be scraped off at all. If there were more women farmers around, things might be done properly.'

'You've got plenty of women to sort you out, Jackson!' laughed Tom Graham from the top of the loaded cart.

'Don't criticise her,' John Tyson said as he swung a couple of sheaves upwards for Tom to place securely on top of the load. 'I rely on my lasses too. A good many farmers around here would be hard put to manage without their daughters.'

'You're right, Mr Tyson,' replied Jane. 'And another thing, I would rather work outside in the fields with all of you fellas . . . simply because it's a darned sight easier than working in the house and dairy.'

While she spoke her father was unravelling one of the thick cart ropes which hung from below the tailboard. 'Catch this Tom!' he called as the thick rope snaked up and over the load, the end swinging downwards to hang neatly beside the horse's gleaming flank, ready to be knotted round the shaft. A second rope was thrown with equal accuracy and arrived close to the Clydesdale's other flank.

'Just make sure you men get those ropes fastened tightly,' warned Jane. 'That last load shuffled about like a pack of cards as Peggy pulled up the station brow. The strain on her shoulders is bad enough when you've loaded it neatly.'

'You hear that?' queried Jackson as Tom landed lightly on the ground. 'Women always stick together. Just watch your big black gelding pull this load. Once he gets them big shoulders settled into the collar he'll be off.'

He turned to Jane. 'You keep your feet moving on that station hill, lass, or he'll walk over the top of you and get home on his own. I've seen it happen before!'

'Come on, Captain.' The powerful neck engaged the collar as Jane spoke and the loaded cart rocked gently as the horse moved towards the distant gate.

'Look at that thieving bugger!' exclaimed Jackson, turning to see Peggy happily nuzzling into some thick corn. She had grazed her way step by step towards her chosen stook as the harvesters were talking. By slowly easing her weight forward as she ate, she had enabled the wheels to turn gently, without emitting the characteristic 'thud' of the block cart which usually warned her master of her intentions. Peggy did not have a pedigree as long as Jackson's arm for nothing!

'What did I just say about women?' Jackson demanded. 'As cunning as a barrowload of monkeys. Just fetch her round between those two rows of stooks, John. Two forking and one loading will soon stop her dancing round the field. I'll take her home; then I can always pick up any sheaves that have rattled off Jane's load. She went up that lane as if she was winning the St Leger!'

'I don't know what you're grumbling about; she's managing well enough.' Tom believed in being fair, even in Jackson's hearing. 'After all, you taught her all she knows.'

'Aye, but it's speed now. It's ever since she went to that college. She tells me they can ride on trolley buses that pass the front door every ten minutes or so. They're training her to be a teacher, and showing her how to lead a lazy life at the same time. God knows what the parents think when they discover what an idle breed of teacher this country is turning out.'

'We've got to move with the times, Jackson. Old Miss Cook must be outdated now.'

'Miss Cook didn't cost anything to train,' retorted Jackson. 'She was the best in her class, so she stayed on and became a teacher. She taught all ours how to read, write and count. And she could clout them good and hard if they didn't do as they were told.' Jackson stopped, leaned on his fork and looked at his friend.

'Now just you tell me, Tom, what else do kids need to learn at school? At that modern grammar school a games mistress used to teach our Esther to jump over hurdles! Have you ever heard of anything as daft as that? She can jump over as many hurdles as she likes when she fetches the calves in. I wonder how many years it took the teacher to learn how to teach that.'

'Oh come on, Jackson. Peggy's dozing off between the shafts. She's tired of waiting for you!'

Peggy plodded and pulled her way patiently at Jackson's side as they covered the mile or so from the harvest field to the farm.

The new corn stacks were sprouting like big yellow toadstools in the yard. Scanning the scene from a fair distance, Jackson could make out Bill's slim outline as he arranged the sheaves, butts towards the outer edge, heads inside to protect the precious corn.

Peggy's nearside ear flicked backwards to catch her master's command. But it wasn't a comment for her.

'I hope he's leaving enough room between the stacks for Kit Rowlands to get his thresher between them,' Jackson muttered. 'But a fella can't be in every spot at once . . . come on Peg, let's have a look and see what's going on.'

Peggy didn't need any encouragement. She was always at her best on homeward journeys. A good feed and a roll in the back field was all she wanted at the end of a long working day. Her back, mane and tail were thick with dust, chaff and corn which could only be efficiently removed by rolling in the grass.

'Good God, Bill!' exclaimed Jackson as he led Peggy towards the half-built stack. 'If that stack leans over any more,' he said, pointing towards the recently completed stack on Bill's left, 'the two of them will be holding each other up!'

'It looks level enough up here,' replied his son. 'It's your eyes, Dad. You've been seeing double since you won that game of dominoes last Saturday!'

'Well if you're going to keep on living here we'd better book the thresher to come as early as possible, before the winter sets in. There might be nothing left if them westerly winds tear round that barn corner.'

'Stop finding fault with the lad.' Edith handed a basket of food to Jane who was standing in the empty cart ready to return to the cornfield. 'If ever Bill does leave home, you'll have a job getting anyone to come and work for you. You'd find fault with everything he did.'

'A typical mother – never lets her son grow up and stand on his own two feet.

'Talking about feet, I'm just about to put the tea on the kitchen table so you can both hurry up and unload Peggy, then turn your feet towards the kitchen.'

* * *

'Don't waste time, Esther,' urged Edith as she cleared the breakfast dishes. 'It seems to take you ages to finish your breakfast when I want you to go to Egremont. Have you forgotten it's threshing day tomorrow? All those fellas will need a good plateful of tatie-pot.'

'Don't worry, I'm going now. What do you want?'

'Three pounds of breast of lamb, six links of black pudding, and a roast of beef.'

'What on earth do you want to waste money buying mutton and beef for, Edith?' objected her husband. 'We've got more pork hanging there than we can eat.

'Don't be silly, Jackson. No one wants ham and eggs on a threshing day. What do you think all the other farmers' wives would say when they went back and said they'd been given a breakfast at dinner time? Maybe you enjoy being talked about and laughed at – but not me. If all those men are good enough to come here and work for a day for nothing, then a good meal is as little as I can give them. Hurry up and get yourself off to the station. I thought you were going there for coal for the engine . . . And keep out of my kitchen if you can; I'm going to be busy baking apple tarts for tomorrow.'

She turned to Bill who had just walked in with a bucket of milk. 'Bill, remember to fill that blue jug on the dairy sconce with cream when you've separated that bucketful . . . I need some to put on my apple cakes for the threshers tomorrow.'

'Cream!' exploded Jackson. 'Beef and cream! Good God woman, we'll never get rid of them! They're not used to being fed like that. Talk about me being laughed at . . . You'll be the talk of the district – spoiling a few farm lads like that. There'll be no feeding them when they get back home. Them two hired lads from Alan's don't even know what proper milk is, let alone cream. They only get porridge and skim milk for breakfast in that house – you give them a couple of spoonfuls of cream on top of a slice of your apple cake and they'll have to spend the rest of the week in the water closet.'

'You do talk rubbish. For a start, the beef is for our own dinner on Sunday – we couldn't afford to feed all those men on beef. Secondly, it doesn't matter to me how well or badly these lads are fed anywhere else; when they come here they'll be given a meal that I would give my own family.'

'Aye, and that's just about all your family do come for. They don't seem to turn up if there's any work to be done, like threshing or picking taties.'

129

'Will you get yourself out of the house and do something useful instead of criticising other people?' said Edith in exasperation as she shooed him out.

Jackson and Bill disappeared to get the half-ton of coal that would be needed to keep the steam engine fed. They would have to make an early start if they were to get all their corn threshed the next day.

*   *   *

The massive steam engine stood against the far corner of the barn wall, its huge fly-wheel spinning – a haze of black and green metal – as its owner shovelled the heap of coal into the fire box, his face blackened and anonymous as he nodded encouragement and cracked jokes with the passing farm lads. At the other end of the racing belt the thresher struggled to digest the endless sheaves of corn which were constantly fed into its shredding jaws.

No matter which farm the thresher visited, the men always occupied the same positions in the complex chain of activity. Any confusion would result, at the very least, in a stoppage of work; at most in injury or even death. The men working immediately above the thresher had to balance precariously on the shaking boards as they caught each sheaf, cut the string, then dropped it expertly into the swaying metal jaws.

The puffing engine, screaming steam-release valve, chattering thresher, shouting men, barking dogs and rustling sheaves of corn produced an amazing cacophony of sound that often drew passersby to the farm gate.

To farm children it was sheer excitement, though dangerous. The outside of the visiting machine was a mass of fascinating wheels, belts, shutters, valves, twine-knotters and spitting teeth.

As the huge thresher digested the sheaves, it ejected the corn, straw and chaff in three directions, replacing centuries of labour with the flail.

The precious corn found its way to the rear to be released through valves into large corn sacks which were clipped on below the taps.

Jackson was always stationed at this corn end. His experienced hand sampled the flowing corn, his brain quickly working out quality, quantity and price per hundredweight. Next year's seed corn would soon be spotted, as he felt the best quality trickle across his palm.

A weighing machine was rarely used in those days – experienced farmers could shut off the valve within ounces of the required hundredweight simply by lifting the sack to feel the correct weight.

The youngest farm lad usually had the job of placing the sacks of corn on a trolley, then wheeling them to a suitably dry storage place – often a loft at the top of a flight of stone steps which had to be successfully negotiated by trolley, sack and boy many times in the course of the day. God help the lad who tipped a bag over on this malicious staircase; the host farmer could reckon any spillage to the last farthing!

'Are you still remembering to put those bags I've marked with my blue pencil on the right-hand side of the corn loft, Alan?'

'Yes, Mr Strong.'

'I hope you are, lad. I don't want to have to move half a ton of seed when I need to take a load of plain corn to the mill.'

'I know that, Mr Strong. I've put all the bags where you said.'

The straw was shunted, then collected in a large bundle called a 'bottle'. Each bottle was tied in two places with string, and ejected by large curved teeth from the opposite end of the machine to that where the corn made its exit. The men would then carry the bottles to a barn to be stacked ready for use as bedding for cows, horses, bullocks and pigs.

Picture the scene, as from the centre of the huge, rocking, chewing machine the chaff spins out and falls to rest in a growing cloudy heap; or if there is a wind, swirls crazily around the workmen and settles in eyes, mouth, collars and clogs.

Dogs and puppies are attracted to the pile of pale yellow chaff. They race inside, disappear, snort, roll, tease, and waylay unwary canine playmates. The powdery snow-like mound has the same fascination for the farm children who throw handfuls at each other until eyes and clothing are full of chaff and angry mothers pack them off to get washed.

The highlight for the threshers and for many of the spectators came as the stack was being reduced to the last few layers of corn.

To keep the corn from touching the damp soil and thus becoming mildewed, the farmer had placed each rick on a base constructed of stones and pieces of wood. When the sheaves settled and sank, small holes were left between the stones and logs. These holes made ideal homes for rats, especially in early October when the females were looking for safe shelter for the winter. The bottom of a corn stack provided warmth and abundant food; dogs and cats had difficulty reaching them; there were numerous exit tunnels.

But the rats' triumph was short-lived. At threshing time many men followed with their dogs, chiefly terrier breeds, and surrounded the shrinking corn stack, watching and waiting for the rats to bolt as their homes disappeared above their heads.

Rats and foxes are both thieves who eat the farmer's profits. But the rat is not a flesh-eater like the fox. He is not a creature of the open air or of the woodland. Whereas the fox is treated as a noble adversary, the rat is a feared and hated pest to be destroyed by any means at hand.

As the rats begin to panic beneath the sheaves, the terriers excitedly take their positions next to their masters: eyes fixed on the base of the stack, nostrils dilated; every muscle, in both man and dog, taut with anticipation. The pause is heard in the farm kitchen and doors are closed. (Desperate, fleeing rats are not welcome.) Women, who enjoy helping with the threshing, usually find this sport frightening or distasteful and retreat to the safety of the farmhouse before the stack reaches its last layers.

Rats are herding animals – instinct tells them that survival depends upon numbers.

A sudden dash, as though by a pre-arranged signal.

Two minutes and the carnage is over.

Squealing, snapping, shouting, flying bodies, spurting blood, whining dogs, escaping rats, chasing dogs and cheering spectators.

Basic, cruel sport – a sport centuries old.

The catch is counted, then bleeding mouths and torn ears are seen to.

A new stack is opened and the rhythm of the thresher

reasserts itself as the laughing men return to their work.

A threshing day always finished before evening milking time; cows being unwilling to settle in their byre near a throbbing rattling monster!

The farmer would check his corn in the loft and be able to reckon how much feed he now had for the winter months.

Everyone returned home to attend to their own livestock. The next morning they would accompany the thresher to the next customer, and their own milking and feeding had to be done very early, before they left home. Meanwhile the thresher had been moved the previous evening to the next farm where coal and water were ready for the engine, and where the farmer's wife had prepared a colossal meal for the threshers.

Most women had a special dish which they liked to serve on threshing day – something which would cook slowly in the oven or in a large pot over the fire. Ideally it was easy to serve, quickly eaten, nutritious, and produced the minimum of washing up.

'Well, how did the crop thresh out this year?' Edith asked her husband as they ate their supper that evening.

'Not so bad. That spell of sun we had in August ripened it nicely. Everybody is getting a decent-quality corn this year.'

He glanced at the clock as he spoke. 'Where's our Jane, Mother?'

'Gone to the pictures,' answered his wife.

'Pictures? She can't have worked hard enough if she has enough energy to bike to Egremont and back tonight! Young folks don't work as hard as we used to do.'

'Oh come on Jackson. Finish your tea and cake. If you men aren't tired enough – I am. I'm just glad we only thresh once a year.'

'It must be a good picture to make a lass bike all the way to Egremont, that's all I can say, Edith.'

'I don't think the film is all the attraction for her.'

'What do you mean, Edith?'

'Well, she's been talking a lot about a young man from Whitehaven. I think she probably sees him at the cinema.'

'But she's too young to be seeing anybody . . .'

'She's nineteen, Jackson. Many a lass is married at her age.'

'But she's still studying at college.'

'Well, she helps you in the holidays, doesn't she? I reckon she can go out a bit as well. You can't keep them at home and rule their lives for ever, you know.'

A disgruntled Jackson drank his tea, then continued uneasily. 'Who is he anyway? Is he a farmer's son?'

'I don't know much about him. I think he works at Sellafield. Our Bill knows him and says he's a nice lad . . . But I don't think it's serious . . . We'll have to wait and see.'

'Another of these chaps who doesn't like hard work,' snapped Jackson.

'You talk such rubbish! Bill says he's from Whitehaven.'

'Whitehaven?' Jackson looked alarmed. 'Just you tell her when she comes home . . .' He shook his finger in Edith's direction.

'Tell her what? Remember – I used to live in Whitehaven.'

'Never mind about that. Folks from Whitehaven are different from us.'

'In what way?'

'You can't trust them; they're used to having buses pick them up and drop them off only half a mile down the road. Soft living I call it . . . Soft living.'

'Well, I hope Jane manages to find some "soft living" for herself. I've never had any. Working all the hours God sends on a farm miles from any sort of civilisation is a thing of the past. I reckon Sellafield will be a grand place to work for a lot of people around here, Jackson . . . and . . .' here she wagged a finger in her husband's face – 'you can call it "soft living" if you like, but I'm all for it.'

135

Edith swept the remaining crumbs from the tea table and stalked towards the scullery door.

'Just you encourage any young chaps Jane goes out with to come here and let me have a look at them,' Jackson called through the open doorway.

'What for? So you can spin one of your cheeky stories. That'll be enough to frighten anybody off. And in any case, who's going to walk all the way from Egremont to see us? It's too far out in the country.'

'He can't be much of a chap if he can't walk this far.' He paused to stir the fire then reflected. 'There's nothing wrong with him, is there? If he can't walk a couple of miles or so to have a drink with me . . .'

'A drink with you?' retorted Edith as she returned to the kitchen. 'If our Jane, or Esther for that matter, ever brings a young man to this house, don't you dare take them to the Grey Mare!'

'Why not? It's been good enough for me for many a year.'

'I'll not have any nice young man who comes here staggering home at goodness knows what hour of the night to tell his mother where he's been. They all know you in Egremont, but I don't want gossip like that to spread as far as Whitehaven.'

Jackson's eyes twinkled as he smiled to himself. 'Don't you worry, Mother. Any son-in-law of mine will be looked after very well when he's in my company . . .'

12

A SHOOTING PARTY

Jackson woke from his doze, and reached for the poker to stir a little more life and warmth into the fire.

'Goodness, it's nearly eight o'clock.'

'Are you going to the Grey Mare?' asked Edith, busily darning a long black sock.

'No, you women always think a man only has the pub to go to of an evening.'

'Where else do you go?' Esther laughed. 'I don't remember seeing you rush off to the pictures or a whist drive!'

'It's true that I've never been to a talkie,' admitted her father. 'Maybe one day I'll go – if I can find time.'

'I can't imagine you going to a whist drive, Jackson,' smiled Edith. 'Your language would be so ripe, a lot of the women would probably walk out. Not everybody is as tolerant as me.'

'Or as long-suffering,' added Esther. 'In any case, you probably can't even play whist, Dad.'

'Now that's just where you're wrong, lass. You ask Tom Graham whether or not I can play cards.'

'Only if you have a good view over a pint of ale,' laughed Edith. 'Why aren't you going to the pub? Are you not well tonight? Or are you short of money?'

'I don't know what all the fuss is about. Most wives carry on if their husbands go out, not if they decide to stay in.'

'Yes, but we all know that a wily old fox changes its habits only when it has a good reason. We're just wondering what good reason you have. Aren't we, Esther?'

'That's right, Mam. He must be up to something.'

Jackson slowly rose from his chair and casually walked

over to the far corner of the farm kitchen. The plates and cups winked and glinted in the firelight as he reached behind the large dresser and lifted out his double-barrelled shotgun.

'What on earth are you going to do with that thing at this time of night, Dad?'

'Clean it, lass, clean it. You should know by now that a dirty gun is a dangerous gun. I've told you that many a time.'

'If you ask me,' retorted Edith, 'the only dangerous gun is the one in the hands of a dangerous man.'

'Oh Mam, Dad is safe enough.'

'Your cousin Jack used to think *he* could handle guns safely, until one day he blew his two fingers off.'

'Stupid bugger,' snapped Jackson. 'No one in their right senses carries a loaded gun, then uses it as a stick to jump down from a gate. He deserved to have his head blown off. In fact he very nearly did . . .'

'I'm just glad he's on your side of the family and not mine,' murmured Edith as she bent her head over her darning.

'Anyway, why are you cleaning your gun, Dad?' asked Esther as her mother went off to prepare the supper.

'I've been invited to join a shoot tomorrow, somewhere near Cockermouth. Tom's calling for me in the morning. It should be a good day. Tom reckons there's always plenty of game over there.'

'I hate plucking little feathers, it makes your fingers ache. And I suppose pheasant will be difficult to pluck – I've never done one before. Geese are bad enough.'

'Tom reckons that some of the pheasants they shot last year were as big as geese, so you'll have no problem, lass.'

'I'll believe that when I see them.' Edith had come back into the kitchen. 'I've heard Tom's stories before . . . Mind you, Esther, they were a good weight when they reached the ground. They were already stuffed – with shot!'

Esther roared with laughter. She liked to hear her mother getting her own back once in a while.

'John Steel's little lad was telling me,' Edith continued to her daughter, 'that last December they all went to Aspatria to a shoot. It was well publicised, so about twenty men turned up. All expert marksmen, I was told.'

Jackson stopped polishing his gun to listen.

'They all set off across the moorland, and they walked and walked and found . . . nothing! Maybe they made so much noise they frightened the game off. In any case, they walked a good hour and were beginning to feel desperate, when suddenly a pheasant broke cover. It flew upwards and the air was filled with lead shot. But do you know what? . . .'

'No,'said Esther.'The bird just flew on. Not one of them managed to hit it . . . I reckon it has to be the size of a turkey before they stand a chance of bagging anything.'

'I wasn't there that day,' said Jackson. 'I've never heard about that pheasant.'

'Well, what man would tell you? You'd only hear the truth from a little lad.'

'Kids shouldn't be allowed to go,' he retorted. 'It's too dangerous.'

'It is,' said Edith emphatically. 'It's far too dangerous. A lot of you men have more ammunition than sense.'

'I don't like picking shot out of my pie, Dad,' Esther broke in. 'Can't you shoot it in its feet or something?'

'What do you take me for? A chiropodist! I've never found shot on my plate. A clean shot through the head every time – that's the way it's done – clean as a whistle. And you needn't bother about the plucking. It'll have to hang above the door till it starts to rot – you'll have no bother plucking it then.'

'Ugh! How awful!'

'That's the proper way to eat it,' Jackson insisted. 'Game has no taste unless it's been well hung.'

'Your dad's right, Esther. When I was in service we were taught the correct way to do things.'

'It's nice to hear I can be right sometimes,' he muttered.

'Sometimes yes – but usually it's all a load of rubbish. Just so long as no one believes a word you say it doesn't matter!'

*   *   *

'What a great day I've had, Mother,' said Bill, sitting down to his tea.

'Why dear?'

'I've finished ploughing that seven-acre field – in peace.'

'What do you mean – in peace? Don't you always plough in peace?'

'Not with Dad around. I'm pleased he's gone shooting today. When he's in the field it's . . . "Tighten those reins, lower the knife . . . Don't hang on to the handles . . . Do you have to hit every stone? . . . Make that mare keep in the furrow . . . Are you going to take all day? The neighbours'll have a good laugh when they look over that bottom gate . . ." '

'Now then, Bill. Your father only says these things to help you. You know he's one of the best ploughmen in the district. He's won a few competitions in his time.'

'Every time he shouts something at me, the horses stop and the plough tips over. Then when we start again there's a nasty bend in the furrow and he's terrified all the neighbours will think he's done it. Anyhow there's not one wiggly furrow in sight.'

Bill smiled with satisfaction as he picked up his knife and fork.

'That's good, your father will be pleased to see such an improvement when he comes home.'

'Improvement, my foot! Our Jane's taken the horses and started to harrow it over – so there won't be a furrow to be seen when the old man comes home.'

'Not so much of the "old man" if you don't mind. Hurry up and eat your meal, then you can finish the milking and

140

feeding before he comes in. And he won't be suited if you've both worked those two horses to a standstill today.'

'Don't worry, Mother. The weather forecast says it's going to rain tomorrow. They'll have a good rest.'

'Let's hope you're right.'

Bill rose from the table and went off to see to the cows. Edith heard their hungry lowing as soon as he opened the back door; while louder, more demanding shouts could be heard from the calf pens when they heard the rattle of the buckets. She cleared Bill's plate and mug, and glanced at the mantelpiece. It was half-past five. Jackson shouldn't be long now – unless he'd stopped at a pub on the way home.

Only Patch rose from the shadows as Jackson's hand rattled the chain on the gate. The farm lay in silence; animals chewed contentedly or slept.

'Anybody at home?' he called as he closed the back door, crossed the scullery and entered the warm kitchen.

'There you are!' he said triumphantly, throwing the pheasants on to the kitchen table.

The shiny, colourful feathers gleamed as the light struck them. Domestic fowl lack the sheer beauty of wild birds, the small heads hanging down over the edge of the oiled tablecloth, the slender dark feet curled upwards – earthbound now.

'Aren't they lovely?' Esther touched the soft feathers gently as she spoke.

'Great sport,' enthused her happy father. 'You should have seen them fly. Old John Barnes could hardly get reloaded fast enough. His poor old retriever was as shattered as he was by three o'clock.'

'And where have you been since then?' asked his wife, glancing at the clock. 'It's a quarter to eleven now. We thought you'd had an accident.'

'With a gun!' laughed Esther. 'Mother always worries if you're off shooting somewhere.'

'I'm all right. You've just got to be careful about standing up too soon. You're likely to get your hat blown off if you have a poor shot too near.'

'So where on earth have you been, Jackson?' persisted his wife.

'Oh, in one or two pubs in Cockermouth Main Street.'

'Doing what?'

'Showing them that the best marksmen come from this side of the County. You should have seen what we bagged – everybody had a brace or two of pheasant.'

'You've only three there, Dad.'

'Well I gave some away. There were folk in those pubs who'd never tasted game – a good meal would do them good.'

Edith took his dinner from the oven and placed it on the

table. 'Sit down and eat your supper, Jackson. It's waited long enough for you. Your tea's nearly ready – if you can drink anything more, that is. It seems to me that you've had more than enough to drink already.'

'I have indeed, Edith. I've had a great day! Mind you, I've walked a good long way to get you all a few decent meals. I hope you two have done some work while I've been out, and not left everything for your old father to do tomorrow . . . But you know, Mother.' He turned contentedly towards his wife as he spoke, and pointed at his treasures on the table. 'If there's a heaven – and a place for me in it – I just hope the good Lord will let me have a double-barrel.'

'But who would you shoot?'asked a bewildered Edith.

13

GRUBBING

Peggy's heels moved at a leisurely pace in front of the narrow grubber which shuffled and occasionally bounced viciously under Jackson's firm hands. Looking rather like a flattened ship, the metal grubber was pulled between the rows of young green potato plants, leaving uprooted weeds on the fine ridged soil which lay in the wake of the farmer's clogs.

Swooping, whirling seagulls snatched the wriggling worms as the teeth of the passing monster brought them unwillingly to the surface. The squealing of the hungry gulls formed a descant against the bass rumble of the spring tide as it crashed against the rocks far below the field where Jackson was working.

Peggy stopped as soon as she had turned back from the cliff edge, the brisk wind blowing her tail forward across her flanks. She knew Jackson could always be relied on to have a few minutes rest at each end of the field. But the other hedge which bordered the country road was a much better bet. Not only could she feed from the long, rarely grazed hedgerow, but there was a distinct possibility that her master would see a friend walking or driving along, and the few minutes would stretch out to a much longer period. Peggy always made the most of such opportunities. The slow dreary walking up and down the rows of green plants which she daren't steal wasn't her favourite way of spending a spring afternoon.

Jackson stood on the exposed edge of his field, running his eye briefly along the edge of the rocks and sand which lay below the single railway line that passed through the small station. In a few hours time he knew that hundreds of workmen would pour out of this tiny station like so many ants. Having returned from the nearby atomic energy factory, they would swarm up the snaking path which reached the far corner of his potato field and cross his carefully planted crop to reach the large dining hall situated near their dormitory huts in the neighbouring field. Contract workers had little respect for a farmer's crop, especially if it came between them and the head of the dinner queue. Jackson knew this well enough, but he still dreaded reaching the far corner of his field, which he knew would be criss-crossed with convenient paths and strewn with trampled young potato plants.

The tide hadn't washed anything up on the shore today. He had once rescued an almost new ladder which he had seen bobbing between the blackened rocks; it must have been washed overboard from a ship far out in the Irish Sea.

'Come on, Peggy,' he said grasping the handles of his small grubber. 'Let's get on with it, lass.'

The obedient mare moved smoothly forward whilst the seagulls too rose from their temporary rest to circle and cry plaintively to each other as they sought their earthbound prey.

A stream of well-flavoured oaths brought Peggy to an immediate halt. She knew from hard-earned experience when the old farmer's outbursts were aimed in her direction. She also knew that, if that were the case, her best course of action was to settle her shoulders firmly into her collar and move very briskly in the required direction. This time it seemed that she was not the cause of his irritation. She was safe – at least for the present.

Jackson quickly wrapped the long thin ploughing cords firmly round the handle of the grubber to prevent Peggy lowering her head to chew the poisonous potato tops. Then he walked ahead to survey the disaster area which formed the far corner of his field.

Careless, hurrying feet had uprooted his laboriously planted potatoes; more hurrying feet had kicked and trampled the inoffensive plants along the myriad paths which individual workmen had made for themselves across his field. The numerous paths led to an equal number of crossing places forced through the hedge which divided his land from what had once been an army training camp, now pressed into service as a convenient campsite for the builders of the new atomic energy factory.

Jackson stood holding the abused plants in his hands. Not being the sort of man to mourn his loss in silence, the air at the cliff top turned a distinct blue with the sound of a very varied and rich assortment of swear words. Peggy's ears moved a little uneasily as the tirade swept close. But no, it wasn't aimed at her.

Jackson's lack of an audience allowed him to extend his oaths across a remarkable range – certainly not suitable for the sensitive ears of the young man who had just reached the top of the path which led from the railway station to the village. Jackson could not – and had no wish to – put his verbal flow into reverse.

The affronted walker remonstrated as the full-bodied language reached his ears.

'There really is no need to use such language.'

Jackson scarcely heard the softly lilting Irish brogue.

'And who the hell are you?' asked the old man, as he bent to replace one of the least battered plants.

'My name is Father Murphy,' replied the young cleric, his words directed at Jackson's broad back.

'Father Murphy! Father Murphy!' retorted the enraged farmer. 'I don't care if you're bloody Father Christmas! Just make sure you walk along the path over there instead of ruining my crops!'

The priest moved quickly along the path to the sound of Jackson's angry mutterings which were still being swept along on the wind. 'That's all I need – a bloody priest to tell me how to be thankful that someone doesn't know how to walk along a well-marked path!'

* * *

'Well, Jackson, did you finish grubbing the station field?'

Edith placed a hot plate of stew and potatoes in front of her husband as she spoke.

'I finished all right,' he replied tersely.

'Why, what was wrong? Were there many rows of poor potatoes?'

'I couldn't find fault with any of the potatoes, Edith. They were growing really well. But you should have seen the destruction at the far end. You know – where the station path reaches the top edge of our field.'

'Oh yes, I know. The workmen tend to take short cuts across the field there. Was there much damage?'

'Yes there was. I've lost a few hundredweight of good potatoes there. A right lazy, bloody lot they are. They go to that factory – they don't know what real work is – they come home in the middle of the afternoon. Then they have the bloody cheek to ruin my crop on their way to the canteen. I don't know what they hurry for . . . Judging by the pig swill Alan Steel collects, they might as well walk the longest way round.'

'Don't get angry, Jackson. Temper never solved any problems. The factory's working now so the contractors will soon be gone. And don't forget how much employment its providing – Esther and Bill have both got good jobs there. Just be thankful that it's brought such good work to this area. We both know that these small farms can't provide a decent living for more than one person in a family. Just remember how many young people had to leave this area before the war to find work in the south. The new factory will be a godsend, especially for girls. Intelligent boys and girls always used to be forced to leave to get decent jobs. No area should be robbed of its clever young people.'

'You read too many books,' remarked her husband tucking into his meal. 'So long as there's plenty of hard workers in this world we'll be all right. I suppose we can carry a few thinkers . . . That reminds me, talking of useless jobs, a priest came through the field this afternoon. He told me I shouldn't be swearing . . .'

'Who on earth were you swearing at, Jackson?'

'Nobody! How was I to know that a sensitive chap like him was coming up the path. Serve him right for creeping about the countryside.'

'Oh dear, I hope you didn't say anything very bad, Jackson. Priests aren't used to rough language.'

'They must be, Edith. You should hear some of those Irishmen when they've had a few drinks . . . They could curse the cross off a cuddy!'

'Now, now, Jackson. He's a very nice young man.'

'How do you know?'

'He's given me a lift a few times when he's seen me carrying shopping back from Egremont. Mind you,' she continued, 'I did tell him I wasn't a Catholic before I got into his car.'

'What difference does that make?' laughed Jackson.

'Well, I just like to be honest with people. Perhaps the young man doesn't like to be seen giving a lift to someone not of his own faith. He has his own parishioners to think about. A priest has to be very careful who he is seen with; it can't be an easy job.'

'If you were twenty-five with silk stockings and one of those blouses which open down nearly as far as the waist he would maybe think twice about stopping . . . but I reckon he's safe with you, Edith. Did you sit in the back seat just in case?'

'No I didn't, you cheeky thing! But next time he gives me a lift I'll apologise for your rudeness this afternoon.'

'How do you know I said anything that would offend him?'

'I know you, Jackson, and I also know the sort of language you can use if you're wrong side out. Poor Father Murphy. He wouldn't expect to hear anyone cursing out in the countryside. It would spoil his walk.'

'Well, he shouldn't have been listening. I didn't think I had an audience . . . Besides, he must hear much worse things in the confessional – unless Catholics are all a bunch of liars!'

'Catholics are much like anyone else,' retorted his wife. 'They lead fairly ordinary lives. I shouldn't think he'll have to listen to anything more exciting than missing mass or cheating at dominoes in the pub. They're nearly all young men working away from home . . . The murderers and swindlers live in the big cities – they'll be far too clever to come up here to this far corner of the country.'

'I don't think this is a backward part of the country to most of these contractors. Most of them come straight from Ireland, and they've never had two half-crowns to rub together in their lives. Going back to Ireland will seem like returning to the ends of the earth.'

'Well, there's nothing much to spend their money on here . . . they can do very little sinning as far as I can see. Poor things – they probably have to send money home to keep their families.'

'Don't be silly, woman! Haven't you seen the brewery lorry going down there? They have plenty of money to spend on drink.'

'They have to confess any drunkenness,' countered his wife.

'Don't be so daft, Edith. Drinking isn't a sin in Ireland. It's only chapel folk who have those sorts of sin – silly buggers! Catholic sins don't seem so bad to me. I'm not likely to steal anyone else's wife – I have enough trouble looking after the one I've got! I'm sure the priest would overlook a bout of healthy swearing, if he knew the damage some of his men had done in my field . . . don't worry, Edith. I'll buy him a drink if he comes into the Grey Mare.'

'If he knows you're in, he'll probably give it a miss,' retorted Edith. 'Come to think of it, the whole district knows when you're there . . . Your voice can be heard clearly for miles around!'

'How about another mug of tea?' Jackson pushed his empty mug across the table. 'It's time I started milking. Those cows have been looking through that gate for the last half-hour. Now that our Bill is working at Sellafield everything has to wait until I do it. A fellow brings his children up to work for someone else these days – it's a changing world Edith.'

'Changing for the better,' replied his wife. 'At least they get a decent wage. The age of slave labour on farms has gone.'

'You're right, Mother,' said the old man, reaching for his cap and stick. 'They won't have to work as long as the light lasts like we had to, just to make a bare living.'

Jackson pushed the gate open against the anxious cows who jostled eagerly for position in case a hungry rival should push ahead to steal a sneaky mouthful of cowcake from their troughs. The farmer went after the herd, his eye sweeping across each beast, instinctively registering any loss of condition.

As Jackson started the milking machine, his thoughts drifted over the day's events. The world was certainly changing, as he had said to Edith. Moving about among his cows, he looked back on the episode in the tatie field. He must have turned into a real farmer now, if he could fly into such a rage over a few crumpled plants. After all, what did a few plants matter?

It was only a few years ago that he had been milking in this very byre, by hand rather than machine, when news had come of yet another terrible pit disaster in Whitehaven. It hadn't been leaves lying crumpled and dead that time – it had been 104 men. He could still remember the previous disasters, Wellington, Haig and an earlier William Pit disaster, all adding up to a death toll of well over 300. He must have turned soft in recent years.

His thoughts rested unwillingly on what he had seen in the pits, when they'd gone down to find the trapped and the dead. Coal gas was a gentle killer. Fathers and sons were found lying close together, unaware that death had no intention of dividing them. It had looked like a macabre waxworks – a death scene but with faces they all knew well. Men clutching their few belongings; workmates who had joked and laughed with them, now unusually silent, waiting for their own personal doomsdays. One or two still knelt in prayer; it seemed an intrusion to lift them on to the stretchers to face the violence of the grief in the world above.

Some passages had been walled up, the men given up for dead, only to be reopened years later and their remains found behind the walls, along with their initials and messages to their families, written in the then soft cement.

Progress, thought Jackson: man's search for a cleaner, cheaper source of power. That's what the atomic power station at Sellafield was all about; a clean pit rising upwards instead of exploring the bowels of the earth. Maybe it was fitting that it should be built here? Who could tell? what disasters might lie in store behind the walls that were rising in the distance?

It was no good thinking about the future – only time would tell. Eventually only the names inscribed on a memorial plaque would remain as silent witnesses to the suffering and loss borne in the name of progress as man sought to bring power and comfort to every household in the land. 'Move over, Belle, and let's get on with this milking,' said Jackson wearily to his unwilling cow.

14

A Visitor

Edith carefully lifted the china cups from their hooks on the top shelf of the huge dresser and dusted each one before placing it gently on its own saucer.

It was rare for the kitchen table to be adorned with a tablecloth, but on this fine late summer afternoon the white cloth sported a small vase of flowers flanked by home-made scones, jam, biscuits and cream cakes. Edith stepped back to admire her handiwork. 'That looks nice,' she said to herself. 'Now I'll just put a clean pinny on before he comes.'

As the sound of approaching clogs reached her ears, she opened the sideboard drawer and reached for her best freshly laundered pinafore.

'What on earth is all this set out for?'

Jackson stared in surprise as he walked into the kitchen. 'Have you invited someone special for tea or is one of the lasses getting married?'

'You never listen to a word I say, Jackson,' retorted his wife. 'I told you last Sunday that Mr Benson had stopped me as I left the church to say that it was about time he called to have a chat. He asked if Tuesday afternoon would be convenient, and of course I said that we would be delighted.'

'Oh did you? Well, you can't expect me to stay in all afternoon just to talk to the vicar. It's all right for a chap like him. He doesn't have to work for a living; he just passes a plate round. I wish I could get my money as easily as that.'

'He's a very well-educated gentleman, Jackson.'

'That's the trouble with this country. Too many folks just sit on their backsides whilst the likes of me have to work hard to keep the lazy buggers, as well as my own family.'

'And since when has half a crown a fortnight taken food out of your mouth?'

'What!' gasped the astonished farmer. 'Half a crown? I can remember the time when a half-crown would have kept us going for a good few days. How long have we been able to throw good money away like that? Living in St Bees parish is becoming an expensive business. There's folk in his congregation who've never had to count their money like we do. That's why one of the kings of England as long ago as the Dark Ages decided to build a public school there. He knew it would be a good spot to send the children of the rich to spend their pocket money . . . and it's been the same ever since. They've always had fancy notions in St Bees.'

'It's been at least twenty years since we've been desperate for a half-crown, Jackson. And, you know, people tend to put the same amount in the collection year after year without thinking that the cost of living is going up for the vicar just the same as it is for the rest of us.'

'He must preach a bloody good sermon if he gets folk to put half-crowns in every Sunday. Remember there's only eight to make a pound. No wonder educated men are clever enough to join the church! No work and plenty of money – it's a fine life!'

'You don't half say some daft things, Jackson. The vicar has to keep the vicarage and the church in good repair as well as feeding himself and his family. It can't be easy living on other people's charity.'

'Some charity at half a crown a visit! He could spend the six days of the week when he doesn't work repairing the church – the same way I have to fix the barn roof if it leaks!'

'The vicar can't be seen mending the church roof! Whoever heard of such a thing?'

'I don't see why not; he's got plenty of spare time. He can do it in the summer months – he doesn't have to get repairs done like us farmers.'

'Well, the day you get up to repair those gutterings that have been leaking for the last twenty years, I'll give you a plaque with your name and the date on it, so that you can nail it to the barn wall as a memento! And another thing,' Edith continued, 'the vicar doesn't have six days off – he's busy with weddings and funerals.'

'We usually only get married once, and we die once, so I can't see that he is obliged to get up at six o'clock in the morning like me. And I can't say I've seen any queues forming at his door, Edith.'

'You didn't let me finish. He has sick people to visit, hospital visits and confirmation classes to take.'

'Which group do we fall into? Or is he coming to size us up to see if he can ask for another half-crown?' Jackson moved closer to the tea table. 'And what's all this supposed to be? There's enough here to feed the five thousand . . . or is it the last supper?'

'Don't you dare speak like that when Mr Benson comes. It's very kind of him to find time to call.'

'Oh he'll find time. When he sees a home-made spread like this, it'll be a job to send him away! I haven't seen a table like this since our Esther was christened.'

'Well he is a new vicar so I think it's up to us to make him feel welcome.'

'He'll feel welcome all right. If he feels like settling in here just tell him that we'll be cutting that ten-acre field tomorrow. A good day's stooking will do him a world of good.'

'I'll tell him no such thing, Jackson,' snapped Edith. 'And just you watch what you say if you're here when he comes, although I don't expect him for an hour or so yet.'

'Don't worry, I'm going out straight away.'

As he spoke, Edith spotted the vicar placing his bicycle against the farmyard wall, and bending down to release his bicycle clips.

'Here he is,' exclaimed Edith, her voice betraying her anxiety.

She hurried towards the door to greet the parson as Jackson made for his favourite armchair. Trapped!

Edith led her visitor into the kitchen and introduced him to her husband.

'A beautiful day,' remarked Mr Benson pleasantly. 'I'm sure farmers must be very busy at this time of year, Mr Strong.'

'Yes, we certainly are. All we need now is a good spell of sunshine . . .' He motioned to the visitor to take a seat at the table as Edith returned from the kitchen with a pot of tea. 'Maybe you can help,' he continued. 'A few prayers in the right direction might bring things along . . .'

'Milk and sugar?' asked Edith in a vain attempt to divert the conversation.

'Both please. You know, Mr Strong, I have just spent several years in Africa, and there the natives come regularly to ask us to pray for rain. Mind you, they ask their own witch doctors the same thing . . .' He smiled in Edith's direction. 'What lovely scones, Mrs Strong. I certainly didn't get home-made food like this in Africa.'

Jackson was intrigued by the visitor's remarks.

'Who got the credit when it rained, Vicar? And who got the blame when it didn't?'

The vicar laughed. 'As always, the witch doctor got the credit when things went well and we got the blame when they went wrong. You know, Mr Strong, when dealing with primitive people, magic and superstition is much more real than a faith that makes no promises and centres round an unseen god; a sophisticated doctrine can be too much for a simple people.'

'Please help yourself to cakes and cream, Mr Benson,' urged his hostess.

'Thank you, these are very tasty.' He continued his train of thought. 'However I shall do my best. I will remember the farmers in my prayers and ask the Lord to bless us with sun and thus ensure a good harvest.'

'I hope you don't get the lines crossed,' remarked the farmer doubtfully. 'He must be used to you praying for rain!'

'Oh I think the Good Lord will recognise my intention . . . But you know, Mr Strong, your prayers are every bit as good as mine. Don't forget to pray regularly yourself for those things you need, and to thank the Lord for all the good things you have received from Him.'

Here he turned, gesturing towards the table. 'Just look at this beautiful afternoon tea – this would feed a black family for many days. It's a pity farmers like you aren't able to go out to these hungry countries and teach the poor natives how to till their land and to feed themselves.'

* * *

The sky was darkening as Jackson returned from his day's work. With the milking finished, he sat down opposite his children as Edith placed a hot dinner in front of him.

'What's happened to the tablecloth, Mother?' he asked in mock surprise, reaching for his knife and fork. 'Are we not good enough to eat off it? Maybe you reckon we might spill something on the rough old table underneath.'

Esther looked up, surprised. 'Why should Mother put a good cloth on the table? I've rarely seen one. Why should you want such treatment all of a sudden, Dad?'

'I don't expect special treatment. But you should have seen the special tea laid out this afternoon – cloth, china and fancy napkins.'

'Who came?' asked Bill.

'The vicar,' replied Jackson. 'Why such a fuss is made of men like that I'll never know! The likes of us who work bloody hard all day only get an oil-cloth on the table, but a chap who can do nothing – and admits it – gets special treatment.'

'Stop talking such rubbish and get on with your dinner before it gets cold,' urged Edith.

'What do you mean by "a chap who can do nothing – and admits it?"' asked Bill, finishing his pie.

'The vicar said that in Africa he prayed for rain, but the natives thought the witch doctor could do better. Then, on top of that, he said that I could pray for what I want myself just as well as he could . . .' Jackson turned to Edith again. 'So you pay him two and six a week to pray for us, when you might just as well give it to me!'

'He's only encouraging you to say a few prayers, Jackson. It would be a change from all the cursing and swearing you do.'

Esther laughed. 'Yes Mam, if God listens to everything Dad says, He'll probably have plugged his ears up by now! And He won't hear when Dad utters a genuine cry for help.'

'I've sent many a cry for help in his direction, lass, but I seem to have to sort it out for myself.'

'Praying isn't all about asking for things,' said Edith impatiently. 'It might be a good idea if you sent up a prayer of thanks every now and again . . .'

'What for?' interrupted Jackson as he settled himself cosily in front of the fire.

'How about saying thank you for your health and strength, and a fine family.'

Edith's earnest plea was cut short by excited barking, followed by the sound of the farmhouse door being opened.

'Come in and take a seat, Tom,' called Jackson, recognising his friend's step.

Tom Graham nodded to the family and sat down opposite the old farmer.

'Well, Tom, what has brought you in to see us today?'

'Nothing in particular, Jackson, except that the vicar called earlier and all I can get out of our Mary is "What a lovely man! . . . Such a nice speaker! . . . A real gentleman!" . . . It's enough to drive any hard-working man to the pub. Can you explain, Jackson, why a woman will marry an ordinary chap like me, then sit around mooning about "a real gentleman"?'

'God only knows . . .' began Jackson.

'God is maybe the reason,' interrupted Esther as she tidied the sideboard. 'As a man of God, he is supposed to be kind, gentle and courteous.' She paused. 'Perhaps a man like Mr Benson is such a contrast to rough farmers that women who are used to hard work and little consideration find him a very pleasant change.'

'Now, now!' scolded her mother. 'Your father and Tom aren't so bad, Esther. They are good men – you can't judge people by appearances.'

'The same goes for the vicar,' snapped Jackson. 'Nobody knows what they are like at home. You can't persuade me that there's never a bad apple in the barrel, no matter what sort of fancy front the barrel might have. Some famous chap once said that all cats are grey at night, and that's true enough.'

'Don't worry,' laughed Esther. 'A vicar with a less than spotless private life wouldn't last long in a small place like St Bees.'

'That's right, lass. It's not like Carlisle, where anything can be going on and nobody knows about it,' agreed Tom. 'I reckon they only send the safe ones to small villages.'

'So, Tom, at least your wife and daughters won't be running off with any St Bees vicars!' laughed Bill.

* * *

As Jackson leant on the gate checking over the rows of corn stooks which he hoped to harvest the following day, his mind dwelt on the strangeness of life. These moments, when the miracle of growth and harvest-time seeped through his very bones, were the times when he felt closest to any kind of god. It was always a good feeling, a feeling of 'rightness' which, for all he knew, might be pagan. He glanced westwards to see the huge setting sun gently dipping its edge into the Irish Sea, as if testing the temperature of the shimmering water, before sliding gently downwards.

He knew it would be a fine day tomorrow, no matter who took the credit for it. Life for Jackson was good – and the questions of why the seasons came round, why the crops grew, and why he had escaped death in the pits when others were only names on a memorial plaque, were mysteries he didn't want to delve into too deeply. Maybe it was a good idea after all, to pay the vicar a regular half-crown to keep things going in the right direction.

15

CHARLIE

'The trouble with you is that you can't say no,' grumbled Edith as she placed Jackson's supper on the table in front of him. 'That is, you can't say no to the rest of the world, but you can always say it to me.'

'But Edith, it's a poor man who can't do a favour for a friend. I've known John McAdam since I was a lad – it's the least I can do to take his pony for the winter. No one will buy ice-cream when the weather's bad.'

'Oh I know that well enough. I'm just wondering why he's suddenly asked you to take his pony. Who had it last winter?'

'Bob Johnson.'

'Doesn't he breed those pedigree Shires?'

'That's right. I didn't think you would remember anything like that.'

'I remember; and even though I was brought up in a town I know that a strange horse can upset those that are on a farm already. I wonder why Bob won't have the pony this year . . . Do you know, Jackson?'

Jackson, who had spent a good afternoon in the pub in Whitehaven, didn't feel inclined to answer his wife's questions.

'We had a great crack, Mother. John reminded me of when I was down the pit, when I used to tell them all that I'd have my own farm one day . . . They all had a good laugh at the time. But I showed them. I spent all my spare time breaking and riding any horse I could find. The rest of them kept pigeons and whippets – but not me. John was just saying how I got a name for being able to handle any horse no matter how cussed it was.'

161

'Has he got a cussed horse, Jackson?'

'I don't think so, Edith . . . You women always think the worst of everything.' He looked up from his plate of cold meat. 'Charlie is an ice-cream pony. Think of all those little kids that must buy ice-cream from John. Have you ever seen an ice-cream pony that bit or was wicked? No, no, lass. A real pet he must be.'

'When is he coming?'

'Tomorrow. Frank Bates is delivering him first thing in the morning on the way to collect Alan Steel's three new calves. Fancy having three bull calves born on the same day. Alan doesn't deserve that sort of bad luck.'

'Well, let's hope he's not dropping off our load of bad luck on his way,' retorted Edith.

'What colour is Charlie?' asked Esther who had been eating her supper.

'White, of course,' replied her father. 'All ice-cream carts are pulled by white ponies, or by ponies with as much white on as possible. It looks good, and clean. Just like, years ago, when I was a lad black horses were used to pull funeral hearses.'

'For those who could afford them,' added Edith sharply. 'The likes of us had to carry our coffins to the churchyard. It cost money to have a fine funeral.'

'But what if the coffin was heavy and the churchyard a good distance from where you lived, Mam?'

'Well,' replied her mother, 'the men just had to carry it and keep putting it down to rest. Country people who had a long way to go had to hire a horse and cart, then carry the coffin the last half mile or so through the village. In those days everybody used to stand out on their doorsteps to pay their last respects to the dead. There wasn't all the rush there is nowadays to push people under the sod as quickly as possible.'

'It wasn't the same up in the fells, lass,' Jackson laughed. 'I remember hearing how a farmer's wife died up in Eskdale and they had to strap her coffin on to a pony to take her over the pass for burial in Wasdale.' Jackson chuckled to himself as he recalled the tale.

'Suddenly the pony stumbled against a rowan tree.' He glanced at Esther. 'You know of course that the rowan tree is magic, don't you?'

'No, Dad, I don't believe in such rubbish.'

'Well my lass, believe it or not, the minute the coffin touched the tree, the old woman recovered and pushed up the broken lid shouting to be let out . . .'

'Oh Dad, what a likely tale! Maybe she'd only been in a coma – she couldn't really have been dead.'

'Dead or not, when she passed away a few years later the old man warned the lad leading the pony to steer well clear of the rowan tree!'

'Mam,' Esther appealed to her mother, who had heard Jackson tell the tale before. 'Have you ever heard such a tale? Is Dad really telling the truth?'

'Goodness knows, he'll watch the rowan tree when it's my turn,' replied her mother.

'The truth isn't always in books, Esther,' said Jackson. 'You young folk think all the answers are in the public library, but strange things have happened that you never read about in books. I bet you never heard about old Lizzie.'

'Lizzie who, Dad? What happened to her?'

'She wasn't the only one, mind you,' continued her father reflectively. 'Anyone who died on a fell farm in those days stood little chance of being buried for a week or so – especially when the snow was deep!'

Esther's eyes grew wide. 'What happened to Lizzie then, Dad?'

'What do you think, lass? They couldn't let the old body rot in her bed now, could they?'

'Don't talk like that Jackson,' begged Edith uneasily.

163

'Remember to speak respectfully of the dead.'

'Go on, Dad. What happened when old Lizzie died?'

Jackson reached for his penknife and slowly began to slice the tobacco and then to place it neatly on his tongue.

'Well now,' he began, 'Tom had taken Lizzie up the valley as a bride, long before the turn of the century, and I don't reckon she ever strayed far from that farm in seventy years. It must have been a lonely life. They haven't got electricity up the valley yet – nor are they likely to for a good while.'

'Yes, but what happened to Lizzie?' asked Esther desperately. 'You said the snow was too deep to get her to the church . . . So what did they do?'

'The did the only thing they could to keep her right for the funeral – they put her on the slab in an outside loosebox and covered her with snow.'

'Oh Dad, that's awful!'

'Why not, lass? Do you know any better way of stopping flesh from going off?'

'Mam, is he telling the truth? Did that really happen?'

'How would your mother know? Town-bred she is. Town life's easy, but up in those fells they had to do the best they could. They couldn't rely on doctors or undertakers in those days – cars and aeroplanes didn't exist either. And country folk have always been thoughtful about putting anybody to any trouble. I remember . . . it must have been thirty years ago, aye, at least that long . . . when old Abe Knowles was near to dying – away up in the fells. Any day he was expected to go. "What day is it today?" he asked his wife one morning. "Saturday and a right cold bitter day it is." "Well then, I'm not going today Mary," he said. "We can't ask them undertaker lads to come all the way up here on their day off." '

'When did he die?' asked an unbelieving Esther.

'Either the Monday or the Tuesday, I can't remember which.'

'I never knew you could choose which day you would die!'

'Wait until you've lived as long as I have, then you'll have a better idea of what's possible and what isn't. Not that everybody can be so considerate with the undertaker . . . Now take Anna Mossop . . . Poor soul, she had no idea what a trouble she would be to them. She'd always been a pleasant, considerate woman.'

'How could she be inconsiderate if she was dead?' asked Bill who had by now abandoned his crossword.

'Crippled she was, from the time she was a young woman. She spent the last thirty years of her life in the tiny front bedroom of her cottage, where she had a clear view up the valley. She hadn't been downstairs for years, when suddenly she died. Like a lot of ailing folk, she had hung on for years – like a broken gate – then suddenly one morning . . . she went!'

'I can't see what's inconsiderate in that.'

'The dying was fine, Bill. It was all the trouble she put them two undertaker lads to when they tried to carry her out of the house.'

'Couldn't they get her into the coffin?'

'No, nothing like that, Edith. It was that narrow staircase. They had the devil of a job getting her coffin down it. Finally they had to lift it up on its end, then twist and turn it like a square corkscrew in a round bottle neck. George told me that every time they gave a twist they could hear her thump against the sides of the coffin. He reckoned she hadn't walked so far since 1903!'

'How can you make jokes about death, Dad?' asked a shocked Esther. 'That sort of thing is tragic.'

'Well now, Esther, death is no tragedy to the likes of me. It's education that's given you the wrong outlook.'

'What on earth do you mean? Surely education's a good thing?'

'No, not always. The trouble is, it makes you ask questions

165

– questions that have no answers. If you have no education like me, then you don't bother about trying to find out the answers. The likes of me just find it easier to accept things as they are – and that makes death a lot easier to live with.'

'Don't waste your energy fretting about people who have been dead for nearly fifty years, Esther. We have enough problems of our own now.'

'What problems, Mother?' asked Jackson cheerfully.

'Well, I have a feeling that this pony of John McAdam's might bring us a few problems,' said his wife.

'Has the pony a nice name, Dad?' Esther asked.

'Charlie.'

*   *   *

Three days later Frank Bates' lorry pulled up at the farm gate.

That evening Esther and Bill went to have a look at their father's latest acquisition.

Charlie looked very tiny in the large stall which was usually filled with one of the large thickset Clydesdales.

'Hasn't he got little feet?' enthused Esther.

'Yes, I'm not used to being able to look over a horse's back like this, observed her brother.

The pony seemed friendly and well-behaved.

'We'll see how well he mixes with the other horses tomorrow,' Bill said.

*   *   *

Peggy accepted the newcomer in her usual placid way. She was the mother of the stable and liked all to be peaceful in her domain. Not so the other two horses.

Charlie had one or two irritating habits. He liked to be first: first through the gate, first into the stable, and first for any titbits that might be going. Perhaps the patting hands and proffered sweets on his ice-cream round had spoiled him. In addition he tended to give a sneaky bite or kick if the other horses came too close to him.

Jackson wasn't happy about the stranger. 'I think you're right, Edith. Charlie must have upset Bob's pedigree horses. No wonder he wouldn't take him again this winter.'

'You weren't to know that, Jackson. It's a great pity if you can't help a lifelong friend like John McAdam.'

'Aye, that's right, Edith,' said Jackson, rattling the coals on the fire. 'But I think I'll have to put him in another field. That gelding is starting to get fed up. He's only a three-year-old himself and I can see the day coming when his patience will snap. If he lashes out he could break Charlie's leg; then I'd have a job explaining to John McAdam why I had to shoot him.'

'Good heavens, Jackson! It mustn't come to that. Not after all our years of farming. I wouldn't like to see you in court for shooting someone else's horse.'

'Don't be daft, woman. I'll make sure that silly little pony doesn't get me into trouble with anyone. I'll put him in the far pasture field this afternoon – that's far enough from our working horses. The few sheep we have in there won't bother him at all.'

* * *

Several weeks later an early morning knock brought Edith hurrying to answer the door.

'Good morning, Mrs Strong. Is your husband in?'

Edith stared in dismay at the tall policeman. 'Come in. He's just finishing his breakfast.'

'What can I do for you, Bill, so early in the morning?

'Have you a white pony, Jackson?'

'Yes, I'm keeping one for a good friend. I keep it in the pasture field near the railway station. It should be there.'

'Well, I'm afraid it was loose on the road last night and a young man ran into it on his motorbike.'

'Is the lad injured?' gasped Edith.

'Only slightly, but his bike is badly mangled. He had to mount the hedge to avoid the animal.'

'What about the pony?' asked Jackson.

'We put it in a field with some cows. It seemed to be unharmed. I'm afraid someone must have opened your field gate, Jackson.'

'Surely I can't be blamed?'

'Oh yes, you are responsible for seeing that your stock does not stray on to the public highway . . .'

'Good God! The lad must have been blind. Of all the stock I have, this pony is the hardest to miss. But any farmer will tell you – a white animal is an unlucky animal!'

168

16

THE FIRE

'**M**y goodness, it's been a long time since we've seen you here, Jackson,' said Jean, announcing the arrival of the popular old farmer to the rest of the customers in the Grey Mare.

'A long time, Jackson,' echoed Bill Brown from the far end of the packed bar. 'We thought you must have died, or left the district.'

'Can't a chap please himself about when he goes to the pub? I can't remember ever asking any of you why you hadn't had a night out . . . Anyway, no one seems bothered enough about my absence to offer me a pint.'

'There's one coming up for you here, Jackson,' laughed Jean. 'Ken Walker was in last week and left the price of a pint of bitter for when you next came in.'

'There's a friend for you – someone who's prepared to put his hand in his pocket for a chap . . . Not that I haven't put some good deals his way many a time in the past. Cheers!'

'You've missed all the fun,' Tom Graham said, making his way to the bar to join the old man.

'What fun? There's never any surprises in this bar,' scoffed Jackson.

'Do you mean to say you haven't read about the fire at Sellafield? There's been nothing else to talk about over the last week or so,' said Harry Jepson.

'Of course he's heard about it. He just doesn't want us to think he's interested,' observed John Steel as he picked up his cards and reached for his winnings.

'So why haven't we seen you down here then, Jackson?' persisted Tom Graham. 'The place has been buzzing with newspaper reporters and suchlike, all asking our opinions about Sellafield, the fire, and what we think about the contamination that has escaped into the atmosphere. You've missed it all.'

'Well, Tom, I don't believe in talking about something I don't fully understand in public . . .'

'I can't say I'd noticed such shyness on your part before!'

'I've never voiced an opinion on any subject that I didn't know something about!' retorted Jackson. 'But I've noticed a lot of rubbish being written in the papers . . . And I believe some local folk have been seen on television, pouring milk down drains and suchlike daftness . . . Anyway who wants to see themselves on television so their grandchildren can laugh at them in years to come when they dig it out and call it history?'

'You needn't worry about that. You're already the oldest monument around here,' mocked John Steel.

'You've missed all the reporters, Jackson,' said Jean, hoping to distract the old man from John Steel's barbed remarks.

'Especially a very pretty, young woman,' added Harry Jepson, laughing. 'Our Robert has been down here every night for the past fortnight. He seems to have taken a real shine to her, but she doesn't bother to look his way.'

'I should think not,' tittered Jackson. 'She'll be looking for somebody with a few brains, not a farmer's son with straw stuck behind his ears! God knows why women come into pubs anyway,' he observed half into his pint and half to a crestfallen Harry. 'It's no place for a well-brought-up girl . . . Just asking for trouble, in my opinion.'

'Times are changing, Jackson. Have you never heard of equality for women?' asked Jean from behind the counter. 'It's been very nice to see a few women in here recently – they're a welcome change from some of the ugly mugs I have to look at year in and year out!'

'I don't think this women's equality will suit the likes of me at all,' grumbled Jackson. 'What does this young lady drink then – a pint of bitter or a glass of rum like the rest of us?'

'She drinks a shandy more often than not, and I can't see what's wrong with that. Everybody wants to buy her a drink – she's certainly changed the atmosphere in this bar . . . Can I get you another drink, Jackson?'

John Steel stood up. 'It's my round, Jean. We can't change our usual habits because of a fire at Sellafield; if we're not careful we'll destroy our whole way of life. I agree with Jackson . . . We've rarely seen a woman in this pub, or any other pub in the district. Next thing we'll have to watch our language – especially you, Jackson – and then there'll be a lounge or some such place for ladies to sit in and drink like they do in a cafe . . . not to mention powder rooms and things like that.'

'That'll be a terrible day.' Jackson shook his head sadly at the thought. 'Can you imagine someone like my Edith coming in here for a drink?'

'You'd have to buy one for her, Jackson. It would be the gentlemanly thing to do . . . And you'd have to brush up on your manners,' laughed Joe Watson who had entered in time to hear the last few sentences.

'She can have whatever she likes to drink for nothing at home, like all our wives . . . I think it was a bad day for this area when them chaps at Sellafield managed to set their chimney on fire.'

'It isn't like an ordinary fire, Jackson. It has something to do with what they call "contamination". There's a lot of it at Sellafield they tell me,' said Harry Jepson knowledgeably.

'So our Bill says,' replied Jackson, equally knowledgeably. 'I was asking him about it when he first went to work there. It seems it's a posh sort of muck . . .'

'Muck! What do you mean, Jackson? Like cow muck?'

'Yes, Harry. Every job has its own sort of muck. It can't be avoided. Even hospitals need to be cleaned more regularly than my mucky byre. Our Bill says it takes him quarter of an hour to get changed before he starts his work and then a bit longer when he's finished to get himself washed and changed and something they call "monitored" before he's ready to go for his bus.'

'It must be an awful dirty place to work in then,' agreed Tom. 'Ten minutes is the most it ever takes to swill my byre!'

'You men don't understand what's meant by contamination,' interrupted Jean tetchily. 'If you bothered to read the papers you would know that it's invisible. The workmen have to rely on instruments and film badges pinned to their clothes to tell them if they're in contact with too much radiation.'

'If the women who come into this pub for a drink have read as much about all this as you, Jean, I think we'll have to find somewhere else to have a quiet pint. All this invisible muck is beyond me. What do you think, John? You've said nothing for the last ten minutes or so?'

'I'm just listening to all you ignorant farmers! It's easy to see that you never read the national papers, but some of us like to keep abreast of modern technology.'

'What do you know about it then?' asked Tom tartly.

'If Jackson had spent a bit of time down here listening to the newspaper reporters like some of us, he would have learnt a few interesting facts about what really goes on at Sellafield. Remember it's all very "hush-hush" down there – that's why the reporters aren't allowed in. They still have to fill their papers with something every day, so they end up coming to interview the likes of us.'

'Well, if folk who work there don't know what's going on – or can't tell anyone if they do – why do they ask us locals who can't possibly know anything?'

'It shows you don't know anything about newspaper

172

reporting, Jackson, when you ask such a daft question.'

'Sounds sensible to me,' remarked a puzzled Tom.

'It's a question of what people want to read in the paper,' explained John. 'The fact that there's been a fire and that there are all sorts of investigations going on wouldn't fill a column. No, people only want to read about ordinary people like themselves. They have to add some human interest to make it a longer article!'

'For once I think you're right, John. After all no one was hurt – not like the William Pit disaster in Whitehaven when over a hundred men were killed . . . There was plenty in the papers then.'

'They're like vultures,' said Jean. 'There's nothing like a disaster to bring them up to this corner of the country in droves. They don't even say much about the Lake District unless there's an accident and the rescue teams are called out.'

'You can't really blame them,' laughed John Steel. 'Jackson's old cow dropping her sixteenth calf wouldn't have the average householder in London reaching for his morning paper, even if it is a miracle to us around here!'

'It's a pity good news isn't the best news then,' snapped Jean.

'You don't understand human nature, Jean. You're like our Edith. Excitement is a frightening thing . . . it might even be sinful!'

'If you ask me, the papers are full of sin . . . and getting more sinful by the day,' retorted Jean.

'And you want women to come and drink in the pubs? You'll make them worse than men . . . We've had a lot of practice holding our drink – it's an art you know.'

'So I've noticed!' she replied as she dried the glasses. 'My guess is that women would have a civilising effect on this bar; at least so I'm told by people in the trade . . . Mark my words, Jackson, you'll see a lot of women in these country pubs very soon, especially as more people can afford to buy motorcars and will enjoy going out to a pub for a drink and a snack. Times are changing . . . and for the better. I'm all for this sort of progress!'

As Jean finished speaking the door opened and a hush descended on the drinkers in the Grey Mare.

'Come and join us, Sarah. Would you like a shandy?' Robert Jepson appeared as if from nowhere, and cleared a place for the tall, slender, red-haired young woman who made her way to the bar with the confidence of one who enjoys her work. As soon as she had tasted her drink, she greeted the regulars she knew and her gaze rested momentarily on Jackson. Robert quickly filled the gap.

'This is Jackson Strong,' he said, introducing the smiling farmer.

'At last,' she smiled warmly as she shook his gnarled hand. 'I was beginning to think I'd never meet you.'

'Has someone mentioned me then?' asked Jackson in surprise.

'Not "someone" Mr Strong, but simply "everyone". Have you any idea how well-known you are?'

'God knows what they've all been saying about me behind my back. It's hard when a chap isn't there to defend himself.'

'No need to worry, but they certainly made me very curious. Would you be good enough to answer a few questions? I think our readers would be interested to hear an opinion from someone who has lived in these parts for a good many years and can throw an interesting light on the changes that have taken place in the Sellafield area.'

As she spoke, Sarah took a pen and a small notebook from her handbag. 'You realise, of course, that we will only print part of what you say . . . that is, the most interesting parts for our readers?'

'I understand, although I can't imagine that anything I have to say will be of interest to folk who've never set foot in Cumberland.'

'You'd be surprised, Mr Strong. People are keen to read something different and my editor always likes to include a human interest story.'

'Well, fire away then, lass.'

'First of all, how old are you?'

'They tell me I'm seventy.'

'You're not sure?' asked an astonished Sarah Elliott.

'Well, the truth is, that when I thought I was coming up towards sixty-five, our Edith, my wife, reckoned I ought to get in touch with the authorities just to make sure that everything was in order, seeing as I am self-employed. And would you believe it, I had always said I was born in 1888, but when they traced my birth certificate I had been born in 1886, so I got my pension earlier than expected.'

'But what if you also die a couple of years earlier than expected?' laughed Alan Steel.

'Edith believes the Good Lord has made his own arrangement . . . My wife is very religious,' Jackson confided in the young woman facing him. 'My birth must have been registered by my father who wasn't very good about small details.'

'No he wasn't,' interrupted Tom Graham. 'He was supposed to be good at starting a job – a painter and decorator he was – then disappearing with the money before it was finished!'

'You seem to know more about my family than I do, Tom.'

'I only know what older folks have told me. Maybe there's no truth in any of it.'

'Tell me, Mr Strong, why did your mother not know the date you were born?' pursued Sarah.

'She died when I was very young . . . But few people had birth certificates in those days, so we had to send to London for a copy. It always amazes me how they can know all about you in London when your own family can't be relied on to remember.'

'Very interesting. Tell me, have you always lived near Egremont?'

'Yes, apart from when we farmed in Gosforth . . . Now there's a nice spot to live, though it's a long way from the auction in Whitehaven. If you couldn't manage to sell your stock when you got there you were faced with a big haulage bill to fetch them back home again. Times were hard for every one in the twenties and thirties, lass. You often had to sell animals for next to nothing if you farmed a long way from the auction.'

'Has Sellafield made any difference to your way of life then?'

'Well, I suppose it has brought better-paid and easier work into this area.'

'What about the scare over the last few weeks? Aren't you afraid of the fall-out?'

'It all depends on how old you are . . .'

'If you *know* how old you are!' laughed Joe Watson.

Jackson ignored the remark. 'As I say, when you have reached my age you know you've won most of life's battles, so it isn't worth complaining . . . Just think of the men killed in the pit disasters and those young folk who died of TB. Even those daft southerners who have died from climbing accidents in the fells would be pleased to be sitting here with the likes of us who know nowt about fall-out and atomic activity.'

'That isn't a very informed point of view, Mr Strong. Surely you realise that not all dangers can be seen?'

'So they tell me; but I'd like a bit more evidence. For instance, when will we see the terrible results of this "fall-out"?'

'Perhaps not for a generation or two. We can't be sure.'

177

'In that case I'm not bothered – I won't be around to see it.'

'But your grandchildren will be, won't they?'

'Well, young woman, I don't remember my grandparents. They died too young; like my own mother. She died young, probably from having too many children too quickly, and trying to feed them on next to no money. So I reckon my grandchildren stand a better chance of living a long, decent life than our families did in the past.'

'You lived in Gosforth, Mr Strong. It's a lovely village – a pity it's so close to the danger area, don't you think?'

'It depends what you mean by the "danger area" . . . a beautiful view doesn't fill stomachs, you know. Apart from the farms and a little domestic service in the big houses, there was nothing for folks to do in Gosforth. I remember a good few having to cycle to Egremont every day to work in the iron-ore mines.'

'There are a number of large houses in that area that would have provided domestic employment,' observed Sarah.

'Yes,' agreed Jackson reflectively, 'lovely houses, built by factory owners at the expense of workers slaving away in the cotton and woollen mills of Lancashire and Yorkshire. You'll see them all round the Lake District . . . They spent their money here in beautiful Cumberland . . . and they paid slave wages to the local folk who worked for them. Yes, Sarah, we know all about the beauty of our area . . . It's just a pity we have to earn money to live, otherwise we could enjoy the countryside without any worries at all.'

'You've gone very political, Jackson,' smiled John Steel as he ordered another round of drinks. 'I didn't know you knew anything about Lancashire or Yorkshire. I reckon it's the *Daily Herald* that I've seen the lad delivering to your house. You should stick to the *Farmers Weekly* and concentrate on improving your milk yield . . . but I'm amazed you're still farming at your age anyway. It's time you packed it in and retired. I'm sure Edith is ready to stop even if you're not.'

'Why should I retire just because someone tells me I'm older than I thought? It's only when you know your age that you think about things like that. If nobody knew how old they were they wouldn't alter the way they lived . . .'

'What rubbish you talk, Jackson,' interrupted Joe Watson. 'I know plenty of folk who would pack in their work long before they should just because they felt old and tired.'

'You're right, Joe. We can all name the lazy buggers around here, but . . .' Jackson reached for his new drink and turned towards a puzzled-looking Sarah. '. . . human nature, or the "Good Lord" as our Edith would say, made everybody different. He had to make some folk stupid and others downright bad, so that we have a fair choice. It stands to reason, Sarah, that if God had filled the world with good people he could have retired himself, and the devil wouldn't have had a look-in at all!'

'Well, I suppose it makes things more interesting, Jackson. They say a life of sin can be more fun than the decent life most of us lead,' suggested a thoughtful Harry Jepson.

'I don't think I'm going to get much material for my newspaper article from this sort of conversation,' said Sarah laughing.

'You haven't enjoyed your evening then?' asked Robert Jepson, sounding disappointed.

'Oh yes I have, I don't think I could have heard more outlandish opinions about Sellafield if I'd searched the entire country. It's been fascinating.'

'So, Jackson, you haven't found a woman in the pub too bad to cope with, have you?' asked Jean with a laugh.

'Certainly not, Jean, but she isn't a permanent fixture. It would be a different matter if our own wives started expecting to be taken out of an evening. Our Edith goes out to the pictures a couple of nights a week as it is. I don't think the funds would stand any more of her gallivanting about.'

'Come on, Mr Strong, women in the rest of England go

into pubs all the time. We have proper equality further south!'

'Where do you come from then, young lady?'

'Liverpool.'

'You can't expect us to copy places like Liverpool . . .'

'What on earth do you know about Liverpool, Jackson, any more than you know about Lancashire or Yorkshire?' asked an astonished John Steel. 'I don't believe you've ever set foot outside this county!'

'All I know is that our Edith's brother Harold catches a liner from there when he takes off looking for work in other countries. Liners can't dock anywhere near here so it must be a pretty big place, eh Sarah? Probably with a lot of foreigners doing the same as Harold, but looking for work in this country.'

Sarah laughed. 'You're right, in a way. A lot of people come to Liverpool looking for work, and it has also seen a great deal of poverty over the years, just like all the big English cities. But many women like to drink in the pubs there, and surely there's no harm in that, Mr Strong. Just because a lady goes into a bar it doesn't make her a loose woman.'

'Quite right, Sarah,' agreed Jean, enthusiastically, seeing her takings going up at a rapid pace in future. 'Things will change around here with the growth of Sellafield; you'll see.' She nodded knowingly at her male customers. The word Sellafield brought Sarah back to the present with a jolt. 'Tell me, Mr Strong, what do you think of the safety measures that have been taken, like ordering all the milk to be poured down the drains?'

'Yes, it was an awful waste of milk,' interrupted Harry Jepson. 'It didn't half hurt me to swill it away when I have so many young calves and pigs waiting to be fed . . .'

'But you'll all be compensated of course,' added Joe Watson cheerfully. 'Farmers always come out on top in any situation like this.'

'It must have hurt you, Mr Strong, to throw yours away?' insisted Sarah, a gleam in her eye.

Jackson rose from his seat, leaning heavily on his stick.

'Well, I must be getting home now. It's a bit late for an old man like me to be drinking and answering difficult questions from keen reporters used to city ways . . . So I'll bid you goodnight, young lady. I hope your visit here was of some use to you.'

Sarah smiled warmly as Jackson made his way to the door.

'Just a minute.' It was John Steel who called after the old farmer. 'Now you have made us all curious . . . You *did* pour your milk down the drain like the rest of us, didn't you, Jackson?'

The silence hung like a cloak over the customers in the Grey Mare as they waited for Jackson to answer.

He turned as he reached the door and scanned the waiting faces . . . Then, after he had reached for his cap, he turned again. 'That would be telling now . . . wouldn't it?'

The door closed quietly behind the old man, as the assembled friends looked from one to the other, the unspoken question hovering in the air.

17

THE CRAB FAIR

'The Cumberland and Westmorland style wrestling is just about to begin in the main ring. Come along, ladies and gents, and support your local champions . . .'

Jackson was only vaguely aware of the message blaring from the loudspeaker as he gazed down on the small market town of Egremont. He had already spent a few hours there, and the atmosphere was electric. Like anyone born in or near Egremont, Jackson had a special feeling for the Crab Fair, which was said to have originated nearly eight hundred years before.

The slight drizzle which always seemed to accompany the fair made little difference to the excited youngsters who milled around the stalls and the ever-popular ice-cream van. When he was their age, Jackson mused, the Crab was always something to look forward to. Even when he was working up in Wasdale he would walk all the way home to join in the fun.

'Have you been watching the judging then, Jackson?' Tom Graham's voice interrupted his thoughts.

'Aye, the embroidery on the wrestling costumes gets better every year. I wouldn't like to choose the best. The women who do the work must have a lot of patience.'

'I'm surprised you take an interest in the needlework, Jackson!'

'It's not so much me that's interested as our Edith. I've got to remember who won – she's a pretty good hand herself with a needle.'

'Did you ever try the wrestling then?'

'No, you've got to be a bit more supple than I ever was, Tom. Besides, handling sheep for a living satisfied any liking I might have had for fighting. Those little buggers of Herdwicks were as slippery as a basket of eels. Just look at them two young chaps over there, there's a lot of skill in that sort of wrestling . . . It doesn't look so hard but by God it takes a lot of strength to turn a big chap like yon on to his back without ending up underneath him.'

'I wonder why this style of wrestling has never caught on in the rest of the country?'

'Probably because here they don't knock the hell out of each other. Most folk like to see blood and skin flying – more like boxing if you ask me. It takes an understanding of the finer points of the sport to enjoy watching this sort of contest.'

'These chaps are good,' said Tom eagerly. 'Some of them have come from as far as Millom, and I saw one fella from Alston . . . Egremont Crab Fair certainly draws the best.'

'Aye, it's the prizes,' agreed Jackson. 'We make a decent job of what we do here; there's no point in half measures. It's like the bike races and the foot racing – everyone comes for the prizes.'

'Did you watch the racing on Main Street this morning?'

'I did, from the steps of the Black Bull. There was a good view of the greasy pole. Do you remember, Tom, how we used to go looking for an old bag to wrap round our knees to make it easier to climb up, hoping to get the leg of lamb that was on the top? Every lad in the town wanted to take it home to his mother.'

'The trouble was, there was only one prize. The best thing for us kids was the apple cart when we could all have something . . . unless we were completely stupid!'

The cheers of the crowd drew their attention – the wrestling had begun.

The afternoon wore on, and Jackson and Tom met friends

they hadn't seen for the last year or more. Eventually the lively chat was interrupted by the howling of dogs.

'Come on let's have a bet,' suggested Tom, making his way towards the hound trailing area.

The rows of betting boards soon came into view. And the cacophony of different sounds rose and fell as the yelping hounds lined up to be slipped, and then returned to a chorus of shouts and rattles, each owner urging their particular dog to race back first to sample the waiting titbits.

'Let's have a look at David's board. He'll have an idea of what might make us a pound or two – he's one of the few people I'd trust with my money.'

'How about a bet from you two old buggers?' called David Wilson the minute he spotted the two farmers. 'I've been looking for a couple of chaps with a bit of money to spare . . . I can recommend a nice little flutter on the three o'clock. There's Flying Lady – she's sure to do well this afternoon – she's been especially prepared . . .'

'You mean she's been starved for a day or two!' laughed Jackson.

'Come on now, gents. Everybody says the same thing . . .'

'You mean everybody does the same thing!' Tom replied.

'The training methods used by the owners are highly secret as you well know, gentlemen. But some of us have a good idea which dogs are likely to perform well today. After all, it's my job to know what's going on. I have a living to make like anyone else.'

'What sort of race will Sunset run today then, David? Her owner is Clem Jackson and he knows a thing or two about hound trailing. He's bred some decent dogs over the years.'

'The odds are a bit long on her, Jackson, but she's a reasonable bet, as an outsider . . . I can't really advise you two chaps. It's best to decide whether you want to take a chance or choose a fairly safe bet – it all depends on whether or not you're a betting man. But come on and place a bet of some sort.'

'These bookies like to see you part with your hard-earned money, don't they?' said a voice from behind.

'You . . . part with your money? I'd like to see the day you part with it willingly,' said David.

Jackson turned. 'Glad to see you, Bill. But you make a fella feel guilty every time you put in an appearance,' he said to the policeman who moved forward to join them.

'Only a guilty man need feel uneasy when he sees me.'

'I'm sure I'm guilty of something – it's just a matter of working out what. I haven't lived a blameless life as you know!' the old farmer chuckled.

'Nothing to worry about, that I can think of. Certainly not today anyway . . . I'm just keeping an eye on folk in general. Most people can have a good time without getting into trouble. The problems usually start with the young uns, and they're pretty well-known to us around here. It tends to run in the family so to speak . . .'

The conversation was suddenly drowned out by the town band's lively rendering of 'John Peel'.

'The maidens will be off soon,' shouted David to his prospective customers. Then, turning to the milling crowd, he called the names and odds of the young dogs in the first race of the afternoon.

'That's a grand tune, Tom,' observed Jackson.

'Aye by lad it is. I've never heard as good an arrangement of it anywhere else in the county – not even the Border Regiment can play it like Egremont Town Band. Yon cornet player can't half do his stuff.'

The two friends both placed bets on the hound trail races, then found a good spot to listen to the band and watch the afternoon's programme of sport. By the time they were settled the sun had come out, and the excited cries of the children mingled with the baying of the hounds as they raced across the fields, noses to the ground, sniffing at the aniseed trail.

Dent Fell looked on approvingly at the activities that had taken place around her for so many hundreds of years. There was a mysterious bond between the local folk who greeted each other every year at Egremont Crab Fair – an unspoken awareness that this event was a bit of history, a link between the living and the dead, and perhaps even the children of the future.

Having collected their modest winnings at the end of the afternoon, Jackson and Tom's next port of call had to be the beer tent. Beer-drinking was always the most popular sport and the competitors had all trained hard for this event!

*　*　*

Jackson reached the end of the stitch of potatoes and stood up slowly and stiffly to get his cold tea and sandwiches.

He gazed at the long row of potatoes lying white and naked on the soil. It was a good crop but, of all the unpleasant jobs on a farm, 'scratting taties' was to him by far the worst. How did anyone in their right mind ever choose to farm at all, he wondered, when they had to dig potatoes out of the ground with their bare hands? The pit paid better money, and at least the weather didn't change underground! Jackson always had the same conversation with himself when he was doing this job.

When the ground was wet, the bits of old meal bags he tied round his knees soon became waterlogged and heavy. Later, the damp and cold seeped through to his legs, increasing the pain of his rheumatism. And when it was dry and windy, like today, the dry soil blew into his face, choking him as he worked, and making him curse the job anew.

Some of his neighbours used a potato digger. In fact he had bought a second-hand one himself and used it occasionally, but it seemed to damage the crop, forcing him to feed too many spoiled potatoes to the pigs. He was certain a good many farmers sold sliced and damaged taties along with the best eaters, but he had never done that before and he wasn't going to start now.

Today wasn't quite so bad because he could allow his thoughts to drift pleasurably back to last Saturday's Crab Fair. In his mind's eye he could still see the owners of the trail hounds urging their dogs on. He heard again the tin-rattling, whistling, name-calling and bucket-shaking, each sound having special meaning for that particular owner's dog. He laughed as he remembered one hound who had been leading the field. She was streaking towards the finishing tape, with lolling tongue and easy swinging gait, when suddenly she stopped – presumably to have a good sniff round – while her owner screamed, yelled, threatened . . . and finally begged her to cross the line. It was all to no avail . . . she sat and watched most of the field race past her. Then, slowly, she decided to amble after her mates, a look of unashamed delight on her face as she spotted her distraught mistress.

But that was part of the fun of this sort of racing – not like the cold intense races of the greyhound track. And not like fox-hunting, where success depended on whether a fox was careless enough to cross the path of a howling mob of dogs, men and horses. Jackson had never taken part in mounted fox-hunting, though he had little sympathy for a fox who couldn't keep clear of a bunch of noisy hunters. In his opinion a bullet was far quicker and did less damage to a farmer's property. Besides, jumping fences and gates spoilt a decent ride.

'You're day-dreaming again, Jackson. I saw you from a long way up the road so I thought I'd stop and have a crack. You couldn't have heard my bike,' said Joe Watson.

'No I didn't hear you, Joe. Where are you off to? It's not like you to stray far from the shop.'

'Annie is looking after things while I deliver a few bits and pieces to old Mrs Bragg. She can't make it to the shop as often as she used to . . . Besides, it gets me out into the fresh air once in a while. What were you dreaming about? You can't be worrying about them potatoes. They look a good crop this year, but they're a bit late, aren't they?'

'You chaps in shops should find out a bit more about the stuff you sell. Everybody thinks the only taties are earlies but folk have to eat them all the year round. These are back taties and a fine crop they are. I just wish someone else would scrat them for me.'

'Aye, it's always looked like a nasty job to me, crawling about on your hands and knees in a wet field. But at least you're out in the open when the weather's good and a lot of folk would fancy that.'

'Yes, just think of them poor souls that have to travel to work on one of those underground trains in London. It must be like shooting along a rat hole. Then in summer they have to work in a stuffy office, while in winter they're obliged to breathe in one another's germs all day – not the sort of life for a healthy fella. It was bad enough down the pit where you had no idea what the weather was like on top. That's why so many miners keep pigeons or dogs – hobbies which take them out into the open air. As for me, I always wanted to farm, so I can't complain about a bit of good soil blowing into my mouth now and again.'

'That's the best way of looking at it, Jackson.'

'I was just thinking about the Crab Fair on Saturday. A good memory always helps to move the job along.'

'You were there in the early part of the day, or so I was told. I believe you were holding forth in the Black Bull. Goodness knows how you managed to keep going for the whole afternoon after the way they said the ale was flowing in the morning!'

'Well, I saw folk I hadn't seen for years, and you can't just nod and say "how do", especially when they offer to buy you a drink. That would be downright unfriendly, wouldn't it?'

'That's what *you* say! What did Edith say?'

'She hardly saw me. I came home to do the milking, then Tom called for me and we went back to watch the clay pipe smoking and gurning.'

'Edith didn't go then?'

'Good God no. If she'd seen me drinking she would have stood a great chance of winning the gurning without the aid of a horse's braffin!'

'Don't let her hear you say that, or you'll have a face you won't dare show in the pub for a few weeks . . .'

'Did you manage to find your way there after you'd shut the shop then, Joe? I didn't see you.'

'Yes I went, though it's always hard to see anybody in the crowd, with it being dark and the spotlights on the stage. But I must say I enjoyed it . . . You know, Jackson, even with the pictures and the television, there's little to beat local folk getting up and making fools of themselves for pure enter-tainment.'

'You're dead right, even when it's the same ugly mugs you see gurning most years, and the same singers and smokers. Little has changed over the centuries. Maybe strangers would think we're all a bit simple . . . and maybe they'd be right!'

'What you say about nothing changing reminds me of a story my grandfather used to tell about the Crab.'

'What's that then, Joe?'

'He reckoned that years ago, well before his time, they used to eat biskeys soaked in treacle.'

'How did they judge a competition of that sort?'

'The competitor who finished eating his biskeys first, and then whistled a tune, won the prize. My grandfather said that one year two contestants finished whistling their tune at what seemed to be the same moment, so they appealed to the judge who gave his decision. However the loser was far from satisfied . . . so he picked up the big bowl of treacle and poured it over the judge's head!'

190

Jackson roared with laughter. 'By God, that's a great story, Joe! If the judges were as drunk and pompous as a few of them are today I can well imagine the cheers that would have gone up from the crowd! We don't get entertainment like that nowadays – more's the pity! It would be a great thing if they could revive biskey eating, don't you think, Joe?'

'I don't think anybody would be hungry enough to have a go at that sort of competition these days, Jackson. But it would certainly be very popular – it might even get on television! Some day them TV chaps should come up to this corner of the country to find out what we really get up to, instead of only coming when something goes wrong.'

'That's human nature,' said Jackson, rising painfully as he spoke. 'And this piece of human nature'll have to get a move on or I'll have these few stitches looking at me next Saturday.'

Joe went back to his bicycle which was leaning against the gate.

'Give my regards to Mother Bragg, and remind her that I'll call with a nice bit of spare rib when we butch later in the year,' called Jackson as his friend cycled off.

If anyone walking along the Egremont road that cold breezy September afternoon had glanced casually over the hedge, they would have seen an elderly farmer crawling along the ground, busily revealing a neat row of un-blemished potatoes. A more observant passerby might just have noticed his shoulders shaking occasionally, as though he was chuckling to himself. No one, however, would have guessed the connection between the shaking shoulders . . . and a bowl of treacle!